THE DIARY OF DANIEL SHEPHERD

THE SHEPHERD CHRONICLES
VOLUME I

———

Jerry Schultz

This is a work of fiction. All of the characters, organizations, and events portrayed in this novel are either products of the author's imagination or are used fictitiously.

THE DIARY OF DANIEL SHEPHERD
Copyright © 2023 by Jerry Schultz

ISBN: 9798386621988 (Paperback)
ISBN: 9798386707071 (Hardcover)

I will give you shepherds who are loyal to me, and they will shepherd you with knowledge and skill. -Jeremiah 3:15

TABLE OF CONTENTS

PART THREE

Forward

Growing up in the Ozarks, there was always an adventure to be had in exploring the woods, taking nature walks or wading around in creeks and springs. Blazing our own trail, we happened upon more than a few creepy, abandoned houses...and we heard our fair share of spooky stories.

From the amazing cooking, to its festivities, legends, entertainments, dreams and disappointments, traditions and small-town idiosyncrasies, you are about to catch a glimpse of life in the Ozarks. It is an astonishingly beautiful place where I still love to visit or go hiking whenever I have the chance to get away. It helps me to feel at peace. I hope you will come to appreciate this part of our country as you experience it through the eyes of these characters.

Faith and family were the foundations of our way of life, but, like everywhere in this fallen world, evil crept in, often catching us unaware. This book, and the series to follow, will address serious life issues in an unflinching way as our characters are forced to deal with the harsh realities of living in a sinful world.

Sometimes this life can become very dark, but there is always the Light of Hope, searching us out and wanting to be found...

PART ONE

OCTOBER

1997

The House on Bald Knob

The vintage Mustang wound its way along the mountainside overlooking the town of Lost Valley. From this vantage point, countless hills and hollows surrounding the town could be seen with houses and steeples nestled between the vibrant fall foliage. The dark red tops of the quaint brick shops of Mainstreet peaked out among the waves of colorful leaves lending a timeless appearance to the living portrait. Out of this landscape of fiery autumn tones, the smoky gray visage of the pony car appeared. Its galloping chrome emblem shimmered in the evening sunlight as it carried three passengers around the treacherous curves of the road.

Daniel Shepherd and his two best friends, Nick Baker and Freddy Fisher, were giddy with anticipation. Nick's parents had just purchased a fixer upper with a river view and the boys couldn't wait to check it out. Rumor had it, the time-worn homestead was haunted. The trio had been dying to investigate and with Nick's parents out of town for their anniversary, this was the perfect opportunity.

"Would you look at that?" Freddy exclaimed as they approached the top of the ridge. Daniel looked left down the hill to take in the spectacular view of Lost River wandering its serpentine path through the valley below as the radiant hues of fall glowed warmly in the sunset.

"Stunning," Daniel agreed.

"We're here," Nick suddenly exclaimed, momentarily removing a hand from the steering wheel to point up ahead at a driveway off to the right.

"Both hands on the wheel," Daniel admonished.

"Sorry," Nick replied as he turned to pass through the stacked stone gateway. Extending away from the entrance were the lichen covered remnants of a split-rail, log fence, its zig-zag pattern distorted over time as it slowly collapsed and rotted into the ground. Daniel noticed a pair of black metal footings on top of the masonry on either side of the entry. He wondered if there had once been an archway here. Perhaps it had displayed a family name. Holes in the sides of the rock walls gave the impression that there might have been a swinging gate as well. Maybe it had displayed the family crest or perhaps a motto of some kind. They appeared to be long gone and forgotten.

The tires crunched loudly as they passed through the once regal entrance and made their way along a crooked, gravel driveway up the hill through the woods. As they emerged from the trees, a two-story Saltbox style house came into view, the vestiges of its former glory still in evidence despite the wear and tear of time. The once whitewashed siding was now weather beaten and grayed with age. Nicknamed a *Farmer's Mansion* when first built, the home would have been small by modern standards, but its size was augmented by an extended lower level and its dimensions had been further enhanced by the addition of a two-story turret protruding from the left side which gave the house a stately, if somewhat strange and spooky appearance.

Adding to the foreboding ambiance was a dry, concrete fountain featuring a cherub standing on one foot, pouring out an empty jar into a birdbath that spilled over into a small pool. A few overgrown juniper bushes and some scraggily boxwoods were all that remained of the landscaping on the bare, neglected grounds. Mossy rocks covered large portions of the sloping bald knob.

In one corner of the backyard, they stumbled upon the remnants of an untended, rotten-wood container garden. A vegetable patch may once have flourished here, but now all that remained was a row of dead grapevines and some wild mushrooms growing on the north side of some decomposing railroad ties.

Daniel jumped when he heard a loud thwack, followed by the groaning of a rusty hinge coming from an old, graying toolshed in the opposite corner of the yard. Faded pastel shutters and flowers painted on the sides of the steps and around the concrete foundation hinted that it may have been used as a guestroom or playhouse, once upon a time. Now it sat empty with the windows covered in dust and grime, the shutters falling off and the door hanging crookedly on its hinges, padlocked in place. A few patches of concrete had crumbled away, revealing a charred foundation of stacked stone from a time well before the current shed was constructed.

"What's in here?" Daniel asked, trying in vain to peer through the filthy windows into the dark.

"I have no idea," answered Nick. "We don't have a key."

A sudden shiver crept over Daniel's body as he turned back toward the house. The extended bottom floor of the home had been leveled up with stacked stones to compensate for the slope of the yard which caused a deep shadow to grow over the boys as the sun sank behind the hills into the west. Altogether, the property certainly looked the part of a long abandoned, haunted homestead.

"Are you actually gonna live here?" Freddy asked as they made their way back to the front of the house.

"What's that supposed to mean?" Nick replied.

"Nothing," said Freddy, "It's just, a little creepy looking."

"Yes, we'll live in the functional parts of the house to save money until the renovation is complete to maximize our profits," Nick answered matter-of-factly.

"If you and your folks pull off this remodel, you'll make a fortune," Daniel replied. "So, what's the story with this place? Why has it sat empty for so long?"

"People say they hear strange noises, see ghostly sights and experience unexplained phenomena in the house and on the grounds," answered Nick.

"But what's the *story* behind it?" asked Freddy.

"No idea. The history of this property is a bit of a mystery."

"It's like we just walked into a scary fireside yarn," Daniel added. "It's kind of awesome. I can't wait to take a look inside."

"Right this way," said Nick, lowering his voice into his deepest basso profundo as he opened the front door. "Welcome. Won't you please come in," he continued as the door whined on its worn hinges.

"That's comforting," Freddy commented.

As they crossed the threshold the boards creaked and moaned under their feet. Most of the carpet and flooring had been stripped down to the original wide, hardwood planks which were badly in need of refinishing. To the right was a formal dining room, complete with wagon wheel chandelier, leading back into a kitchen that looked like it was straight out of an old farmhouse with its simple white cabinets and patterned linoleum floor.

"The place certainly has good *bones*," Freddy joked.

"Yeah. Check out the wainscoting. Whoever built this really knew what they were doing. The craftsmanship is amazing," Nick added, feigning obliviousness to Freddy's sarcasm.

Freddy looked at Daniel and widened his eyes in amusement.

"Can we come help with demo day?" Daniel asked.

Nick just chuckled and rolled his eyes in response as he stepped straight ahead into the spacious living room. Everything in it was covered by sheets due to dust from the renovation, further lending to the haunted house vibe. The view of the room was partially obscured by a large, sheet-covered bookcase which created a small hall leading to an ornate staircase positioned along the left wall. Across from the bookcase were French doors with glass inserts leading into the protruding bottom level of the turret. The hexagonal room was arranged as a formal sitting area and furnished with priceless antiques which were currently covered in plastic. The furniture had come with the house, value added, but Nick's mom had been utilizing the rotund room as her temporary sewing space. Wraparound windows sent light dancing across the room, giving it the appearance of a sun room by day...by night would be a different story. The upper level of the turret contained a bedroom with a spectacular view of the valley below while the main section of the upstairs contained a newish bathroom and two additional bedrooms, one of which was being used for storage.

An eerie quiet settled over the property as sunset gave way to twilight. Only the occasional rustle of leaves in the evening wind broke the pervasive silence outside. Those same wind gusts whistled through the attic, putting the boys on edge as each crackling sound of the old house settling brought their nerves to high alert. The trio began to rethink their decision to spend the night in this strange, shadowy domicile.

They comforted themselves by heading into the kitchen to raid the ice box. Inside, they discovered a veritable smorgasbord of leftovers. As Freddy chowed down on a mouthful of Mrs. Baker's famous meatloaf, he said "Wow, Nick, your mom can really cook."

"Thanks," Nick replied as he and Daniel filled their plates with the rest of the meatloaf and heaps of cheesy chicken casserole.

"Talk about comfort food," Daniel agreed, "This meatloaf *is* amazing."

"Do your trick, Chef Daniel," Freddy requested.

Daniel just smiled.

"C'mon man, let's have it," Nick insisted. "What flavors do your discerning taste buds savor this evening?"

Daniel obliged, replying in his most pretentious food-critic voice, "Well, I detect hints of cumin, paprika and cracked black peppercorns cooked into the poultry which really brings the cream of mushroom and chicken to life in this casserole. The green chilies give it a bit of a kick which is softened by the sweetness of the diced tomatoes. The texture of the crushed and moistened tortilla chip crust is superb. The grated marble cheese is the perfect finisher for this dish."

"And the meatloaf?" Freddy asked through a mouthful of mashed potatoes.

"The consistency is sublime," Daniel continued. "It contains the perfect amount of breadcrumbs flavored by the natural juices of the beef. I note hints of garlic and onion powder with just a shake of red pepper flake, but it's really the chopped green bell pepper paired with the tomato sauce that makes this recipe so delectable."

"The super sampler strikes again," Nick complimented.

"You should be a professional taste tester," Freddy suggested. "It's like your secret power. We'll call you *The Terrific Taster*."

The boys shared a great laugh as they dug into the delicious dinner. By the time they finished feasting, darkness had overtaken the murky haze of twilight. Only the faint glow of an old pole farm light kept the black of night at bay as whisps of fog began to form in the cool, hilltop air.

After the meal, the boys headed upstairs to Nick's room, the turret bedroom, its view now limited to the darkened tree line at the edge of the yard and the very faint twinkle of streetlights in the town far below. Nick shut off the light at the bottom of the stairs. Daniel and Freddy looked at each other and shrugged in the faint blue light before heading up into the blackness. As they entered the room and began to look around in the dim light coming through the window, suddenly a shadow flashed across the wall causing Freddy to jump and Daniel to let out a frightened yip. Nick held a finger to his lips for quiet and motioned for them to sit down in the middle of the floor. As they sat there, silently observing, more shadows crossed the room, travelling from wall to wall. Daniel thought it looked like a vampire cape flitting

17

across the room. Freddy loudly whispered that it looked like a witch flying on a broom. Nick put his hand to his lips once again and motioned toward the window. After tip-toeing their way across the floor to begin looking for the source of the shadows, they discovered bats flying in and out of view, dodging back and forth, eating bugs drawn to the light emanating from the pole in the yard. Each time a bat circled the upper room of the turret and fluttered past the window, its wings, magnified by the glass, cast an enormous shadow across the wall.

"At least that explains the moving shadows," offered Freddy, breaking the silence.

"Somehow that doesn't make me feel better," said Daniel.

"Did you see the size of the ears on those things?" Freddy asked.

"They're huge," Daniel agreed.

"Those are Ozark big-eared bats," Nick explained. "There must be a cave nearby."

"Tomorrow, we've got to find it," Freddy insisted. "We can go spelunking."

"Tomorrow's Sunday," Nick replied.

"So?"

"We've got church," Daniel answered.

"Can't you just skip?"

"There's no way I'm missing service to go crawling into some dark hole in the ground. I'm going downstairs to get a soda to settle my stomach."

"I'll come with you," said Freddy.

Daniel flipped the light switch, but nothing happened.

"Some of the wiring is faulty," explained Nick. "The only way to turn the light in the tower on or off is with the switch at the bottom of the stairs."

"Great," Daniel said, as he began descending the steps, clinging to the rail, for a quick cup of bubbly comfort. While Freddy helped himself to a few more homemade chocolate chip cookies, Daniel headed back upstairs. As he made his way in the pitch-black darkness of the stair well, he could swear he heard footsteps behind him.

"Freddy, is that you?" he whispered. There was no answer. He continued, and the footsteps in the dark trailed right behind. The hairs on the back of his neck stood up and he felt a touch just below his hairline that sent a chill right through his spine. After slapping at his neck and swiping back wildly to feel if something was there, he ran up the stairs as fast as he could, the sound of someone chasing him following closely behind.

Entering the room, he could not see Nick. Turning around, he didn't see anyone else come in. Feeling his way down the hall, hoping to find a light switch in the unfamiliar house, he entered Nick's parent's room, but it had blackout curtains preventing any light from entering. Disoriented, he paused for a moment, waiting for his eyes to adjust to the darkness. A pointy eared shadow-form seemed to appear on the wall, staring right at him. Freaked out, he sprinted toward the door...and the shadow fled in the opposite direction across the wall, fading into the blackness...without making a sound of any kind.

As Daniel ran into the hall he bumped into Nick and both boys screamed. "Why are you trying to scare me like this?" Nick bellowed.

"Trying to scare *you*, why are you hiding down this hallway?" exclaimed Daniel.

"I was going to the bathroom. Where's Freddy? I heard him following you up the stairs," said Nick. At that moment, Freddy came walking up the stairs, his loud, stomping steps echoing through the house. Nick turned to Daniel, inquiring "Whose footsteps were those behind you earlier then?" Both boy's eyes widened.

"What's going on?" asked Freddy.

His friends just stood there, looking as if they had seen a ghost, or at least heard one. After explaining about the phantom footsteps, the boys stood still, listening for a few minutes until they heard voices downstairs. No car tires had been heard crunching to a halt in the driveway. No rusty door hinges had squawked open. No creaky floorboards had cried out to alert them to the presence of others. Yet the sound of voices murmuring in the living room drifted up the stairs and into their ears.

Cautiously, they made their way down the stair well, Daniel bravely leading the way. As he reached the bottom floor, he found himself facing the sitting room. A few scattered rays of light found their way through the windows. As he peaked into the room, Daniel was suddenly unable to draw breath as he saw a full-bodied apparition floating about a foot off the ground, her white dress billowing in the moonlight. Shrieking in terror, he jumped back and fell into his pals, who caught him and stood him up. The others quickly glanced inside before fleeing into the living room as fast as their feet could carry them. As they rounded the sheet shrouded bookcase, they expected to see...something...anything. But there was no one in sight. Huddling together, Daniel was the one to motion for silence this time. As soon as they became quiet, they heard the voices, right there among them. At the slightest sound of steps or whispers, the voices disappeared, but when they got quiet, the voices were present again.

The moon was high in the sky by this point, shining over the treetops and through the windows, providing enough illumination for them to see. They began lifting sheets, looking underneath for some type of stereo or boombox. Nick threw up his hands in offense when Freddy looked inside the pocket of his hooded sweatshirt, as if to see if he had a remote control hidden in there. They opened the windows to hear if the sound could be coming from outside, but it was not and they closed them back. Using his highly trained musician's ears, Daniel pinpointed the source of the sound. It appeared to be emanating from a coffin length object covered by a sheet on the left side of the room. Daniel and Freddy drew deep breaths and slowly peeled back the sheet. They could never have predicted what they would find underneath.

Completing the haunted house ambience was a classic Hammond organ. It was a bit more hip than your average haunted instrument, but nonetheless, the sound of an indistinct murmuring of humanoid voices was clearly emanating from within the instrument. They discovered that when the power switch was in the "on" position, the voices could be heard. When it was in the "off" position there was no sound.

Nick couldn't contain himself any longer and burst out laughing. Freddy flipped on the light switch.

"Alright, spill. What's so funny?"

"We believe the organ is picking up radio waves. It gave me quite a fright our first night in this house. Mom and Dad noticed that sometimes it sounds like music and sometimes talking. If we turn it off and unplug it, the instrument remains silent."

Daniel readily accepted the theory. The explanation was certainly plausible enough to give the boys some peace of mind but Freddy expressed his doubts.

"Are you sure this old organ isn't broadcasting some sort of supernatural soundwaves?"

"I'm sure," Nick replied.

"Why do you have an organ in your house anyway?" Daniel inquired.

"Mom and Dad used to sing in a Gospel group. Mom played this organ."

"Ok, but what about the footsteps on the stairs?" Daniel made his way over to investigate. With Nick at the top and Freddy at the bottom and all the working lights in the house on bright, Daniel slowly ascended the staircase. With each step that he took, the ghost steps echoed in return. They discovered that the newel post was loose at the bottom of the balustrade. Each step on the old, bare-wood staircase caused the beautiful railing to vibrate and the post to knock against the floor.

Suddenly remembering the spectral figure in the sitting room, Daniel glanced at Freddy, then at the doors to the turret. "Who wants to go in there?"

Freddy dramatically flung the French doors open wide, flooding the room with light, and then fell to the floor, laughing. Nick chuckled as Daniel made his way over to the room where he discovered a white wedding dress, mid-alteration, hanging on a headless mannequin, right above a floor vent.

"My mom has been hemming this gown for my cousin's wedding."

Daniel glared.

"Trick?" Nick suggested.

"I'll show you a trick," Daniel growled as he tackled him to the ground. They wrestled until he pinned Nick's shoulders to the floor before flashing his teeth in a wide grin.

"Happy Halloweeeeeen!!!" sang Freddy as all three boys erupted into uncontrollable laughter.

"Halloween isn't until Friday," corrected Daniel.

"Happy Halloween *week*," offered Nick.

"Well, this should be interesting," Daniel responded as he laughed and shook his head.

Sunday, October 26

The boys popped popcorn and stayed up watching spooky movies until the wee hours of Sunday morning. By the time they finally crawled into their sleeping bags to get a little shut-eye, Daniel was too tired to notice as Freddy's leg swept the cord to the alarm clock and unplugged it...

Two deacons, J.C. Jones and Lester Crow, stared daggers at Daniel as he and Nick tiptoed into church, their tardiness betrayed by the squeaky door hinge Daniel forgot to oil. The deacon's sons, Reed Jones and Aden Crow, smirked from the back row as Reed lowered a burly arm behind the pew and irreverently extended his middle finger. Daniel's father glanced up and simply raised an eyebrow to his son...before continuing on with his sermon.

Ghost Faces

Daniel was the newest member of the trio, having moved to Lost Valley in middle school when his dad was called to be the pastor of Riverside Community Church, located down in the valley near the river in the center of town. Daniel was a contemplative young man. His dark brown hair was always carefully kempt and his warm, brown eyes reflected a genuinely kind soul. A fashion tee, blue jeans, high top sneakers and a brown leather bomber jacket were pretty much his standard attire. That jacket was his prized possession. He mowed dozens of lawns to pay for it and wore it everywhere he went when the weather was cool.

Freddy was a character, the comedian of the bunch and always up to something. His untamed, sandy blonde hair, mischievous steel-gray eyes and a few light freckles gave him a happy and carefree appearance which was matched by his worn-out tennis shoes, frayed jeans and the untucked t-shirt of his favorite country band.

Nick was a good balancer between the seriousness of Daniel and the goofiness of Freddy. His stylish, gelled black hair and kind, honey-brown eyes gave him a distinctive look that matched his personality. Nick was a solid, steady and trustworthy friend, the firm, but gentle type. As always, his neatly tucked shirt and dark jeans were impeccably laundered. The collar of his bleached denim jacket was popped and his bright white sneakers seemed to never get dirty.

All three boys entered the school week with a high level of optimism, but Monday would turn out to be a wet blanket, extinguishing everyone's good spirits.

Lost Valley High students prided themselves on their maturity and a general sense of coolness. LVHS pupils cultivated an atmosphere of collegiality and had become accustomed to interacting like adults and equals. They showed respect to their teachers and they expected to be treated with trust and respect in return. So, when it was announced that the week prior to Halloween would be devoted to discussing the dangers of doing drugs and drunk driving, it not only dampened the Spooky Week spirit, it felt like a straight up slap-in-the-face.

That morning, the news was broadcast over the school intercom that throughout the day on Thursday, students would be pulled out of class at random and their faces would be painted white to represent the thirty people who are killed by drunk drivers each day. The conscripted pale-faced students would be required to sit silently in the back of each classroom, forbidden from uttering a single word. In fact, no one was allowed to speak to or interact with them in any way for the rest of the day. The students were instructed to treat them like ghosts. It would be as if they had suddenly departed this life. No one could have realized just how haunting those images would become.

Daniel was livid. Normally compliant, he became suddenly defiant. He told Nick and Freddy, "I'd like to see them *try* to paint my face white. They can't make me do that."

"This is ridiculous," agreed Freddy, "A girl we've never met from over in Lake City gets into a car wreck and now all the teachers are going crazy on us."

"I agree. It's like seventy miles away and in a different state," Daniel added.

"What was her name?" asked Nick.

"Lindsey something," said Freddy.

"It was Lindsey Cobble," finished Daniel, "and what happened to her last spring is tragic, but it doesn't make this ok."

"I've heard kids talking at work and it sounds like all the schools in the area will be having assemblies and stuff this week too," offered Nick. I agree they're going a bit overboard, but what are we supposed to do about it?"

"I'll tell you what I'm gonna do. I'm gonna walk right out of this school and leave. I ain't walkin' around in white face paint all day. They have no right to treat us this way," Daniel asserted.

Freddy asked "Where will you go?

Nick asked "Aren't you afraid you'll get in trouble?"

"I don't care," Daniel answered with determination, a sudden light coming into his eyes. "Let's make a pact, right here and right now, that if they attempt to paint any of our faces white, we'll all three walk out. We'll go hang out at Burger Barn. We can get some chubby-dubby burgers with cheese and onion rings, maybe have some root beer floats and bring your quarters boys, we'll spend the day in the backroom arcade."

"Nah, man." Nick Interrupted. "I work there. I don't want my boss to see me skipping school. I want him to think I'm responsible. I'm hoping he'll make me a manager when I graduate so I can work there, or at his Ridgeview location, to pay for college. Bring your bats and baseball gloves and we can go over to the lot."

"No way. It's right next to the church. If dad catches me cutting class, there will be no Halloween for me," Daniel objected.

"We could explore Deer creek," Freddy replied. "Nobody will be out there. Bring some old shoes and fishing poles."

"Yeah," agreed Nick. "The weather's been really nice for this time of year. We should definitely head down to the creek to see if the fish are biting out by Miller's Bridge. Plus, we won't get busted."

"Right on," Daniel laughed. "That's what I'm talkin' about. So, you're in?"

"We're in!" they enthusiastically replied, the morning's tension broken by their happy, but unlikely, daydream of a plan.

Thursday, October 30, 1997

Thursday came and Daniel hesitantly made his way to school. The acid of anxiety churned in his stomach making him feel sick. He made it through the first few classes of the morning without any face-painting incidents. A few students were called out of class from the music building, but did not return.

As he entered the long main hallway of the school, he felt an eerie sense of quiet. Only the sounds of whimpers, sniffs and the chink-crunch of light blue locker doors shutting broke the creepy silence. He smiled at Gabby Shoemaker as she made her way toward him and thought to himself that she seemed rather sad lately. As he got closer, Daniel could see tears welling up in her eyes as she reached up to brush away the drops already glistening on her cheeks. He tried to think of something to say, but was distracted by a familiar mane of teased blonde hair trailing behind her. As Gabby passed by and Hannah Farmer appeared, Daniel jumped back in shock. Her face was whited out like a ghost! As he stood there gasping with his mouth open, she glanced up at him sadly before continuing down the hall toward the science lab with a rapid slurp of air meant to stifle the sobs building up within her. Daniel was upset with himself for not knowing what to say or do.

As he continued down the crowded corridor, with the carpet absorbing the sounds of footsteps, Daniel suddenly heard a sniffle and felt heavy breathing on the back of his neck. Turning around, he leaped back and gasped as his heart nearly jumped out of his chest to see another ghost-white visage, the face of Annie Wheeler, stained with tracks of tears streaming from her bloodshot eyes, carving out rivulets as they made their way down her chalky painted cheeks. Daniel's heart went out to her, but there was little he could do other than tighten the corners of his mouth and offer a grim look of support. He thought to himself, *what a twisted thing for a school to do to kids.*

"Are you ok?" he asked, breaking the established rule of the day.

"No," she mouthed, shaking her head as she began to veer off into her next class, her head downcast. Daniel reached out his hand, gently laid it on her shoulder and gave her an empathetic pat. Looking back, Annie reached up and placed her hand on top of his, looked up into his eyes, gave his fingers a squeeze and mouthed "Thank-you," before patting his hand and going into the classroom.

As Daniel turned around to go to his Spanish class, Reed Jones pushed him into the wall. "Watch your step, Shepherd."

Daniel glanced up to see if any teachers were watching, but their faces all seemed to be turned, looking away. A few minutes later, his class began to practice their daily Spanish conversation questions with their eccentric teacher, Mrs. Maxine Cartwright. The momentary calm was shattered as Cindy Spicer was dragged, sobbing hysterically, out of the special needs classroom next door. Crying loudly in the hallway, she begged them to take the white goop off of her face, wailing "Take it off. Take it off. I don't want to wear it anymore."

She didn't understand why she was being punished by not being allowed to talk to anyone all day long. She complained that the face paint felt hot and made it hard to breathe. The teacher kept telling her to stop talking and another educator came down to tell her that she had to be quiet and wear the horrible mask.

That was the last straw. The Spanish class, growing angrier by the second, begged Mrs. Cartwright to do something about it. In response, she walked over and closed the door to muffle the sounds of the girl's anguished pleas.

"NO," they shouted in unison. "We meant HELP HER."

Mistreating a student with special needs was the lowest thing a person could do at Lost Valley High. It was a disgusting display. Daniel mumbled, "How could these teachers not show even the slightest hint of compassion or empathy?"

Mrs. Cartwright didn't hear as she was already walking out the door to speak with her colleagues in hushed tones as she placed her arm around Cindy who asked, "Can we please call Dr. Blumenthal?"

"Yes, honey," Mrs. Cartwright promised, but it was too late. With classroom doors being left open up and down the hallway, nearly the whole school had heard the incident which rapidly escalated the situation, putting the mood of the student body into a state that can best be describe as a volatile combination of enraged and upset. Friends wept at the thought of losing each other and their pain was magnified by not being allowed to speak words of comfort to help one another through it. Resentment toward the faculty rose minute by minute, though most of them had nothing to do with the scheme.

By lunchtime, Principal Potter ordered that no more students be whited out. He called counselors to come over from the middle school and elementary and asked them to join the high school counselor in the library to meet with students who were distraught by the ill-conceived tactic. Yet, he made the questionable decision to follow through with the assembly planned for that afternoon.

Right after lunch an announcement was made for all students to proceed to the gymnasium for an assembly. On the way there, Daniel asked Nick "Why is Cindy Spicer in special needs classes? She used to be one of the smartest kids in the school."

"Brain damage from a massive seizure or cardiac event, maybe oxygen deprivation or something. I'm not sure. I heard a rumor that it might have been drug or alcohol related. That's another reason we're enduring this dreadful day."

As they entered the small gymnasium, their eyes were instantly drawn to the center of the basketball court where each of their whited out, dead faced classmates sat silently, cross legged, in a morbid line. As faculty and law enforcement lectured the student body on the consequences of drunk driving, the ghost faced classmates just sat there in awkward compliance, several of them in tears. This was a scene few would soon forget, and others would come to regret.

Daniel was done at that point. He'd just plain had it. As the assembly dismissed, he, Freddy and Nick slipped out the back doors by the locker room and took off. To keep Nick in his boss's good graces, Daniel got three root beer floats from the pick-up window at Burger Barn and met them out at Miller's Bridge. They spent the rest of the afternoon fishing and as far as Daniel knew, his dad didn't find out. They figured that so many students were in and out of class going to the library to see the counselors that it would be hard for the teachers to keep track and the three got away scot-free without being missed at school, as far as they knew.

The Last Day, of October

The next day things began the journey back to normal, or so it seemed. The students of Lost Valley High were still deeply resentful over the previous day's heavy-handed haranguing, but at least the corridors weren't crawling with ghost faced teens or filled with the sounds of gasps and tears. It's probably a good thing costumes weren't allowed. Excitement crept back into the air as the kids began looking forward to the festivities and the scrumptious treats that awaited them come evening.

As he entered the main hallway, coming in from the music room, Daniel was shocked to be grabbed by Annie Wheeler. She playfully pulled him over to her locker exclaiming "Daniel Shepherd, do you realize we have never had a single class together since you moved here?"

Daniel had never thought of this, but quickly picked his jaw up off the ground, exclaiming "You're right. How is that even possible?"

"It's like fate is conspiring against us." Annie joked. "Tell you what. You and I are going to sit down and figure our schedules out so that we can take at least ONE class together before we graduate next year. Heck, we'll take them ALL together, or at least have the same lunch shift so we can eat with each other every day."

Daniel replied, "Yeah, I would like that."

"So, it's a plan?"

"It's a plan."

"Promise?" Annie inquired.

"Promise." Daniel answered back.

Annie queried, "When can we get together?"

Daniel answered, "Maybe next week? You check your schedule and I'll check mine and we'll definitely find a time to do it."

Annie agreed and Daniel continued on down the hall thinking *Why does Annie even care?* And then: *She's really cute. Maybe I should ask her out...* and also: *Why is she wearing bowling shoes?*

His thoughts were interrupted when Aden Crow shoulder rammed him saying "Watch where you're going, Shepherd."

The guy was a real jerk, glaring back at Daniel with those beady black eyes, but even he couldn't dampen Daniel's spirits today. It wasn't just that he and Annie had never had a class together. They even went to the same church, but she rarely took part in youth group events. He would see her across the sanctuary on Sunday mornings sitting with her family, but Daniel was often busy helping in the children's ministry and they rarely had the opportunity to speak. The two barely knew each other, yet he felt so hopeful, brimming as it were, with fresh optimism.

His good mood only continued to improve. After classes let out for the day, Hannah Farmer and her best friend Gabby Shoemaker came running through the hallway tossing orange flyers and handed him one directly. It was an invitation to a Halloween party.

Hannah said "Hope you can come, Daniel!"

"Wait. It's Friday. Don't you have to cheer for a football game tonight?" Daniel asked as he furrowed his brow.

"Nope. It's our bye week. No Friday night lights tonight," Gabby replied.

"There's no game this evening, so the team has an extra week to get ready for the District Championship next weekend," explained Hannah.

"But wouldn't they have had to plan that far in advance?"

"I guess they were...confident," Gabby answered.

"The pre-season polls all had them ranked top five in the state," Hannah added.

"We're hoping they win it all this year. It would be so much fun to cheer in a state championship game," Gabby said.

"Anyway, having a Friday night off makes this the perfect night for a party, doesn't it?" Hannah asked, elbowing Gabby.

"Yeah, sure," Gabby added. "And Annie will be there," she suggested with a knowing grin as Hannah locked elbows with her and pulled her along, skipping down the hall, saying "Hope to see you there," over her shoulder.

The invitation contained a map with directions to a costume party and hayride out in the flats West of town at Hannah's house from 8:00 pm until midnight. Mixed feelings of excited anticipation, nervousness and concern flooded his brain. Daniel's devout family generally frowned on All Hallows Eve soirees and he knew his parents wouldn't be happy, but Annie would be there and he couldn't miss this opportunity. And then there was that unsettling feeling gnawing at his insides that evil was brewing in Lost Valley and something bad might happen if he wasn't there to stop it. He needed to be there and was determined to go. *And Annie would be there.*

Daniel left school that afternoon soaring high on the winds of wishful thinking, his feet barely touching the ground. All concerns were momentarily shoved to the side like ballast in a hot air balloon.

Jarred awake from his fanciful reverie, he abruptly slammed on the brakes in his tricked-out truck, narrowly avoiding a collision with a jacked up white 4x4 as its teen driver, Reed Jones, whipped around the corner, speeding down the block with his engine roaring. Aden Crow was riding shotgun and made an obscene gesture through the back window.

Had they just intentionally tried to hit him? Or scare him? Daniel wondered as he parked for a few moments to regain his composure.

His cool mini-truck with the high luster aluminum wheels and the sweet indigo blue metallic paintjob was nearly destroyed—not to mention the life that flashed before his very eyes. His parents had the truck painted for him as an early birthday present and he had just gotten it back from the shop. His dad figured that it would prevent the pick-up from rusting as it was getting older and would help it to last longer.

"It was a decent investment," he had said, but Daniel knew it was a sacrifice. His parents couldn't afford to buy him a new car, but fixing the old truck up was a much-appreciated gift. Daniel had to be careful to wash it by hand for a month while the paint cured, but it was incredibly beautiful. He had picked out the color himself.

After taking a few more deep, calming breaths, Daniel set out across town to pick-up his traditional Friday afternoon thin crust Pepperoni from Mr. P's Brick Oven Pizza. Nobody could bake a pie quite like Mr. P.

As he pulled into a parking spot, Daniel recognized Reed's full-sized 4x4 in the lot by its mud-streaked white paint, sports bar with off-road lights and the matching black grille with which he had a close encounter just minutes earlier. He was glad the restaurant had a pick-up window.

Treats and a Trick

Daniel and his little brother Benny polished off their half of the delicious pizza before changing into their Halloween costumes, leaving the rest of the wood fired masterpiece for their parents. They didn't want to pig out, so as to save room for sweets. Daniel had plans for later that evening, but Benny was expecting his big bro to take him Trick-or-Treating and he wouldn't let the little guy down.

Benny was proudly outfitted as a cowboy, complete with boots, spurs, blue jeans, a tasseled shirt, matching cap-gun six shooters in holsters, and an oversized yard sale rodeo buckle. The ensemble was topped off with a ten-gallon black felt hat. He was so effervescently happy that his eyes were alive with green fire dancing out from the pupil and into a blazing blue circle to complete the iris.

Daniel's hastily conceived costume began with faded jeans and an old pair of his dad's western boots. Rummaging through the front closet, he found a full-length gray duster coat and a battered brown, pinch front cowboy hat with a dark leather hatband decorated by turquoise stones. He fetched an old-fashioned sheriff's badge out of his childhood toys, placed it on the duster and then pinned a replica deputy badge on his little brother. As they prepared to walk out the door, he put the hat on, took a quick look at his reflection in the mirror, smiled, and then grabbed a toy rifle pop gun to carry, just for fun.

Benny hummed happily as his big brother proudly paraded him around the block and into the surrounding neighborhoods collecting candy in a black, plastic jack-o-lantern with a bright orange glow-in-the-dark face. They were venturing a few blocks over to the riverfront where the houses were a bit larger, hoping to find some full-sized candy bars, when Daniel bumped into his new crush Annie Wheeler, taking her little sister Lucy on the rounds, apparently having the same idea. Lucy invited the boys to come with them and Daniel quickly agreed. Benny gave his brother a big wink and played along, sharing some candy with her (a few pieces of the good stuff). Daniel smiled at his pint-sized wingman, thinking, *maybe I'll take him out for a waffle cone at Aunt Polly's Old-Fashioned Ice Cream Parlor this weekend.*

Annie and Lucy were dressed in lavish Renaissance dresses. Annie's was an elegant floor length gown sewn from emerald green velvet and trimmed with white satin and lace. The stitching was exquisite. Her sky-blue eyes danced when she spoke and her Auburn hair was styled in soft waves and curls that gleamed in the moonlight.

Lucy's dress was a light pink satin, contrasted with the same white lace and satin as her sister's. Her blonde hair was curled into spirals with a pink satin bow and ringlets of ribbons that matched her dress and she had the same blue eyes as Annie. Lucy had on comfortable white tennis shoes, hidden when she was standing up.

Daniel complemented Annie on her gown. "Your dress is amazing. Did you rent that from a costume shop?"

"No, Annie laughed playfully. I made these from some old curtains and leftover flag fabric the Band Director put beside the trash can in the music room to be thrown out. I snatched it up after choir. I found some lace in my mom's scrap drawer and created my own pattern.

"Wow. You're really talented. This is skillful work. It's incredible, and an awful lot of effort for Halloween costumes."

"Thanks," Annie blushed. "We'll be able to wear them to the madrigal dinner this winter at Riverbend Junior College and again next Spring when we go to the Renaissance Fair in Lake City."

"Sounds like fun," Daniel hinted hopefully. Annie just grinned mischievously.

Just then, as Benny and Lucy were gabbing along pleasantly and starting off toward a promising looking house across the street with a steaming cauldron on the porch, an old brown Chevy Nova came speeding down the block. Daniel and Annie had to grab the two kids and practically tackle-pull them back over the curb and out of the way.

"What's with that lunatic?" Annie asked.

"That Frank Evans is a real menace," Daniel answered.

Lucy started to cry a little bit, but Benny put his arm around her and comforted her as they sat up.

"What a sweetheart," Annie whispered to Daniel.

Benny's hat had been knocked off revealing his blonde hair, curled up around the edges of the hat ring. Pretty soon he and Lucy were chatting excitedly about the possibility of candied apples or his favorite popcorn balls. It was adorable. Annie and Daniel just smiled at each other, eyes glancing at the kids and then back toward one another as he offered her his hand, helping her to her feet. She placed a hand on his chest to balance herself and they lingered there for a long moment, before awkwardly stepping back.

Daniel picked Benny's hat up off the ground and put it back on his head, saying "Giddy up cowboy." Benny laughed as his brother lifted him up and sat him on his feet. Annie helped Lucy up and dusted a few stray leaves off of her dress. As the group walked down the block, a mouthwatering scent wafted toward them. "What do you think that smell is Benny?" Daniel asked.

"Mmm. Smells yummy, but I don't know," answered Benny.

"I do. I know," chimed in Lucy. It's the cinna-pecans."

"What are those?" wondered Benny.

"Roasted pecans glazed with cinnamon and sugar. They're amazing. Doesn't it smell wonderful Annie?"

"I don't know, Lucy," answered Annie. "I still have parosmia from that strange cold I had. I can't smell much of anything so I'll have to take your word for it. At least my taste buds are beginning to come back."

"What's purr-nose-mia?" Lucy asked.

"Puh-ROSE-mia," Annie chuckled. "It's where your nose doesn't work quite right. Some things smell really weird, others have no scent at all."

"I'm sorry," said Benny.

"No worries, Benny. I'll be alright. I caught a cold from Hannah, who got it from Gabby who came down sick after a girl sneezed on her at the doctor's office. When she went back, the doctor said it was nothing to worry about and should only last a few weeks," assured Annie.

"Can we get some cinna-pecans now?" begged Lucy.

"You bet," said Daniel. "My treat. Look, I see where that smell is coming from!"

He used his pop gun to point up ahead toward an impromptu snack stand where they were delighted to find the aromatic pecans, sweet candied apples and hot apple cider. They took their treasures and sat on some hay bales sharing the delectable treats.

Daniel commented "This block doesn't mess around."

Benny asked Lucy "Are you coming to the Harvest Carnival tonight?"

"Maybe," Lucy replied.

"If you come, we can ride the train together."

"I like the train," Lucy said with a smile.

Man, the little guy is a natural, unlike myself, Daniel thought. He was quite shy, sometimes awkward and rather hesitant around girls.

After a few more candy stops, it was time to head back to the house. They said their goodbyes, bashful looks were exchanged and the boys set off toward home. It was nearly dark by the time they arrived at the parsonage but the night was still young.

Benny hugged Daniel and said "Thank-you for taking me Trick-or-Treating."

"You're welcome, buddy. I had fun," Daniel replied.

Benny munched on a few pieces of candy while they waited for their parents to get home. Daniel took the opportunity to indulge in one of his favorite pastimes, writing in his diary, though he preferred to call it a journal. He had just finished recording the events of the day when his parents announced their arrival. They would walk Benny across the large, vacant double lot next to their home and over to the very kid-centric Harvest Carnival at church where games, goodies, and golf-cart train rides with Lucy and Benny's buddies, the twins Coop and Mason, awaited. This year, Daniel had different plans.

His Dad gave him a bit of a *look,* when he brought up the party, but Daniel was a good kid who practically never got into trouble and in his opinion, attending a simple hayride wasn't too much to ask. Mr. Shepherd told him it was his decision if that's what he *really* wanted to do. Daniel said "Thanks," and flew out the door before the good Reverend could change his mind, or impose a curfew.

The Party of the Decade

On the way to the party, Daniel swung by Freddy's house to give him a ride. Burger Barn had called Nick in at the last minute to take an extra shift so he was working the pick-up window and would have to miss out on the evening's festivities. Freddy was decked out in full pirate regalia, accessorized with a captain's hat, eyepatch, a plush toucan on his shoulder, a plastic scimitar and a white rum bottle, which he swore contained only water. Daniel smelled it to verify. Freddy was also carrying a roll of duct tape. "What's that for?" asked Daniel.

"Aaarrrrrrr, you'll see," answered Freddy.

You'll see, mimicked the parrot on his shoulder

"Aye. That he will," said Freddy.

That he will. That he will, mocked the parrot, as the corners of Freddy's mouth twitched suspiciously.

"Hey, you missed your turn," Freddy said, breaking back into his normal voice. "It'll take an extra ten minutes to go the long way around the sticks."

"Yeah, but this road is safer," Daniel replied. "We've got plenty of time."

"Whoa," said Freddy as they finally pulled into the drive. Cars were parked in the grass along the lane, so Daniel backed his little pickup truck into a spot to make it easy to get out when they were ready to go home (and to show off his brand new blue paint job).

"Whoa indeed," echoed Daniel as they entered the back yard through a side gate.

The front half of the yard was done up like a street fair with lights strung back and forth between the full, covered, wraparound porch of the house and an elevated pergola with a wooden deck in the middle of the yard. In the back half of the lawn, the warm glow from the traditional incandescent bulbs gave way to the purplish glow of black lights running between the pergola and the t-shaped post of an old clothes line by the fence. In the corner of the yard under the black lights was a three-sided shed which had been repurposed for the evening to host some do-it-yourself DJ equipment. Two rotating colorful lights shot through the purple darkness to reflect off of a large disco ball hanging from the front of the shed. There was another disco ball hanging in the pergola for good measure.

Under the pergola was a magnificent spread of food. Giant bowls full of mini-chocolate bars, brightly colored candies and snack mix were perched on stands in each corner. A long table was placed in the center with pinwheels, finger sandwiches, orange & black tortilla chips and colorful popcorn balls. There were three fondu pots filled with cheese sauce, chocolate dip for fruits and melted caramel for apples. There were skewers for the apples but if you wanted one, you'd have to bob for it from a big metal tub in the remaining corner. The rule of the game is that you have to take the apple down to the very bottom of the tub and bite into it, but most people just cheated and grabbed one or pinned the apple to the side to get their teeth into it. At one end of the table was a large punch bowl filled with orange, frothy goodness. There was a large water trough at the edge of the deck filled with old-fashioned glass bottles of soda on ice. Daniel put a popcorn ball in the pocket of his duster to take home with him for Benny.

"You've got to ask Annie to dance," urged Freddy.

"What?" asked Daniel, taken aback. "Why would you say that?"

"Oh, Come on man. It's obvious from the way you've been talking about running into her earlier...You *like* her. Look, there she is by the punch bowl. Go for it, ask her," insisted Freddy.

"But she's talking to Tripp Barber," Daniel protested. Graham Henry Barber the third, or Tripp, as he was known, was the resident pretty boy of Lost Valley. All the girls swooned over him and those wavy blonde locks, though his exes seemed to harbor a particular hatred for their former beaux. He tried to hand Annie a glass of punch and nearly spilled a few drops on her dress as he gestured along with whatever self-aggrandizing story he was telling.

"I'll distract him," insisted Freddy.

"How are you gonna do that?"

"I'll ask him about his car. He won't shut up about it. The other day he was like 'My new Beamer will beat any car in this lot' and then Aden Crow was like, 'Wait until I get my Firebird back and we'll find out.'

Aden had gotten two tickets in a week, so his dad grounded him from the car for a month. Apparently, he had yet to learn his lesson.

"I'm tellin' you man," Freddy continued, "One mention of that car and Trip will forget Annie's even at the party."

"No one's dancing," replied Daniel.

"Be the first," suggested Freddy with a grin. "At least go talk to her," he said as he gave Daniel a shove in Annie's direction.

Distant thunder rumbled ominously.

47

"Duhn. Duhn. Duhn," sang Freddy. Both boys laughed.

Freddy's plan worked like a charm. He picked up a popcorn ball in one hand, put the other on Tripp's shoulder and hooked him in like a fish, slowly walking him across the yard to go have a look at the beautiful new BMW. *What a great wingman,* thought Daniel. As Tripp droned on and on about his extravagant ode to German engineering, Daniel took a deep breath and made his move.

"Hi Annie," started Daniel.

"Hi Daniel," replied Annie. "Did you get Benny off to the church party alright?"

"Yeah, my parents took him over. I'm sure he's ate his weight in candy by now."

"My parents took Lucy down too. I bet they're having a marvelous time on that silly train. That was crazy about that car earlier, wasn't it? I can't believe he would speed like that through a street full of trick-or-treaters."

"No kidding, I can't believe how dangerous that was."

"You should try the cheese dip, it's amazing," Annie said, dipping a chip straight into the pot and handing it to him.

"Mmm. You're right. This is delicious," responded Daniel, "But whoa, hot, the afterburn, though." Fanning his mouth, he grabbed a soda and took a big gulp. "How can you stand eating that? It's got like, ghost peppers in it or something."

"My messed-up taste buds, I guess. The spiciness is probably the only reason I can taste it at all."

"It doesn't feel hot to you?"

"Not a bit."

They both laughed and Daniel was about to ask her to dance, but just then, with comically awful timing, Hannah and

THE DIARY OF DANIEL SHEPHERD

Gabby came over to interrupt. Hannah had gone full teen rock star for the party. Her huge, tightly permed blonde hair now had pink streaks sprayed into it, her sapphire eyes were surrounded with glittery blue eye shadow and her cheeks sparkled with glitter infused make-up. She was wearing bright pink canvas shoes with 4 different colors of socks layered over each other and white tights underneath an acid-washed denim skirt with a matching jean jacket. She had the collar popped and the sleeves rolled up and a hot pink t-shirt on underneath. Her arms were covered in glow stick bracelets and she had on luminescent necklaces in a variety of colors. With a toy guitar slung across her shoulders like a backpack, she looked like she was ready for her upcoming shopping mall concert tour.

Gabby seemed a little bit happier than Daniel had seen her recently. Her warm, chestnut eyes shone and her typically teased dark brown hair was straightened and woven into a single elegant braid down her back, held in place by a ponytail hook inset with a beautiful turquoise stone. Adorning her feet were tasseled moccasins with colorful, beaded patterns across the toes and around the ankles. She was decked out in a buckskin leather skirt trimmed with an elaborate bead design ringing the fringed bottom. She wore a matching buckskin blouse with fringes around the waistline and underneath the leather sleeves. Tiny beads had been painstakingly stitched into an intricate pattern across the chest. There were turquoise stones set into the beadwork on her clothes and she wore turquoise rings on her fingers as well as bracelets, earrings and a necklace to match.

"Hiiii Annie," Hannah said with a sparkle in her eyes, a raised eyebrow and an impish grin.

"We Looooove your dress," added Gabby.

"Thanks, you both look fantastic," Annie replied.

"Hey Daniel, great costume. Would you take our picture?" Hannah asked, handing him her camera.

"Sure," Daniel obliged, carefully framing the shot to get all of their awesome costumes while showing their exuberant, smiling faces.

Suddenly, a large raindrop landed directly on Daniel's nose, another on Annie's ear. One by one, ice-cold raindrops began to fall...then there were more, getting closer and closer together. Suddenly lightening split the sky, followed immediately by a thunderclap so loud it shook the pergola and the rain began to fall steady as the kids teased each other for jumping at the thunder. "Quick," shouted Hannah in a panicked voice, "Grab the food." Everyone close-by grabbed a bowl or tray and ran as fast as they could across the yard and up under the cover of the porch as the rain began to pour.

The partygoers enjoyed some food while waiting, hoping that the storm might pass. The lack of stars in the night sky wasn't a promising sign.

"This is certainly gonna dampen your plans," said Freddy, as he elbowed Daniel in the ribs. "Man, you should have seen Reed giving you the stink-eye. Him and Aden showed up while Tripp and I were looking at his car and you were talking with Annie. Reed looked like he was gonna blow a gasket when he saw you two together."

"Oh really? What did he dress up as? A horse's rear-end?

"A horse-*man* actually. They were both dressed as civil war soldiers. Aden wore a Kepi hat like an infantry soldier and Reed had on a Hardee Cavalry hat."

"Where are those jerks at, anyway?"

"I saw Hannah talking to them, pointing toward the cars as if she was telling them to leave. I'm not sure if they're still around or not."

"Good. What's Reed's deal anyway?"

"Maybe he has a thing for Annie."

"You don't think she'd go out with a guy like that do you?" Daniel asked.

"I don't know, I think you'd better worry more about Dracula over there," Freddy warned.

A sketchy looking nightstalker with greasy black hair named Charles Carpenter had whisked Annie away to the porch underneath his vampire cape to keep her dry while Daniel was busy responding to Hannah's plea for help carrying the food and was now chatting her up, offering her a cupful of punch. He was saying something weird about smells as she smiled bashfully and laughed.

"That guy really *is* a vampire," Daniel said. "The weirdo just moved in a few doors down from us."

"You missed your chance bro," interjected Freddy.

"Not helping," replied a very annoyed Daniel.

The porch was a little narrow for hosting much of a party and Hannah's mother refused to allow the guests to come inside. She had just gotten new carpet installed and would not have it ruined by a bunch of teenagers with muddy feet. Anytime someone tried to go inside, she came after them with a broom. "Shoo teenager, shoo. Go away," she'd say as she mimicked sweeping them off her porch. Her twinkling blue eyes gave away the fact that she was at least half joking and actually quite enjoyed having the young people around. She had the same shade of blonde hair as her daughter, though Hannah was taller than her mother, taking after her father who was a classic tall, thin, farmer with brown hair and kind eyes that sparkled with amusement at his beloved wife who eventually compromised, allowing one person at a time to remove their shoes and go inside to use the bathroom, "but just for emergencies."

The rain had lightened from a downpour into a steady drizzle with no signs of stopping anytime soon when Hannah came up with an idea. She and Gabby had carefully planned a route for a hayride later that night which was to be a major attraction of the party. Two small flatbed trailers were prepped, ready to go and sitting out in the pasture beside the house hooked up to tractors. They were next to worthless right now, but beside them, power washed and "clean" was a large box cattle trailer hooked up to her father's antique semi-truck. This party was going on the road.

After some begging, Hannah convinced her dad to let one of the hired hands back the box trailer up to the barn and put a row of hale bales down the middle to sit on. As the rain slowed to a drizzle, she and Gabby set up a small table and portable speakers in the front while Daniel and some others helped move the food from the porch and into the trailer. Annie transferred half the sodas into a rolling cooler and somebody poured the punch into a couple of empty gallon jugs. The girls hung a disco ball from a hook with bailing wire and plugged in a few strands of lights which they duct taped to the ceiling.

As the party prepared to embark upon this rollicking Halloween adventure, several people were having difficulty locating their shoes after they returned from the bathroom. Freddy, who had declined to help carry food to the trailer, wore a very satisfied grin across his face.

"What did you do?" Hannah accused.

Freddy quickly shuffled around the corner of the porch and then came back with all of the missing shoes...duct taped together into a giant shoe ball with all of their laces intertwined. "Arrrrr," he roared, "I be a shoe-pirate and these aarrrr my treasures." The shoe pirate was soon pelted with unwanted candy pieces and ice cubes by the booing, annoyed attendees. He narrowly avoided having fondu dumped on his head, with Hannah stepping in to prevent the waste before sending the mouth-burning cheese out to the trailer.

Daniel mumbled "Freddy's a pretty cheesy pirate, it would only have been fitting." Annie laughed as she *slowly* began to walk across the porch toward the trailer.

Daniel resigned himself to helping Freddy untangle his mess so they could get this show on the road, but Freddy said "No. While you were carrying food to the trailer, vampire boy had to go to the bathroom." Changing to pirate voice, he said *"His shoes are buried in the middle of me treasure.* Here's your chance. Walk Annie to the trailer while Charles waits for his shoes, and I'll take my sweet time untaping my masterpiece."

"Brilliant, Thank-you!" Daniel said as he gave Freddy a fist bump and winked before hurrying off to catch up with Annie...who hadn't managed to get very far. Daniel used his hat as a rain shield over Annie's head as they rushed across the yard and into the pasture.

Spooklight Road

Once the revelers reached the trailer and trampled in like livestock, they slowly pulled out of Hannah's driveway onto a patchy blacktop road. As they traversed a labyrinth of bumpy backroads, the rain eased, alternating between periods of clear skies and light drizzle. The moon peaked out from behind the darkened clouds from time to time, casting an eerie glow onto the dreary lane. A low cloudbank moved in creating a fun, spooktacular atmosphere as they drove through the fog.

The group danced some country line dances and a few brave souls tried two-stepping in an oval around the haybales in the middle of the trailer. Then the tunes slowed down. The fiddle sang and the steel guitar twanged as a country ballad began to play and Daniel Shepherd cowboy'd up the courage to walk over to Annie Wheeler. He was glad that he left his toy gun in the truck.

"Howdy, ma'am, would you like to da'yance?" he asked in his best western drawl, in perfect character with both the music and his costume.

Replying in the Queen's English, Annie said "Why yes, good sir, I would be delighted," in a manner befitting of her stunning dress.

They both laughed, then swayed in silence for a few minutes just listening to the song until Annie broke the quiet.

"Thank-you for the other day."

"For what."

"For looking at me, for noticing I was upset and breaking their stupid rules to ask if I was ok. It meant a lot. That was kind of you," Annie said.

"You're welcome. I can't believe they did that to us. It wasn't right," Daniel replied.

"I just wish they would treat us like adults instead of little kids."

"I agree. It would have been so much more meaningful to open up some sort of dialogue, like a classroom discussion, or even to let the students lead the assembly."

"That would have been so much better than the shock and awe, freak show approach."

"That sort of thing just triggers everyone's defense mechanisms and ends up doing no good anyway."

"Wow. Look at you. Daniel Shepherd, psychologist. I'm impressed. What do you want to do for a living when you get older?"

"I don't know, something where I can help people. I want to work somewhere that I can make a difference. Maybe like a teacher, or possibly even a preacher, like my dad."

"You would make an amazing teacher, or preacher. You are so compassionate. You'd be incredible at either one."

"What about you? Will I be seeing an *Annie Wheeler Designs* label in the stores one day, or perhaps your own boutique store?"

"I love to sew, but that's just a hobby. I've thought about being a choir teacher or maybe working for a church, leading the music. I really want to work with people. Kind of like what you said. I want a job where I can make people's lives better, where I can help them."

"Maybe we'll work at the same school one day."

"Or church."

"Speaking of church. How come you never come to youth group events Annie?"

"I can't stand to be around Reed and Aden. I hate to talk bad about people, but they are just too much. It makes me miserable."

"Oh, I understand, those guys are bad news. They're so awful. That's part of why I spend more time working with the children's ministry and teaching and do less with the youth group. Pretty sad isn't it."

"Yes, Daniel, it is."

After a brief quiet pause, Annie continued "It's hard to believe we've never talked like this before."

"Well, let's not let anything keep us apart anymore."

"I agree," Annie said softly as she looked up into his eyes. Almost on cue the trailer lurched, throwing the two into an embrace as Daniel caught her to keep her from falling when the truck turned from blacktop onto a gray gravel road. Chuckling with delight, neither pulled away. Nor did they notice Hannah and Gabby high-fiving in the corner, grinning ear to ear as they played ballad after ballad, watching the new couple with glee as they toasted their success, clinking soda bottles together. Annie and Daniel slow danced song after song while the rest of the world disappeared. Conversation turned into swaying cheek to cheek and then heart to heart as she laid her head on his shoulder. Daniel could hardly believe it was real. They barely noticed as the old truck cab turned from gravel onto red creek rock and from creek rock onto brown dirt. Suddenly the brakes squealed, empty soda bottles tingled, something went rolling across the floor and the hay shifted forward as the trailer came to a stop. They held onto each other for dear life until the floor stopped moving.

"We're *hee-re*," sing-songed Hannah.

"Where's *hee-re*?" Annie inquired.

"You'll *see-ee*," replied Gabby.

As they climbed out the back of the trailer, they found themselves at the beginning of a desolate, darkened, dirt road. The rain had stopped and the fog bank was beginning to lift. The moon emerged from behind the clouds, bathing the road in a soft light, it's reflection shimmering in puddles of water.

Someone in a werewolf costume howled at the moon. A few members of the party echoed in response. An eerie, distant howl echoed through the forest; the high-pitched cry of a coyote separated from his pack. Somewhere across the prairie, the pack called back.

Annie reached for Daniel's hand, interlacing her fingers with his and pulling close to his side. It was the greatest feeling in all the world. Daniel could make out the shadowy silhouettes of his peers and see the outline of trees lining either side of the road. The wind blew gently, rustling through leaves as the branches swayed. The group walked along a slight downgrade to a point where the road plunged sharply into a steep ravine. Hannah directed them to sit down and watch the top of the hill across the gully where the road reached a peak before disappearing into the downslope. As Daniel stared at the gap between the trees created by the road, he saw a dog scamper across the apex and disappear into the woods. Then suddenly, the tiniest pinprick of light appeared, slowly floating toward them, little by little becoming larger. It was just below the treetops and above the trunks. The white light began to dance around in mid-air, glowing ever brighter and larger. Some of the kids were unphased, but Daniel was astonished. The light began to zigzag back and forth and then to make an odd hum-buzzing sound and then it POPPED. Recoiling in surprise at the tiny explosion, Daniel almost fell over backward. Annie laughed. His jaw hit the ground as he saw an orange light shoot out from the original sphere and bounce across the air forming tiny semi-circles with each hop before floating back toward the source. The two lights encircled each other from a distance, then began to play, zinging and whizzing to and fro before floating away into the distance like two long lost lovers reunited at last, becoming ever tinier until disappearing from view.

"What *was* that?" Daniel asked in shock.

"That...is the Spooklight," answered Annie, "though some people call it the Ghost Light or the Will O' the Whisp. It's been around for ages. Pioneers wrote about it in books. There are all sorts of legends about what it is. One story claims that the light is the glow from the lantern of an old shepherd that died over a hundred years ago. They say he came out here from the city, searching for his lost son and when he couldn't find him, he never left. Legend has it that he still roams the hills at night, watching over his sheep to protect them from coyotes, hoping the light will draw his prodigal son back to him. When you see the two lights come together, that's father and son reunited and celebrating."

"That's not what I heard," Hannah interrupted. I've always heard that the white orb is the helmet light of a lost minor and the yellow light is a lantern, carried by his wife as she searches for him to deliver his lunch pail."

"Yellow? I thought it looked orange," Daniel argued.

"It was totally yellow," insisted Hannah.

"That was orange," he said, laughing.

59

Ye-llow, Hannah singsonged.

O-range, Annie sang back, giggling as Hannah gave her a light, playful shove.

"That's much too recent though. The light was seen long before there were minors around here," Annie protested.

"Well, I've always been told that the lights are the spirits of star-crossed lovers from rival tribes, a strong young brave and a beautiful maiden, whose fathers were chiefs that refused to allow them to marry," Gabby contributed. "The couple tried to flee so they could be together, but her father sent a hunting party to track them down. As the chasers closed in and it looked like they were trapped, the lovers took a leap over the bluff and into Lost River in an attempt to escape, but the current was up and they were swept away and apparently drowned. Their bodies were never found."

"And the lights are their souls reunited," Annie interrupted. "I really like that one. Anyway, scientists have studied it. Some claim it's swamp gas."

"But this isn't a swamp," Daniel protested.

"Exactly," Annie agreed. "No one knows what it is...only that it's *real*."

"Does it always look like that?" Daniel inquired.

"I've heard it comes closer to people sometimes. They claim it gets really big and bright and will come right through the windshield of a car. But I've never seen it do anything like that."

"We're moving closer to get a better look when it comes back," Hannah said, taking Gabby's arm. "You coming?"

"Maybe in a minute," Annie answered. Hannah gave her a not-at-all-inconspicuous wink. Gabby gave a little wave and said "Bye-ee."

Lowering her voice, Annie whispered to Daniel "Hey, my throat is still a little sore from my cold and I'm really thirsty. Do you want to head back to the trailer and get something to drink?"

"Absolutely," Daniel whispered back. "I don't know about the stories, but whatever that was is fascinating. I'm really glad I came tonight."

"Me too," Annie said.

Hell's Half-Moon

While the rest of the group lingered to see if the orbs would return, Annie and Daniel made their way back to the trailer. All of the sodas were gone and there were no water bottles left, so Annie dug out the gallon jugs from under the table and poured them a couple of glasses of punch. They sat down on the hay bales as Daniel rambled on telling her the story of his adventure at Nick's house, while Annie drank her glass of punch, coughing and choking every now and then, apologizing that her throat was really dry. She had poured a second glass by the time Daniel finally took a sip from his cup and immediately spewed it out on the floor before knocking the cup out of Annie's hand and spilling its contents on the deck of the trailer.

"Don't drink any more of this."

"What are you doing?" Annie asked, offended. "What's wrong with you all of the sudden?"

"The punch is spiked. Someone must have messed with it before it was loaded onto the trailer. Couldn't you taste that?" Daniel asked.

Annie replied "Not with my messed-up senses. I taste very little, only certain flavors. It seemed really sweet, like it had a lot of sugar in it, though I couldn't tell you what flavor it was."

"The taste was a bit off, like something a little hot and peppery that shouldn't be in punch was in the aftertaste," Daniel explained.

Annie had quickly jumped up when Daniel grabbed her glass, but was now regretting it. "I'm starting to feel a little dizzy." She grabbed on to Daniel for support as she sat back down. "What do you think is in this?" She looked scared.

63

"I don't know," said Daniel. "But you'll be ok with me. I promise I won't let anything bad happen to you and I'll make sure you get home safe."

Freddy was the first of the others to arrive back at the trailer and he helped Daniel pour the jugs out into the ditch while Annie sat on a bale of hay.

As the rest of the party slowly made their way back up the hill, Daniel sat down beside Annie tenderly placing his arm around her. Upset because she had never drank before and would not have willingly consumed alcohol, Annie laid her head on his shoulder and softly cried. She shivered in the coolness of the evening air, so Daniel put his duster coat over her shoulders.

As they rode back, Daniel noticed that Gabby was sitting on a haybale and crying. Hannah was comforting her. He wondered what happened. She seemed so happy earlier.

By the time they made it back to the Farmer's house, Annie was having trouble standing. She fastened Daniel's duster around herself for warmth and allowed he and Freddy to help her to her feet. Walking was difficult, so she clung to Daniel as he helped her across the yard but her legs began to give way so he gently placed one arm under her knees and one under her arms, picked her up and carried her around the house and toward his truck. Freddy caught the popcorn ball Daniel had saved for Benny as it rolled out of the duster pocket and then he opened the door, placing it in the console before Daniel carefully sat Annie down in the passenger seat. He was glad the mini-truck had a low stance and was easy to get in and out of. This had been the greatest night of his life up until that stupid spiked punch showed up to ruin a perfect evening. He was sick at his stomach to think of what might have happened to her or others if he hadn't been around. It was a good thing that he came.

He was so sick to death of people pulling this stupid never-ending garbage. Daniel fought back the tears, suppressing the fury welling up within his soul. Was this righteous, protective anger, or just burning rage? He resolved to prevent this from happening to anyone else ever again. His head swam with questions. What should he tell her parents? Had she driven her own car here or ridden with someone else? Should he take her to the hospital? What would his own parents say? He hadn't done anything wrong, but would they see it that way? Who did this and why? What had Annie ingested? Was something sinister going on? How many times had something like this happened to other girls?

Daniel thought back to some other suspicions he had been harboring. He knew there would be a time to seek answers and justice, but for tonight he had to remain calm. Annie needed him and he needed a clear head to get her home safely on the dangerous, curvy road ahead as they made their way down from the flats, through the hills and back into the valley below. At least he wouldn't have to pass Hell's Half-Moon, an infamous bend where the rocky hillside came right up to the edge of the road on one side and there was only a few feet of shoulder on the other. The turn off to Bethel Road, which would lead them down a longer, but safer route, was before the lethal loop. He started the truck and then took five deep, tactical breaths, in for a four count through the nose, then out for a four count through the mouth. He decided to take her home to her parents first. They would take her to the hospital if necessary.

As he reached the end of the driveway, Annie curled up in the passenger seat and fell asleep...or did she pass out? She was breathing ok. Daniel reached up and turned the radio off so as not to disturb her, thinking to himself, I might be in love with this girl. I'll take care of her. She'll be ok, she just needs to sleep it off in the safety and comfort of her warm bed under her parent's watchful eye. He stole one more quick glance Annie's way just to make sure she was alright, then pulled out of the drive, fixing his eyes on the shoulder-less road with his hands firmly gripping the steering wheel at ten and two. There were perilous curves up ahead and he needed to be paying full attention to the road...

FIVE MILES AWAY: After passing by the turn off to Bethel Road, Daniel saw what appeared to be a beam of headlights coming into view, shining straight through the curve known as Hell's Half-Moon and off into the night sky over the deadly drop-off down the hillside. Suddenly, a blinding white light streaked around the bend and flashed through the windshield. Instinctively turning his head toward her, Annie Wheeler's sleeping face was the last sight Daniel Shepherd ever saw. Annie never woke up.

PART TWO

TEN YEARS
LATER

2007

Ambush

Benny Shepherd sat down alone in the upper left corner of the old gymnasium and pulled on his favorite worn-in coat, popping the collar up for warmth. Grimy filth from decades of neglect covered the windows, but at least they could still be pushed open to let in some fresh air. The smell of new wax, soured socks, flowery perfume and scorched popcorn mingling together was more than he could stand, so even though there was a bit of a nip in the breeze, he was grateful for the relief the window seat provided. He hoped the damp, cold air would dissuade anyone from sitting too close. He noticed his pals Cooper (Coop) and Mason Hunter entering the gym late. They had walked all the way from the music building at the far end of the school and hastily grabbed seats near the door just before the assembly began. He could see them craning their necks to look for him, but he averted his eyes and feigned obliviousness. He wanted to be alone today. He needed to be alone today.

Benny shuttered, not at the cold, but at the realization that the ten-year anniversary of the crash was approaching. Halloween week, once Benny's favorite, had become the worst time of the year. On this particularly morose Monday, the county sheriff's office and local police department had sent representatives to the high school to give a special presentation to kick off red ribbon week. As Sheriff Andrew Smith droned on about the dangers of driving under the influence, his speech took a turn for the worse. Benny's stomach lurched as Sheriff Smith recalled the time ten years ago when young Annie Wheeler had taken her seat on this very gymnasium floor, her face painted white as a symbol of solemn remembrance for those killed every day by drunken drivers, not knowing she would soon become one of them. He detailed of how young Daniel Shepherd drank for the first time in his life on Halloween night, and how his selfish decision to drive under the influence had caused the tragic death of Annie, a bright light snuffed out much too soon. Benny wondered if the tear that Smith wiped from his eye was real, or just theater for added effect. He could feel eyes burning into the side of his face as his peers searched to see if he would react to the Sheriff's accusation, but Benny didn't budge, he just kept his eyes straight forward, emotionless...at least on the outside.

It wasn't fair, Benny thought. Daniel had been such a kind, thoughtful and loving brother. Why wasn't his life viewed as a tragic loss? Why was he always the villain in this story? Why couldn't anyone show the least bit of compassion or sensitivity? Did they really need to keep using Daniel as a cautionary tale, over and over again? He had lost his brother that night...and it seemed like people hated *him* for it.

Benny hunched his shoulders forward and scrunched his neck down into his coat collar, staring at the gym floor for the rest of the lecture.

After the assembly, he slung his backpack over his shoulder and bailed toward a shortcut out of the gym. By using the doors near the locker rooms, he could avoid the judgy stares, pointy comments and claustrophobic chaos of the crowd leaving through the front exit. He'd heard enough of that already. Benny never even noticed his friends trying to wave him down, but he stopped dead in his tracks when he felt a tapping on his shoulder. It was his brother's old friend Nick Baker, wearing a pair of khaki trousers, a white polo, a black jacket and black duty oxfords with non-slip soles.

"What's up Benny?" Nick asked. "Where are you off to in such a hurry?"

"I'm just trying to get out of here. Do you mind?" retorted Benny. He was not in the mood.

"I just wanted to see if you were alright."

"I'm fine. Where's your uniform...*officer?*"

"I just made detective. No more uniforms for me. They gave me the badge on the one-year anniversary of my transfer from the Ridgeview police department back home to Lost Valley"

"Lost Valley is big enough to have detectives?"

"I'm the one and only."

"Congratulations," Benny offered with a weak smile.

"Thank-you, I'm really enjoying being back in town," replied Nick sincerely, unphased by the rudeness of his old pal's little brother. "Look, Benny, if you ever want to talk or if I can do anything for you, if you ever need my help with anything at all, here's my card. It's got my cell phone number on it and I always have it with me. Don't hesitate to give me a call."

"Thanks," Benny mumbled halfheartedly as he tucked the card into his front pocket before shuffling out the door and into the misty, overcast haze of a chilly, fall day. He had hoped to escape from the parking lot before anyone else made it out of the gym, but Nick's interruption had ruined that plan.

He was almost halfway to his car when he heard them, a couple of senior guys, Riley Jones and Jason Simmons, loud-talking at him as he rushed down the sidewalk. Riley projected, "I wonder what it's like to be the brother of a drunken letch that preyed on girls and got one killed?

71

"Or to have a disgraced former preacher as a dad? What a loser, living in that creepy haunted house," Jason piled on.

Benny knew he should just walk on by. He knew they were fishing for a fight, but it was not the day for it. He'd had enough and he just couldn't take anymore. Spinning to face them he looked Riley square in the eye and said "Shut Up," before trying to continue to his car and stumbling on a crack in the concrete. Seizing the opportunity, Jason ran up and grabbed him from behind, putting him in a full nelson hold while Riley came around front, punching him repeatedly in the stomach and once square in the eye.

Then they began trying to drag him away. Benny knew where he was being taken. He had seen it before. They were going to throw him into the spit pit. They would stand at the top of the stairwell leading down to the old locked basement door, forcing him to stay in the concrete prison. If he tried to leave, they would hit and kick him back down. He would be lucky if he didn't break an arm falling on the concrete stairs. Even if he avoided physical injury, he'd be trapped down there as passersby hurled insults while hocking lugies on him. It was a disgusting ritual. Benny was revolted at the thought. This was more humiliation than he could bear. As they began pulling him through the scraggily bushes of the school's landscaping, he tried to escape but they grabbed and pulled on his front pockets, and his coat was torn in the struggle. As the material ripped, all three boys were sent tumbling to the ground. Benny jumped to his feet and drew his fist back ready to inflict swift damage to the next boy who came within reach as the two began slowly inching toward him, snarling like rabid coyotes.

"Close your mouths weirdos," Benny said.

"Oh, you're dead," Riley threatened.

Just as they lunged toward him, Officer Nick Baker appeared, standing right in the middle of them. Grabbing both boys by the front of their shirt collars to hold them back, he ordered "Break it up boys. It's all over."

"You can't touch me. Get your hands off me," Jason protested.

"Let go and get out of the way or I'll go through you," Riley said.

"Are you *trying* to get arrested?" Nick questioned. "Benny, take my wallet out of my back pocket and show these gentlemen my badge." As Benny flashed the badge, Nick looked at Riley and asked "Do you want to go to jail?"

"No."

"No, what?" Nick demanded.

"No Sir, Officer."

"Then don't take another step toward Benny Shepherd. I'm going to let go and the two of you are going to leave." Releasing them from his grip, he admonished them "Now get going." As they lingered for a moment, he brandished his handcuffs their direction and then ordered them "Move it. Now."

"We'll see *you* tomorrow at school," Riley sneered, glaring at Benny as they slowly backed away.

"Oh no, you won't. The two of you are suspended for three days," said Principal Gary Potter, who had just arrived. They froze instantly at the sound of his stern and commanding voice.

"Are you alright?" Nick asked as he picked up Benny's jacket and handed it back to him.

"I'm fine," insisted Benny, looking down at the ruined coat. The pocket was hanging off and it was ripped apart at the seams, destroyed beyond repair.

"If they give you any more trouble, or if you ever just need to talk, you've got my number, give me a ring," instructed Nick, holding his hand up like a phone.

"Thank-you," replied Benny. "I will."

Principal Potter escorted the attackers around the corner of the building to their vehicles, ensuring that they left promptly without causing further trouble. As Nick moved to provide back up for Principal Potter in expelling the criminal element from the parking lot, Coop and Mason came running up.

"You alright?" Coop inquired.

"I'm fine," muttered Benny.

"Where were you in the assembly?" We looked for you," added Mason.

"Sorry," Benny mumbled, "I was way up top."

"Well don't take off on us like that again."

"You know we've got your back."

"I know," Benny replied, finally lifting his head.

"Wanna go for a slice of pizza?" Mason invited. "We haven't got to hang out much since you were working so many hours over the summer."

"C'mon. It'll be fun," Coop insisted. "I figured you would have more time to chill once your summer job ended, but we haven't seen much of you outside of school lately."

They really are the best friends a guy could ask for, thought Benny. They were always inviting him to youth group events at their church as well, but he just couldn't go back there. At least he had two guys he could really count on, two buddies he could always trust.

"Maybe another time. I've got to get some ice on this." Benny answered, pointing to his eye. "Thanks for the invite though. I'll see you guys later," he added, before turning to unlock the door of his ten-year-old tan sedan and climbing in. It started right up with a peppy vroom. Old faithful. His dad always kept the car tuned up with a careful maintenance schedule. Benny had even helped his pops wax the old car by hand to protect the paint job. Mark Shepherd was nothing if not a faithful steward of his resources.

No one was home when Benny arrived. Figuring his mom must have had an afternoon showing, he stopped by the kitchen, grabbed a bag of frozen peas out of the refrigerator and stomped up the stairs to his room. "Hello stairway ghost," he joked as each footstep was echoed by the loose newel post at the bottom of the railing. It was funny now, not so much when he was a little kid in a strange old house, just six months after Daniel passed away. When they first moved in, between the whispering wind, the scary shadows and the phantom footfalls, Benny thought the house was haunted. He pretended the footsteps were his brother's ghost so he wouldn't have to be afraid. He was so sad and lonely, he would sit in his room having one-sided conversations, until one day his mom heard him. She was very sweet and gentle as she explained to him that the noise was just the loose railing and Daniel was in heaven, happy and at peace. Deep down, Benny already knew that.

Back-Fence Talk

Benny Shepherd looked out of his bedroom window, surveilling the picturesque valley below. The panoramic view from his turret bedroom was one of the few things he really liked about this old house. As he cracked open the window to let in some fresh air, he glanced down at the yard. At least his parents had gotten rid of that hideous fountain with the creepy cherub. It looked so out of place.

Benny's brother had always been his hero. He loved Daniel and looked up to him. Now, even after all these years, his heart still ached with a deep, insatiable grief that was tearing him apart.

This evening, his head was swimming with thoughts as the rumors of the past ten years swirled around in his mind like a whirlpool. The echoes of taunting voices from school pulled at him, sucking him down into the depths of further despair. Throughout the day in the hallways, the locker room, the lunch line, people had been whispering behind his back, repeating the same old slanderous comments about Daniel. Avoiding those voices was the main reason he sat so high up in the corner of the gymnasium for the assembly that afternoon.

Tears filled his eyes and ran down his face as he thought: It just wasn't right, what the sheriff had said. It was unnecessary and unprofessional to smear his brother's memory. The whispered rumors and seeds of gossip that were planted ten years ago continued to bear their poisonous fruit.

Everyone knew the *story* of what happened that night, or at least *thought* they did. Benny had grown up under the shadow of it. Life in Lost Valley could be divided into two parts, before and after crash. Two teenagers getting killed in a drunk driving incident shook up their little small-town world. The wreck had been horrific. Both funerals were performed with closed caskets. The sheriff's department had Daniel's truck towed away so their family wouldn't have to see it.

The hard facts of the case were very few. Daniel's truck had collided with the same brown Chevy Nova that almost ran over Benny and Lucy Wheeler earlier that evening. The truck rolled over the embankment and into the tree line where it smashed into a large oak and stopped. Daniel Shepherd was pronounced dead at the scene. Annie Wheeler suffered massive head trauma and blood loss due to internal hemorrhaging. She slipped into a coma and passed away the following afternoon. The other driver, Frank Evans, survived.

Beyond these few facts, rumors made it difficult to distinguish truth from fiction. People believed whatever they wanted to believe. Gossip is a favorite small-town pastime. Folks lean over their backyard fences to get the latest scandalous news from their neighbors or stop their pick-up trucks in the middle of the road for a quick catch up. From barber shop to bowling alley, grocery store to café, the small-town scuttlebutt never stops spreading. Accounts of the crash contained conflicting information, but that didn't stop them from repeating the stories anyway. The most common tale among the townspeople was that Daniel Shepherd was clearly intoxicated when he got behind the wheel of his truck. They believed that he came around the bend of Hell's Half-Moon at high speed with his wheels across the center line, hitting the Nova and causing his truck to flip over and roll off the road.

Annie's presence in the vehicle was a source of scandal and outrage. Her car had been left behind at the party adding fuel to the fire of speculation. Some of the teen revelers reported that Daniel and Annie were very clingy at the party, snuck off alone to drink and were all over each other walking to his truck after the hayride. They assumed the couple was leaving early to go park somewhere in the dark. This rumor gained traction because one of the officers at the scene allegedly noticed a blanket in Daniel's truck. He declared that the only reason Daniel would be carrying a blanket around in his truck was if he planned on having an illicit encounter.

A few teens noticed that Annie appeared to be practically falling down drunk by the time they left the party. Others claimed to have smelled alcohol on Daniel's breath, but said the pair surprised them by leaving the party so early and so quickly they didn't have a chance to stop them.

The most vicious rumor started small and gained traction in the weeks following the crash. The story caught on and began to spread like wildfire that Daniel slipped something into Annie's drink with the worst of intentions which is why she was acting the way she was. The detail that really threw gasoline on the flames of the small-town gossip inferno was that nearly an hour had elapsed between the time they left the party and the time the wreck was reported to have happened just five miles away down the hillside. Hannah Farmer's party ended at Midnight and many people heading back toward town saw the flashing lights of the ambulance and the county sheriff's cruisers at the scene. Local police helped divert traffic around the crash from both directions. No one leaving the party had seen Daniel or Annie for nearly an hour. The speculations about what happened during that time, when some believed Annie to be incapacitated by a spiked drink, sent a sharp, stabbing pain through Benny's stomach.

The rushing thoughts in his mind reached the top of their crescendo, threatening to drown him under the pressure. He couldn't believe it. He wouldn't believe it. He didn't believe it. He knew the truth. Daniel and Annie were friends. His brother was a kind and caring soul, a protector who would never intentionally hurt anybody. The crash wasn't his fault and he would never have hurt Annie. His brother was no rapist. He just couldn't be, but it would take some sort of shocking new evidence to convince *this* town otherwise.

The deliberations of Benny's mind returned to his bedroom and the peaceful view of the distant river before him as a gentle breeze blew in through the open window. He wiped the tears away from his eyes.

Benny pondered the fact that he had not set foot in a church building in a decade. He had been baptized as a six-year-old when he professed faith and asked Jesus into his heart the summer before the wreck. He was earnest about his decision and excited to tell everyone he met about Jesus, but what happened to his brother shook him to his core. He still believed in God, but he had some serious doubts about the church after the way his family had been treated. He had questions about the accident that had never been asked and questions about the Bible that needed to be answered but he didn't have a lot of people to talk to. Being a Shepherd made him feel like something of a pariah at school. At least he had Coop and Mason, his only close friends.

Discovery

Feeling a sudden chill, Benny closed the window, looked down at his torn coat and then into the mirror, lowering the frozen bag of peas from his eye long enough to see the shiner already forming from the beating he had taken after school. If there was one thing that never changed, it was bullies. Growing up in a disgraced family without an older brother to look out for him made Benny an easy target.

He knew that money was tight and he didn't want to ask his parents to buy him a new coat but he had a thought...his brother's old brown leather bomber jacket.

Being forced to move only six months after Daniel's death, his parents were not yet ready to cope with going through their son's belongings, so they had the movers pack up the contents of his room into boxes. These boxes had been stored in the large shed in the back yard. Even after all these years, they still couldn't bring themselves to get rid of Daniel's stuff.

Benny walked down the stairs and out the back door to the shed. Its grimy windows had been cleaned and the shutters and door were properly hung, though it still had the faded flowers along the sides as it had never been repainted. As he entered, the smell of fresh soil met his nose. His mom had been using this as a makeshift greenhouse. Slotted shelves sat underneath a window on the left side of the shed, allowing light to fall upon a few seedlings she was nurturing before incorporating them into the landscape and some tomato vines she brought inside from the garden. The back wall and part of the right side of the shed were stacked with boxes. One by one he took his pocket knife and cut the tape on the front row of old, dust covered boxes, looking for the jacket. Inside a large box marked "CLOSET," he found the coat. As he lifted it out of its resting place, underneath he saw a shoebox marked "KEEP OUT." He put the coat on, breathing in the authentic cowhide scent and the faintest hint of his brother's cologne. It fit just right and the smooth lining felt really good. His curiosity peaked by the warning to keep out, he removed the lid from the long-forgotten container, figuring Daniel wouldn't mind anymore. Inside was an impromptu time capsule containing an eclectic variety of boy treasures. There was a colorful wrist watch, a couple of hot wheel cars, a gold chain, some rare coins, a few baseball cards, newspaper clippings of his brother holding a trombone, a few pesos he brought home from a mission trip, a well-worn Bible, pictures of Daniel's friends and then he saw something that made his heart skip a beat.

Benny reached into the box and pulled out a brown leather journal with rough cut, cream-colored parchment pages. Benny unwound the leather strap binding the book and slowly fanned the pages with his thumb. It was Daniel's diary. There were entries all the way up through the last week of his life...

Benny had never believed the lies swirling about his brother for the past ten years and after that morning's assembly, he felt a renewed sense of urgency to clear his brother's good name. It wasn't right for people to remember him as an abusive, drunk driving predator. It simply wasn't true. It couldn't be.

As he was finishing up restacking the boxes, Benny heard the sound of tires crunching their way up the driveway. It was a little too early for his dad to be home from work, so Benny knew it must be his mom. He didn't want to her to be upset by seeing Daniel's diary in his hands, so he quickly put the journal back into the shoebox, clutching it under his arm to carry up to his room.

Perhaps he might be able to find something to restore his brother's reputation and vindicate their family within the pages of Daniel's diary. Nothing could have prepared him for what he was about to uncover.

He slipped in the back door and crept up the stairs to his bedroom, but before he had a chance to read, his mom called him to wash up and then come downstairs to set the table for dinner. When Benny reached the kitchen she said, "I hope you're hungry. I showed a house over in Ridgeview this afternoon, so I picked up some cashew chicken and eggrolls from Bonsai Gardens." This Ozarkian take on Asian cuisine was one of Benny's favorite dishes. Delectable chunks of white meat chicken breaded and deep fried in peanut oil, then topped with cashews and green onions with a savory brown sauce poured over fried rice smelled so good it made his mouth water. Somehow moms always know, but she asked anyway.

"Benjamin Levi Shepherd, what happened to your eye?" she inquired softly, holding her hand over her mouth in shock.

"Did you get in a fight?" his father asked as he sat his keys down on the counter. Benny's mom gave her husband one simple sideways headshake while raising her eyebrows.

"No, I didn't fight anyone. A couple of Seniors jumped me after school today."

"For no reason?" asked his father.

"They were saying awful things about Daniel and about you and I told them to shut-up and they attacked me."

"Who were these boys?" Mr. Shepherd demanded.

"It was Riley Jones and Jason Simmons. Principal Potter kicked them out of school for three days."

"Jones. That family," his mother sighed.

"I'm going to call J.C. Jones right now," Mr. Shepherd said as he slammed his wallet down on the counter.

"Don't. It'll only make things worse. Nick Baker was there to stop it and the principal caught them. Just let it go. Please. It's embarrassing. I just want to forget about it."

"Does it hurt? Do you need any medicine?"

"No mom, I'm fine."

"Well, be sure to keep ice on it."

Benny waved the bag of frozen peas. His mom quickly changed the subject and began talking about her landscaping plans as Benny dug into the delicious feast. He felt much better as the food settled into his stomach.

"Why do we live here?" Benny asked.

"What do you mean?" replied his father.

"Why do we stay in this old house, in this town?"

His parents exchanged a grim look. His mother spoke first. "When your father was fired from the church, we were only given one month of severance pay and we only had thirty days to vacate the parsonage in town."

"Why did they only give us one month to move?" Benny inquired.

"They said they wanted the house available for the new pastor immediately," his mom answered.

"But instead, when they hired one, they moved his family into a luxurious new home out in River Glenn Estates, a development owned by one of the deacons...J.C. Jones."

"Riley's father," Benny mumbled.

"Anyway, most ministers live paycheck to paycheck," his father explained. "We didn't have any savings and my position at the lumberyard, now called Baker's Home Improvement, was the first job I could find."

"Our finances were really tight," Mrs. Shepherd explained, "and the Bakers have always been very kind to us. Mr. Baker hired your father and they had this home they were renovating when the housing market collapsed."

"People want to move to a safe, idyllic small town, not a community embroiled in scandal. With the recent...tragedies and rumors of risky adolescent behavior going around, no one wanted to buy a house near Lost Valley and prices dropped very, very low," Mr. Shepherd expounded.

"Donna Baker was helping me get my real estate license and showing me the ropes," Mrs. Shepherd continued, "The real estate market was much heathier in the surrounding towns and it was a good source of income. She and her husband Josh had been saving up for their dream home and one day we went to look at a house that was exactly what they had been hoping for. The owners wanted to move away from Lost Valley and the price of the property had just been drastically reduced."

"They offered to sell us *this* house at a fraction of what they had planned to make after finishing the renovations," Mr. Shepherd continued. "They had brought the plumbing and electrical work up to code and they had refinished the floors and painted the outside. By saving on the rest of the renovation costs, they were able to let us have it for a modest profit, just enough for them to be able to purchase the home they wanted."

"They really did us an extraordinary kindness. And with the short time frame we were working with, they were willing to let us move in right away, even before we closed escrow," Sarah

Shepherd explained. "I felt that a place like this outside of town would provide some privacy and an opportunity to heal."

"And a place to escape from the sideways glances, malicious whispers and judgmental attitudes," Mark Shepherd added.

"People were very unkind," Benny's mom said, wiping a tear from her eyes.

"But why didn't we ever move away?" Benny persisted.

"We could never afford another place with this much potential," his dad answered.

"And I wanted you to grow up close to your grandparents. I wanted you to see your cousins at family gatherings and to be able to keep your school friends, especially Mason and Coop." his mom explained.

"I know it's been difficult, Benny. It's been hard on us all," his father empathized. "But sadly, life is difficult wherever you go. At least here we have family and a few close, loyal friends. It was Josh Baker who convinced the other deacons to allow us to keep that tan sedan you're driving now as part of my severance package from the church."

"Not that they wanted the car. One of the deacons, Lester Crow, was already planning to sell the church a shiny new luxury SUV to help them lure in a new pastor," Mrs. Shepherd commented.

"Very true," her husband conceded, "but if Josh Baker hadn't stepped in, they might have held on to the car just for spite. With our truck wrecked, we would have been in real trouble without it."

"God has been so gracious to us. He has always provided for our needs," his mom added.

"I believe he worked through the Bakers to show us compassion and the love of Jesus when we needed it the most," Mark Shepherd added.

"Just like he did today with Nick showing up right when you needed him," Sarah Shepherd concluded.

After supper, Benny went up to his room and closed the door. A strong breeze whooshed loudly through the trees and he looked out the window to see branches bending back and forth under the gale as heavy drops of rain began to beat against the window. After lowering the blinds and closing the curtains to muffle the sound, Benny picked up Daniel's diary. The binding was broken in such a way that when he unwound the leather strap holding it shut, the diary fell open to Saturday, October 25, 1997. He smiled as he read about his brother's haunted adventure with his two best friends, right here in this very room. Daniel had been recording his deepest thoughts, personal secrets and grandest excursions for nearly a year. There were so many memories to sift through. As Benny thumbed through the pages, he came upon an entry where Daniel had documented a disturbing observance.

Tuesday, September 2, 1997

Another girl was crying at school today, uncontrollably. Since last spring, it seems like at least once a month a different girl is sobbing in the hallways. At first, I thought it was just relationship drama. Now I'm starting to think that something else might be going on. These girls seem beyond sad and more like despondent. I think something bad may have happened at a back-to-school party over Labor Day weekend.

Benny closed the diary and flopped down on the bed in shock. He ran his fingers through is hair and just held his hand there on the back of his neck for a minute. What on earth had his brother stumbled onto?

Tuesday, October 30

Gotcha Day

The next morning, Benny awakened to the heavenly smell of breakfast in bed as his mom gently patted his shoulder, "Benny wake-up. Happy Gotcha day."

She had made a feast of his favorites. Benny's mouth watered at the sight of fresh baked apple, peach and cherry Kolaches with cream cheese and thick, smoky slices of bacon. She even cooked up her signature scramlets which were cubed potatoes sautéed with bell peppers, chopped white onions and country sausage, held together by scrambled eggs, crumbled over with white corn tortilla chips and topped with sharp cheddar cheese.

The family ate together on TV trays around Benny's bed. It was a cherished Gotcha Day tradition. Benny, had been adopted by the Shepherds and brought to the United States when he was still an infant. Each year on the day that he was adopted, they celebrated his Gotcha Day (because that's the day that the Shepherds *Got Him*, and made their family complete).

After breakfast, as they sipped hot chocolates topped with marshmallows, Mr. and Mrs. Shepherd presented Benny with his traditional Gotcha Day gift. Each year they would give him something special from his birth country, the former Czechoslovakia. This year's present was extra special, a gift that had been planned far in advance. His parents explained: "When we first met you, Daniel came with us. He was so excited to finally get to have a little brother...and to fly in an airplane. Daniel cherished the gifts he had received from Eastern Africa on his own gotcha days. They helped him feel connected to his Ugandan heritage, so he insisted on helping pick out one of your future gotcha day presents. Daniel went from shop to shop throughout the town square, searching for just the right gift. We saved this one especially for this year when you would be driving."

Benny gingerly removed the wrapping paper to discover a beautiful, hand carved and vibrantly painted toy truck. "It was your brother's favorite souvenir from the trip, but he didn't keep it for himself. He chose it for you and insisted on paying for it with money he earned from a lemonade stand."

Daniel had always been so thoughtful, so others-oriented. This was a truly heartwarming gift. Benny was momentarily speechless at the love expressed from his brother to select such a present, and the fact that the truck was blue, like Daniel's.

With a tear in his eye, he thanked his parents and told them how much he loved the gift. Between this carefully chosen present and the diary, Benny was even more certain of his brother's unimpeachable character. A new resilience, a stubborn determination began to set in. He resolved right then and there that he would get to the bottom of this. He would clear and restore his brother's good name. Somebody...or somebodies, lied...and Benny was going to find out who and why. But not today, this day was for family celebration.

The trio of Shepherds took the day off from work and school to go hiking. In contrast to the thundershowers from the night before, it was a crisp, fall day and perfect for nature and fresh air as the sun played peek-a-boo behind the clouds. Rain has a way of cleaning and renewing things.

Mr. Shepherd ran a hand through his once black hair which had grown salt and pepper over the past decade, though he was still fit as a fiddle. He dealt with his grief and stress through exercise, turning something awful into something healthful. He wore a broken in pair of white high-top leather sneakers with relaxed fit jeans and a navy-blue parka with the collar popped.

Mrs. Shepherd's dark hair was highlighted by a few distinguished gray streaks as well. For today's nature walk, she exchanged her typical business casual attire for hiking boots and comfortable jeans, borrowing one of Mr. Shepherd's heavy flannel shirts as a jacket for warmth. She often accompanied her husband on his evening walks and by all appearances was in good physical health as well.

After a brief walk down through a gully in the woods, they came upon a rough trail at the top of the next hill. "Our families were among the first settlers to arrive in this area. They helped to found the town of Lost Valley," Benny's mom commented as they followed along the path.

"I was just a toddler when my birth parents passed away," his dad reflected. "I was so blessed to be adopted by your Granny June and Papa Floyd, but I didn't grow up around here. That's part of the reason why I chose to attend Vista Point Bible College nearby in Ridgeview. The chance to move back to this area felt like an opportunity to connect with part of my lost heritage."

"And thank goodness you did, since that's where we met," Mrs. Shepherd added.

Smiling, Mr. Shepherd continued "It has been fascinating to learn a little bit about the history of this place from your mom. She's something of an expert."

Sarah Shepherd smiled, "Believe me, I'm no expert. But there are some interesting things about this area. The path we're following is a remnant of an old wagon trail from the pioneer days. It once crossed the grasslands of the plateau and followed along this bare ridgetop until it sunk enough into the earth to allow the wagons to safely wind back and forth down the hill and into the vast hollow we know as Lost Valley. This trail once led weary travelers past a fresh water drinking spring and across the prairie North of town to ford the river. They would traverse the waters at the shallowest point where the bed consisted of small, smooth stones, the water was clear, the bank was wide and the slope was gentle."

"Rain runoff and little springs trickling down from the hills feed the river as it flows through the valley, swelling it deeper and deeper which was unsafe for a wagon to cross," his dad cut in.

"Once they made it safely through the water," his mom continued, "they would cross the valley to enter a pass between foothills on the journey out west."

"Most of the trail has been reclaimed by the woods or long since disappeared into farmland and neighborhoods," his father added. "Game trails that twisted and turned with the landscape became horse paths which became meandering hillside roads which were eventually paved over."

"But hidden in the woods of the Ozark mountains, if a person knows just where to look, remnants of this old pioneer trail can still be found," his mother concluded.

As they hiked along the top of the crest, they came to a protruding look out from where they could see the whole valley with all of its familiar landmarks. There was the old mill out south of town, Mainstreet, the restaurants of the Riverwalk, the rusted metal water tower bearing the town's name (now only a decorative landmark) and the iconic City Hall with the county Courthouse inside.

The view was spectacular, and Benny enjoyed the peacefulness of nature along the trail. Despite getting a late start, it turned out to be a great day for spotting wildlife as the animals prepared for the coming winter. Gray squirrels scurried up Oaks and jumped from limb to limb, tucking away acorns into hollowed out trees as red-tailed hawks soared overhead riding the breeze. The family spotted a couple of cotton-tail rabbits and even startled a white-tail deer out of a thicket of wild blackberry bushes, a six-point buck that went bounding away when Mr. Shepherd got too close to its hiding spot.

They enjoyed a picnic lunch on the mountainside overlooking the pastures on the north side of town before heading back. Mrs. Shepherd had packed bologna and cheese with ridged potato chips, apples and for dessert, the leftover fruit kolaches from breakfast. It was as fine a lunch as Benny could imagine.

As he looked out over the prairie north of town, Benny noticed two coyotes snaking their way through the grass. "Is it normal for coyotes to be out in the daytime?" he asked.

"No, it's unusual," his mother responded.

"They hunt primarily at night and in the twilight hours of the evening. Anytime you see a coyote out in broad daylight, you need to be careful because there's a chance it could have rabies," his father added.

"Did you know that their name means *trickster*?" his mom asked.

"And beware, because they often hunt in pairs," his dad added. "Some people call them prairie wolves."

Benny thought of Riley Jones and Jason Simmons.

"They basically *are* little wolves," his mom continued. "They're so closely related to wolves that they interbreed. The offspring are called coywolves. I always thought that was a cute name."

"With *coy* used as a prefix that way, it sounds like you're calling them timid wolves," Benny observed.

"Well, coyotes often appear cowardly or coquettish when confronted by humans. They will shrink back and keep their distance, but never turn your back on them, they're deceitful and will circle in to catch you off guard, especially if they're rabid," his father added.

"In fact, even when healthy, coyotes are more aggressive than wolves," his mother explained. "Someone came along rather recently in history and gave them this very descriptive and clever name, but when I think about people being compared to vicious and crafty wolves in the Bible, this is definitely the type of animal that is being described."

The coyotes disappeared into the woods as the family finished their lunch and started the return trip home.

"Is that Daniel's old jacket?" his dad asked.

"Yes. Mine was torn up yesterday when those guys jumped me."

"It looks good on you," his mom hinted.

"Yeah. It fits pretty good there," his dad continued. "Did you come across anything else while you were out in the shed?"

"A box of Daniel's keepsakes. Pictures and baseball cards and *stuff*." Benny wasn't ready to tell them about the diary just yet. He didn't know how.

"Daniel used to love coming up here," his dad reflected.

"He really enjoyed being outdoors," his mom added.

"I love it too. This was a great idea," Benny concluded.

Changing the subject, his mom asked "Have you ever thought about inviting a friend to Bible study?"

The Shepherds hosted a gathering in their home each Sunday, but did not attend formal church services anymore. Josh and Donna Baker and about four other couples consisting of friends and relatives came to worship and study the Bible each week and Benny sat with them, but it's different when you're a preacher's kid, even a former preacher. He felt awkward about asking his parents certain questions and without church friends his age, Benny felt isolated and frustrated. Apparently, his mother could sense it.

"Coop and Mason really like going to the big youth group over at Riverside."

"Well, your friends are always welcome," Mr. Shepherd said hopefully.

"Cool. Thanks."

Mrs. Shepherd had optimistically brought her binoculars along, hoping to get some bird watching in though it really wasn't the prime season for it. Come springtime the forest would resound with a symphony of songbirds, but today, it was quiet, the calm after the storm. The swirling winds had blanketed the path overnight with soft, damp leaves so the families' footfalls were nearly silent. Only the peaceful sound from gentle wind waves rushing through the trees and the occasional caw-caw-caw of a lonely crow interrupted the stillness, but Sarah Shepherd remained undeterred. As they hiked back, the sun rose high in the sky, dissolving the darkened clouds into wispy white fluffs, causing a few birds to stir from their slumber.

"Most birds are heard more frequently than they are seen," Mrs. Shepherd explained, as she identified the cooing of a dove from somewhere down below. Benny thought it sounded more like *ha-WHOO-oo-who-who*, than a coo sound. He'd always assumed that was an owl hoot. They watched overhead as a gaggle of geese flew south in a wedge, while off in the distance, a woodpecker drummed into a tree. Further down the trail, Mrs. Shepherd pointed out the rusty red breasts of a pair of robins, preparing to spend the winter here, and a while later she spotted the best find of the day in Benny's opinion. A beautiful Blue Jay was hopping across the ground swallowing acorns whole. Then it cleared away a few leaves and began scratching away into the dirt. It emptied its crop of four acorns and buried them before flying up into the lower branches of a nearby tree. He would be spending the winter too. Blue jays remember where to come back for their cache, though they are also known to leave some acorns in the ground which helps the Oak trees spread around. Benny's parents were most excited about seeing a small brood of four wild turkeys, a rare find indeed.

Sarah surmised "It looks like a hen and her nearly grown poults."

Mark mentioned, "It's good to see them making a comeback. These hills used to be teaming with turkeys when the land was wild."

Mr. Shepherd was also interested in the various types of trees and explained them as they walked along the edge of the forest. The woods at the top of the hill consisted mostly of white Oak trees, their falling copper and red leaves covered the trail and more wafted down with each gust of wind, rocking back and forth before settling to the forest floor. The bright yellow fronds of the occasional black walnut tree provided a stark contrast as their seeds blackened on the ground beneath. A few honey-colored hickories and a couple of old growth, short leaf pines added depth of color to the scene while scattered sycamore trees and multi-colored maple leaves added variety. Looking over the side of the hill, Mr. Shepherd pointed out that the understory of the canopy was dotted with the heart shaped yellow leaves of the much shorter redbud trees, scruffy dark green cedars and the purple-red hue of the native dogwood. Down in the valley, near the river, a variety of yellow, orange and red maples combined with the goldenrod leaves of the ever-peeling birch trees to complete the kaleidoscope of color.

Benny reached out to touch the sticky sap oozing from the trunk of an old maple tree. "Can you get syrup out of these trees?"

"Yes," replied his dad.

"How do you get it?"

"You have to use a special tool called a spile to tap the tree."

"Where can we get one?"

"Your grandparents actually have a few antique spiles," his mom replied. "They are family heirlooms. My forebears used to sell and trade maple syrup way back when."

"How do they work?"

"Well, you tap it, then sap it. They used to tap the tree by boring out a hole with a handheld bit brace and then pushing the spile in there. They would hang a bucket underneath the tap and wait for the water to come trickling out. Once they gathered enough liquid, they would pour the buckets out into a cast iron pot over a fire and boil it down until it was syrup."

"That's pretty neat," Benny replied.

"Syrup season is so much shorter in this part of the country than it is up north that most people don't even bother with it, but these sugar maples are the right type of tree and by working diligently, our family was able to make some extra income in the past."

As the Shepherd's marched on, his parents commented from time to time about the beauty surrounding them, but Benny was too lost in his thoughts to pay much attention. That was the best part about being in nature, time to think, time to process, time to heal.

That evening, they enjoyed barbecue from Spicer's Family Smokehouse on the river. It would have been nice to eat inside the restaurant, but the Shepherd family usually attracted stares if they went out together, so Mr. Shepherd went down to pick the food up while Mrs. Shepherd called in the order and Benny set the table. They feasted at home on ribs and chicken with that sweet, smoky sauce caramelized right onto the meat. Benny's mom and dad splurged for *The Family Feast*, a two-meat combo with three family style sides. The Spicers combined country cooking and a smokehouse into one restaurant which meant that really primo side items were available. The Shepherds devoured twice-baked potatoes, savory, slow-cooked pinto beans and the best home-style macaroni and cheese west of the Mississippi. Having eaten an apple kolache for breakfast and a peach kolache with lunch, Benny had the last of the authentic Czechoslovakian pastries, a cherry kolache, for dessert. The food tasted incredible after a long day of hiking. It was the perfect ending to a glorious day.

Before bed that night, Benny pulled out Daniels' diary to do some more investigating. As he continued reading through the pages of his brother's journal, he found a mix of funny mishaps and happy moments, but there was also darkness. Daniel had expressed serious concerns over events that occurred during those first few weeks of his Senior year.

Saturday, September 13

On the pep bus on the way home from the game Friday night, some people were playing a game of 21 Questions. Someone creates a list of 21 questions then you go around the room, asking each person the same question, one at a time. The goal is to ask super embarrassing questions and if a person refuses to answer, they're out of the game. The person who lasts the longest out of the 21 rounds, or answers the most questions, is the winner. First Prize was a gift certificate to the movies. One of the most humiliating questions was how long did your first "time" last? Two girls said that they blacked out and could not remember their first-time having sex because they had no memory of the evening at all. Neither girl had ever drank before. One had consumed a wine cooler, the other a glass of spiked punch. I wish I would have made them stop the game earlier.

Monday, September 15

Today at lunch some guys were talking about the game of 21 questions Friday night. They questioned whether girls could really have blacked out from such a small amount of alcohol.

99

I don't have a clue, but Alcohol is frightening. I wish people wouldn't drink.

Daniel knew that something was going on that was causing pain and despair to the girls of Lost Valley High. Benny needed to find out what it was.

The Flower Shop

The next morning, Benny carefully removed a spray can from his chest of drawers and concealed it within his backpack. He didn't want his parents to know...

After school, he went by the local flower shop, Water's Edge Floral Designs. Every available surface was covered with white, grapefruit sized flowers in clear, plastic boxes. They were wedged onto shelves in between baskets, bouquets, centerpieces and fresh cut stems all around the shop. In the middle of each white blossom was the logo LV in offset purple letters with golden piping. Each flower was surrounded first by a ring of purple ribbon and then by a circle of gathered golden fabric.

The florist/owner, Gabby Shoemaker, was standing behind the counter holding a tube of purple glitter glue, carefully applying the letters to another bloom, preparing the Homecoming Mum in much the same manner as one would decorate a cake. Her daughter Maggie was sitting on a stool, swinging her feet back and forth, munching on a pink popcorn ball. She was already in her Halloween costume, attired as a fairy princess in a light blue dress with royal blue trim and white mother of pearl buttons, a pearl necklace and clip-on pearl earrings. She wore clear slippers and a shiny pink tiara in her hair. Seeing Benny, she picked up her pink, glitter covered wand and gave it a swish and a flick right toward him saying "Smile."

Benny grinned his cheesiest, showing the pearly whites to oblige her.

Gabby looked up for a moment to say "Hi Benny."

"Good afternoon," he answered, before proceeding to investigate the various floral arrangements. He picked out two colorful bouquets of fall wildflowers, the largest they had, made with yellow sunflowers, orange roses, wild berry stems, and a variety of mums in shades of yellow, orange, purple and burgundy, contrasted with straws of wheat in place of baby's breath. They were sitting on a cart so he asked "Are these for sale?"

"For you they are," Gabby answered, "I made them special. How are you doing...*today*?"

"I'm fine."

"These are on sale, 100% off and buy one get one free." She didn't have to ask what they were for. She knew. From the time he was old enough to ride his bicycle alone, Benny had been coming into the store every year on this day.

He had heard the rumors floating around about Gabby Shoemaker, that she was something of a wild child in her younger days. She had been disfellowshipped from Riverside Community Church her Senior year as a result of her reputation as a party girl, but that happened after the Shepherds had already been run out of the church themselves. Gabby had always been extraordinarily kind to Benny and he didn't put much stock in gossip.

"I remember the first time you came in, back when I was working here in college," Gabby reminisced. "You were just a little older than my daughter is now. I watched you from the window, riding over from your grandparent's antique store. You were so cute pedaling away on your little bicycle, trying to hold those flowers. Then you came back half an hour later, red in the face and soaked through with sweat, asking what you could get for two more dollars."

THE DIARY OF DANIEL SHEPHERD

"And you gave me a bottle of water and sent me on my way with another beautiful bouquet, a piece of Halloween candy and both dollars still in my pocket."

"Well, Annie was one of my best friends and your brother was always nice to me. It wasn't hard to figure out what you were doing. It broke my heart. Here you go," she said as she handed him the flowers.

"Thank-you."

On his way out the door he nearly bumped into Nick Baker on the sidewalk, holding a brown paper sack.

"Hey Benny. How's that eye feeling? It doesn't look too bad.

"I'm fine."

"Are your ribs ok?"

"I'll live. What's in the bag?"

"A care package. This is Gabby's busiest week of the year, making all these Homecoming Mums, plus she's designing the floral arrangements for our class reunion. She'll be working late tonight, so I brought by some enchiladas and apple empanadas. After we eat, I'm gonna watch the shop for a while so she can take Maggie trick-or-treating. You be sure to let me know if you have any more trouble with that Jones kid, alright."

"Will do."

"Take it easy Benny."

"See you later Nick."

The Graveyard

As Benny drove out to the old Shady Hill Cemetery where Daniel was buried, he jerked the steering wheel, his tires kicking up gravel as he swerved to avoid being sideswiped by a white 4x4 hogging the road as it came flying around a corner.

Each year on the anniversary of his brother's death, he put fresh flowers on the grave. The cemetery was old but well-cared for, mostly. Some graves dated back hundreds of years. Generations of Lost Valley residents had been mourned and laid to rest here beneath the peaceful shadow of vibrant orange maple leaves. Benny slung his backpack over his shoulder and carefully placed a bouquet in each hand to carry as he walked through the aging graveyard. Daniel's burial plot was near the tree line with a simple flat marker reading:

DANIEL JOHN SHEPHERD
NOVEMBER 11, 1980 – OCTOBER 31, 1997
BELOVED SON AND BROTHER

Benny knelt down and retrieved the can of graffiti remover from his bag, along with a few shop towels. He slowly began to erase the profane and hate-filled words that always managed to find their way onto his brother's headstone. It was good that his parents never visited the grave. It would break their hearts even more to see Daniel's burial site desecrated this way. A few tears filled his eyes.

"There you go big bro. Good as new," he said after the task was finished. He then gently placed the flowers in their holder and spoke these words. "I don't care what they say. I know you are innocent and I promise I am going to prove it. I love you, Daniel."

After a few deep breaths, Benny wiped the tears from his eyes with his shirt to avoid getting chemicals from the graffiti remover in them. He then proceeded to Annie Wheeler's grave to repeat the ritual. He was only ten years old that first trip when he rode his bicycle out here and saw that she and Daniel's tombs had been vandalized. He cried hard. He had placed his brother's flowers in their holder and peddled as fast as he could back to his grandparent's store to get some damp towels and then returned to the flower shop to get a bouquet for Annie. He had scrubbed and scrubbed, but the ugly words just wouldn't come off. Now he knew better.

Annie Wheeler's tombstone was of the upright variety, larger than Daniel's and more elaborate, which made the graffiti much more noticeable...and horrible. He carefully removed every trace of the spiteful, vulgar words that had been spray painted onto her grave marker and then placed the beautiful fall floral arrangement into its holder. Just as Benny stood up to turn around, he heard a short gasp. It was Lucy Wheeler. She had watched the whole scene as she walked across the graveyard.

"Hi Benny."

"Hi Lucy. Sorry, I was just, uh..."

"Removing the graffiti? I've seen it before. I know what they say."

"I'm sorry."

"Why are *you* sorry? Thank-you for cleaning it off."

"You're welcome."

"Did you bring these flowers too?" Lucy asked.

"Yeah. I just felt like they should be shown some respect, especially today."

"For what it's worth, Benny, I've never believed the rumors, not any of them. My sister was not promiscuous and I don't believe your brother would have ever done anything to intentionally hurt her either. Annie talked about Daniel after we finished candy collecting together...*that* night. She really liked him because she thought that he was a genuinely good person and she knew he was a Christian. You saw them together. He was shy and a perfect gentleman. He saved us from that car, and bought me cinna-pecans. He was kind and sweet."

"Thanks for saying that, Lucy. It means a lot."

Lucy had always been gracious to him. She never blamed him for their sibling's accident and untimely deaths. Unfortunately, he rarely got to see her. After what happened with her sister, Lucy's parents had chosen to homeschool her.

"Do you remember the train rides that night?" Lucy asked.

"I'll never forget it. Those were so much fun. That was my last night of childhood innocence."

"You kept hollering, 'More, more, one more time,' and your dad would take another loop around the parking lot."

"Zooming around the curves," Benny laughed.

"Look," Lucy handed him a small photograph in a frame with a stand on the back. It was of Annie, that night at the Halloween party. "Do you remember those dresses Annie made for us?"

"Yes," they were fantastic.

"I still have them. About a week after we laid Annie to rest, Sheriff Potter, who was a deputy back then, had that dress cleaned and repaired and brought it to our house along with her personal effects from the hospital after the police were finished with them. If I have a daughter someday, maybe we'll wear them together."

"I'll never forget the day he came to our house to deliver Daniel's tool box and the contents of his glove compartment: safety glasses, mowing gloves, a tire gauge, an ice-scraper, a stocking cap and a pocket-knife. Daniel was always very practical. How was the dress..."

"Not stained?" Lucy finished. My mom asked Sheriff Potter the same question. My sister was wearing your brother's full-length duster over her dress when he found her. It was ruined, but that also shows that Daniel cared enough about Annie to give her his coat. I didn't know much about your brother, but I trust my sister's judgement. That's why I've never believed the rumors."

Looking down at the frame she asked "Don't the girls look happy in that picture?"

"Yes. I recognize Gabby Shoemaker, but who's the pop star?" Benny queried.

Lucy gave a little laugh, "That's Hannah Farmer. She and Gabby were the hosts of the party that night."

"Ok, now I recognize her. The giant pink-streaked hair and blue eye make-up just threw me off. I haven't talked to Hannah since I was six years old when she helped me create Noah's Ark out of popsicle sticks for Arts and Crafts time during Vacation Bible School."

"Aw," Lucy responded. "Hannah's back in town, staying at her parent's place for a few days. She couldn't stand always being thought of as the girl who hosted the notorious party the night of the accident so she lives over in Lake City. She owns a boutique, Sissy's Closet, where she re-sells gently used fashions, vintage clothing and jewelry. She prefers the anonymity of big city life.

Anyway, they were going through some photos for their upcoming class reunion and found this picture that Daniel took. Hannah thought I might like to have it, so she brought it by the house. I made a copy to bring down here to put on Annie's grave today. I'm hoping it might discourage the vandals. It makes me happy to think of her this way, so vibrant and full of life."

Benny handed the picture back to Lucy and she solemnly placed the frame on the flat block at the base of the tombstone, angling it slightly so as not to cover up any of the engraving.

"Was there anything else...*strange* with Annie's belongings when Sheriff Potter brought them by?"

"What a bizarre question to ask," Lucy replied, furrowing her brow. "Come to think of it, yes. There was a red bandana. He said it had been wrapped around her head, like someone tried to stop her wound from bleeding. He washed it and brought it to us so we would at least know that someone tried to be a Good Samaritan and help her. By the time he arrived at the scene, no one else was there. He figured they might have gone to look for help."

"Wow. I never heard that before."

"We never found out who it was."

For a minute, the pair simply stood there, observing a moment of quiet reflection, breathing in the cool, autumn air and listening to the breeze sing through the trees. Breaking the silence, Lucy said "I miss seeing you at church, Benny, like when we were little. We don't go to Riverside anymore," she quickly added. "We've started attending services over at Hilltop Bible

Church. I've been going to youth group on Wednesday nights and I really like it. It's a small group, just twelve to fifteen people and everyone is super friendly."

"That sounds cool."

"It is. You should come visit sometime. Supper is at 6:00 and then we have worship and a lesson. Afterwards we play Foosball or hangout, drink hot chocolate and listen to music. It's pretty chill. You'd like it...and *you'd be welcome*," she said with raised eyebrows and a little extra emphasis.

"I'll think about it."

"You should come tonight. There'll be special treats...but without all the Halloween hoopla."

"That might actually be kind of nice. But I'll have to ask my parents, they won't be too keen on the idea of me going out on Halloween night."

"Mine are the same way, but surely they'll make an exception for church?"

"Maybe," Benny shrugged. "It was good to see you Lucy," he said taking a few steps toward his car.

"It was nice to see you too," Lucy exclaimed as she bounced over and leaned in, giving him a short, awkward hug. "Thanks again for taking care of Annie's grave."

"You're welcome, Lucy. See you later."

"I hope you mean that. Promise you'll ask your parents?"

"I promise," Benny replied with a sheepish grin.

"Here, Hand me your phone. Let me give you my number...in case you need directions or something."

Benny smiled and happily granted her request.

"There," she said as she handed the phone back to him. "Now you've got my number if you need to call. Goodbye Benny."

"Bye."

The Stone Chapel

"Hi Benny. How was your day?" his mom asked as he walked through the door."

"Fine."

"I made a batch of scotch-a-roos this afternoon. Would you like one?"

"I'd love one."

Benny bit into the heavenly confection, closing his eyes to savor the flavor of crispy rice cereal magically transformed into bars with melted butterscotch chips and peanut butter, topped with a generous layer of chocolate. "Thanks mom. These are amazing."

"You're welcome. I figured since you won't be going out...on this night...you should at least have some nice treats. I'm going to make..."

Benny interrupted. "About that. I ran into Lucy Wheeler today while I was putting flowers on Daniel's grave." He paused to gather his courage. "She invited me to come to youth group tonight, over at Hilltop Bible Church. I know you don't like me going out on Halloween, but she thought, and I hoped, maybe you could make an exception? Since it's for church. It's not very far."

Just then his dad walked into the room, he had heard. He and Mrs. Shepherd exchanged an eyebrow raise and a little grin. "I think that would be fine."

"Thanks!" Benny exclaimed. "I'm gonna go get ready. They'll feed us supper there. Is that alright?"

"Yes, that's alright," his mom replied.

"I'll drive you," his dad added, his eyes pleading.

"Sure Dad," he accepted the compromise. "Thanks."

"You're welcome, son."

Thirty minutes later, after a shower and a bit too much cologne, Benny was ready to head out the door. He had exchanged his typical t-shirt for an untucked navy-blue button-up with rolled sleeves. In place of his cross-trainers were a pair of light brown leather shoes and he was wearing artistically faded jeans. His normally free-blown hair was air-dried and styled with a bit of mousse and a bunch of hairspray.

"Dad, why haven't you ever tried to find a job as a pastor again? Benny asked as they drove down the road.

"Son, I wasn't just fired from Riverside. I was defrocked, so to speak. Not that I would ever wear actual robes, but they revoked my ordination. No church wants to hire a pastor without a ministry license."

"But how could they do that?

"During Bible college, I worked as the part time youth pastor at Riverside. That church ordained me into the Gospel ministry. After graduation, before we had you kids, I accepted a full-time position as a pastor and we moved away. Whenever the senior pastor position opened up back here in Lost Valley, Josh Baker reached out to your mom and I and asked us to consider applying, so we moved back. Because Riverside Community Church ordained me, they had the power to retract their endorsement of me."

"But that isn't right. Why did they do it?"

"The deacons were grumbling about your brother coming in late to church and then they heard rumors about Daniel playing hooky from school and skipping out on a church event to go to a wild party where he was allegedly seen dirty dancing. Once the story circulated that he had been drinking and driving, they declared me unfit to be a pastor. They cited 1 Timothy 3:4 to claim that a parson whose son was so obviously out of control was disqualified from ministry."

"He was late for church like once, ever and you can't blame him for ditching school. They were making students walk around in white-face all day. Besides being really creepy, it was racially insensitive." Benny winced at his overshare, hoping his dad wouldn't ask how he knew about that. He wasn't ready to reveal the diary yet.

"I know son. That's why your mother and I let it go. We figured if drinking some root beer floats and fishing with his friends was Daniel's idea of rebellion, then we had raised a pretty great kid. I'm impressed you remember that."

"Do you believe the other things they say about Daniel?"

"Your brother might have made a few mistakes, but he was a good boy, a fine young man. No, I do not believe the majority of what they say."

As they pulled into the church's gravel parking lot, the pastor came walking over to meet them. After introducing himself as David Miller, he shook Benny's hand and motioned toward a stone building where a door marked *Chapel* showed him where to enter to find the rest of the youth group. As Benny made his way to the entrance, Pastor Dave stayed behind to speak with Mr. Shepherd.

Benny was nervous as he approached the door alone. He rarely attended social functions and when he did go out, he was always flanked by Mason and Coop, whom he had known since they were toddlers together in the nursery at Riverside Community Church.

Lucy greeted Benny with a quick hug and a cookie as he entered the youth room. Her silken blonde hair had been released from its ponytail into an attractive side part. She wore dress jeans that flared over a stylish pair of suede boots. A skillfully stitched, V-neck, periwinkle peasant blouse completed the outfit.

The chapel had been a small country church once upon a time. Years ago, before the church went into decline, they had built a larger sanctuary and this space had been converted into a dedicated area for the student ministry.

To the left, a few students were drinking sodas while lounging in a sitting area on well-used and comfortable looking couches. There was a small bookshelf filled with books, games and music.

On the right was a coffee and cocoa counter where students were holding steaming mugs while sitting on tall stools at the bar top or at one of the few scattered tables with mismatched chairs. Burgundy area rugs tossed over knotty wooden floors added warmth to the spaces by the couches and the counter.

On the far end of the room was a small, step-up platform. In the center of the wall was an archway inset with a stunning stained-glass window depicting sunrise over the Sea of Galilee. Antique lanterns were mounted on either side of the glass with dimmable modern bulbs burning within them. The remainder of the wall displayed the craftsmanship of the skillfully selected stacked stones. The other interior walls had been updated and covered with dry-wall which was painted a warm taupe color and carefully framed to showcase the original windows and lantern holders. Each side was adorned with two stained-glass windows and three evenly spaced lanterns. Each window displayed a

Biblical symbol. One featured a cross, one a dove, one the outline of a fish and the last one had a shepherd's crook. Matching lanterns were suspended from the vaulted wood-beam ceiling, preserving the historic charm of the chapel, while providing abundant light.

In the middle of the stage was a cross-shaped pulpit carved out of age-darkened wood. To the left was a keyboard on an X-stand hooked up to a large tube amplifier. There was an acoustic guitar on a stand, a couple of microphones and a percussion station that included some congas, a cajon and a trap table full of accessories. In the back corner was an old eight-channel mixer with quarter inch cables running to speakers placed at the front corners of either side of the stage. To the right was a bass guitar on a stand with a kickback amp behind it and next to that was an electric piano. Behind them, in the corner, was a drum set.

"Isn't it cool?" Lucy asked.

"It's awesome," Benny agreed. "This is a pretty large room for such a small group."

Lucy replied "The church that used to meet here had dwindled down and almost died as older members passed away and young families flocked over to Riverside, drawn in by the amenities a large church has to offer. Pastor Dave is diligently working on a replanting strategy which includes our new name, Hilltop Bible Church."

"I like it," Benny replied.

"Come on, I'll introduce you to the group."

About half the students were from Lost Valley and the others went to school in Grainfield, eight miles to the Northeast, as the crow flies. Some of them only lived five or six miles from the church. Everyone was really nice. Benny was glad to eat his cookie while they talked, giving him an excuse to listen without having to think of something to say.

They opened with an awkward ice-breaker game which gave Benny the opportunity to learn everybody's name. As the students made their way to seats near the little stage, Lucy excused herself from Benny's side and took her place behind the keyboard.

They sang worship songs for about thirty minutes, a combination of familiar hymns and newer favorites. Tonight, the praise band was using the left side of the stage. Benny really dug the sound of the acoustic rhythm guitar run through the sound board and thought it was cool to hear Roger, a student from Grainfield playing it. Lucy alternated between piano sounds and soothing synth pads to create a beautiful and worshipful atmosphere. He had no idea she played at all, let alone so well. The percussionist, Kent, sat on top of the cajon using it to create an eclectic variety of sounds from snare drum to bass with a shaker nearby for contrast. All three of them contributed vocals. Lucy and Roger took turns leading, along with two other students from Grainfield, Tony and Bella, whom Pastor Dave had helped prepare Bible verses and points of reflection to share in between some of the songs. It had been ten years since Benny attended a service in a church building. He loved it.

After the time of worship was over, Pastor Dave walked up behind the pulpit and delivered a sermon about the importance of truth, and not bearing false witness. It really resonated with Benny. It felt like God had brought him here just to hear this message. Truth matters.

After the service portion of the evening ended, as the group dispersed to the various entertainments around the room,

Benny walked up to the front to speak with Pastor Dave. Lucy came down from the platform to join them. They shared their grief and sadness over the way the memories of their brother and sister had been disparaged and spoke of their desire for truth. Pastor David laid a hand on each of their shoulders and prayed over them. He prayed that truth would be revealed, that God would guide them to ask the right questions of the right people and he prayed for special protection over both of them on their quest.

By the time they finished praying, the foosball table in the back was pretty busy, so Benny and Lucy sat down at a table with Tony and Bella to enjoy some colorful popcorn balls and homemade goodies. There was carrot cake with cream cheese frosting, a moist two-layer chocolate cake with vanilla icing and someone had brought the most delicious homemade fudge Benny had ever eaten. Tony and Bella made themselves a couple of fancy caramel lattes and Lucy had a mug of hot apple cider. She said it was her favorite. Benny created for himself an artisan hot chocolate, complete with the leaning tower of whipped cream decorated with chocolate shavings and topped off with a chunk of fudge. Trying to fish out the fudge before it sank, he got a little bit of the cream on his nose which Lucy whisked off with her finger and put in her mouth. Everyone at the table thought it was hilarious. Roger kept staring over at them from the couch, looking particularly unamused.

Since it was Halloween night and other kids their age were prone to be out partying, no one minded that they stayed at church a little longer than usual. They played a few games. Lucy was the champion of charades and Benny was a star at a drawing and guessing game. It was the most fun he'd had in a long time.

119

He didn't even mind when his parents arrived to pick him up and hung out for a few minutes, talking with Pastor Dave. It was good to see them being sociable. His father and Dave were so chummy, they looked like they could have been old friends. They enjoyed some cider and a popcorn ball while Benny finished up his game. His mom loved the fudge. Everyone said it was nice to meet him and invited Benny to come back. He assured them that he definitely would, and took a purple popcorn ball for the road.

After church, Benny came home and plopped face first into his mattress. His body was tired, but his mind was racing. Church had been great, but he couldn't stop thinking about Daniel. After a few moments of brain clearing deep breathing, he rolled over and off the bed onto the floor where he knelt down and did something he hadn't done much of lately, he prayed. He agreed with Pastor Dave's petition for the truth to be revealed. Then he asked God to not only lead him to the right people, but he also asked the Lord to bring the right people to him. He prayed for wisdom, for discernment and for protection for himself and for Lucy. He asked for wrongs to be made right, for justice to be done and then he finished by praying for restoration for his parents. After Benny's prayer was completed, he reached over, opened the drawer and fished Daniel's diary out of his nightstand to read a few more entries. One would push Benny's investigation to a new level.

Tuesday, October 7

Several boys at school have become obsessed with what they call Aphrodisiacs. Today in the library, I heard them whispering back in the stacks searching through books trying to find out about herbs or substances that will make a girl want sex so bad that she can't say no. They snickered and yipped like a pack of hungry coyotes when someone asked "You heard who lost her virginity at that back-to-school party didn't you?"

After a few minutes of looking, one of them said they should forget about herbs and find something more powerful called AROUSAL or another substance called EASY. "Yeah, but it's illegal to buy that stuff," a voice replied.

They didn't know I overheard the first part of the conversation so when I came around the bookshelves and asked them what EASY and AROUSAL were, they stuttered and stammered and one of them blurted out:

"We didn't say EASY, we said E C. His friend elbowed him in the ribs and gave him a dirty look before one of them interrupted and said, Yeah....errrr, E.C....Buxton---they're, uh...this type of pretty yellow flower my mom likes to plant. And NO, you guys can't pick flowers off our lawn. If you want to give your girlfriends flowers on your date, go to the flower shop, cheapskates."

What about AROUSAL? I asked. What is that?

"It's, umm, uhh....chocolates, Yeah, they're these special imported chocolate liquors that girls really love. It helps get them in the mood you know. They're super romantic. You're supposed to be 21 to buy them, that's why we were whispering, but we aren't doing any harm. We're southern gentlemen, we like to woo girls with flowers and chocolates. Don't they do that where you come from? Are you some kind of heathen? Who doesn't buy a girl flowers and chocolates when they go on a date? What's wrong with you?"

They were lying through their teeth, but they were so slick, I didn't know how to respond to that. It's sick. This is so twisted. It is so difficult to be surrounded by evil like this. Surely such substances are urban legends, but I have to wonder if this could be related to the girls who said they blacked out and couldn't remember their first sexual encounter.

Benny closed the book, rewound the leather straps and put it away, quietly closing the drawer as if someone might hear it shut and realize what he was up to. He still hadn't told his parents about the diary. Someway, somehow, he had to get to the bottom of this. He needed help...and resources. He hopped up, reached for the card on his dresser and telephoned his brother's old friend, detective Nick Baker.

The Old Mill

Nick Baker had the next day off from work, so he and Benny made plans to meet up right after school underneath Miller's Bridge over Deer Creek on the outskirts of town. In the springtime and summer, out-of-towners came to fish in Lost River for smallmouth bass, but for a few locals in the know, this quiet spot was the preferred fishing hole. This late in the year, as the weather got colder it was usually abandoned.

After school, Benny drove out to the little stone bridge, parked his car in the dirt turnaround and walked down to the creek, finding a large, dry boulder to sit on while he waited for Nick to arrive. He skipped a smooth, flat rock across the creek and watched a school of minnows scatter as the stone broke the surface of the crystal-clear water. He spotted a pair of tiny, young bluegills drifting precariously close to the watercress where a yellow striped turtle lay in wait, hoping for a meal. "I think your eyes are a bit bigger than your stomach there little fella," Benny said as he turned to look upstream, watching the waterfall down from the old mill pond.

The mill was a testament to the erstwhile craftsmanship of days gone by, but after years of abuse and neglect, the long-abandoned gristmill was badly in need of restoration. The water wheel no longer turned. Most of the windows were broken or missing. Some of the lower planks of siding needed replacing and the thick, wooden shakes on the roof were rotting away, but there was still a certain charm to the place. Surprisingly, the stacked stone foundation appeared as strong as ever. Benny was amazed it hadn't sunken into the soft ground surrounding the creek or been washed away by a flood, but there it was, solid as, well...a rock.

Benny heard the sounds of tires turning off the road and crackling over a bit of loose gravel before coasting to a halt in the dirt. The engine stopped and the door shut. He glanced around to see Nick headed his way, fishing poles and a cooler in hand as he walked away from his old Mustang.

"What's with the fishing poles?" Benny asked

"Your brother and I used to come fishing here all the time, Freddy too, back when we were still friends. I figured its high time I showed you our favorite spots."

Benny shrugged and nodded agreeably. "What's in the cooler, worms?"

"Yeah, I picked some up at the gas station on the way." But that's not all I've got. I brought subs and sodas. Thought we could eat while we fish. You hungry?"

"I could eat. Wait. What? You put the food in with the worms?"

"Yeah. They're in their own little container with a lid on it. I don't see many fish here under the bridge. Let's try up in the mill pond."

Benny heard a splash and looked back to notice a muddy cloud in the stream where the turtle had been. He saw the two little fish darting away toward the safety of the open water beneath the double-arched bridge. The slider must have missed his supper.

"Would you prefer the rod and reel or do you want to try the cane pole?" Nick asked.

"The rod and reel."

They quietly fished catch and release out of the pond for a while, eating the sandwiches between bites. Nick lifted his bait and dropped the line of the cane pole back into the water, jiggling the juicy worm right in front of a fish. Within seconds the cane bent and the tip took a nose dive into the pool. He promptly pulled it back out of the water with a striped logperch attached. While Nick moved a little further up the bank, Benny's bobber took the plunge and he reeled in a good-sized green sunfish. "Nice one," Nick complimented.

"Thanks," Benny replied.

A few minutes later, Nick hooked a half-pound goggle-eye near the bank under the roots of a great big Elm tree. "Did you know this type of rock bass is sometimes called an Ozark bass?"

"Nope. I've never heard that before. Interesting. Your fishing pole's bending so far it looks like it's about to break," Benny warned.

"Ol' trusty here can take it. This pole always catches the most fish," Nick replied as he gently released the bass back into the water.

Nick had patiently waited for the right moment to bring up the subject and with the silence broken, he asked "So, Benny, what was it you wanted to talk about?

Suddenly, it was like the dam burst and the questions came spilling out of Benny's mouth. "Is there anything more you can tell me about my brother's accident? Are there, maybe, some details that I should know, something about that night that wasn't reported in the news? Is there any important information that wasn't public knowledge, anything that was kept secret?"

Nick shifted uncomfortably and bit his lip. "Well, there is something that has always troubled me. On the night of your brother's wreck, I was working at the Burger Barn and missed the party. I got off work at eleven o'clock and by eleven o' three I was in my car and pulling out of the parking lot. On the way home, I thought I might swing by to see if Daniel and Freddy were still at the party. We weren't part of the in-crowd and didn't normally get invited to stuff like that, so I drove out that way and came upon the crash. I only saw it from a distance. I could tell there had been a wreck, but I didn't see your brother's pick-up. I swear I didn't know he had been involved in the accident. I couldn't see very well in the dark with headlights shining in my eyes. There was a guy signaling for me to turn around. I rolled down the window and asked if I could help, but he waved me back, claiming help was on the way so I turned around and went home. I passed a tow truck and assumed it was going to help clear the wreckage. I figured the ambulance would be coming from the other direction, heading in from Ridgeview.

Benny, the site of the crash is a twelve-minute drive from Burger Barn. I diverted around the wreck at 11:15, but the newspapers and the six o'clock news reported that the accident occurred around Midnight. It always seemed strange to me that they reported the wrong time for the crash."

"Why would they do that?" Benny inquired; his brow furrowed.

"I've asked myself the same question a thousand times. The answer is because people lied to the reporters."

"Why?"

"Because they were trying to cover something up."

"What could they have been trying to cover up?"

"That is what I've been trying to figure out for ten years. It's one of the reasons I became a police officer. I wanted to be able to investigate these kinds of situations and bring justice and closure to the families. Something fishy went on after that wreck, and possibly before, and I've never quite been able to catch on to it."

A thought came into Benny's mind. Much had changed in ten years. Most people had cellular telephones in their pockets now. Benny often wondered if it would have made a difference. What if someone at the wreck-site would have been able to use a cell phone to call for an ambulance? If help from the hospital over in Ridgeview could have arrived sooner, maybe the lives of his brother, and sweet Annie Wheeler, could have been saved. He thought about it all the time. "Who was it that called for the tow truck and the ambulance?" Benny asked.

"Reed Jones and Aden Crow always took credit for it. Reed said they drove upon the wreck and immediately went searching down the hill, stopping at each and every house, frantically knocking on doors until they found someone willing to let them come in and use their phone to call for help to save their friends. They painted themselves as quite the heroes."

"But you have your doubts?"

"Your brother had just been given that truck by your parents when the church got your dad that tan sedan you drive. Daniel was so proud of that new blue paintjob. Your father's old car phone was still in the truck. So, I asked Aden why they went searching all over for a place to call when they could have called from the car phone and saved precious minutes. He told me the phone had been thrown from the vehicle in the crash, smashed into a thousand pieces and totally destroyed. But that doesn't explain why someone lied about the time of the accident. If you ask me, something smells fishier than this pond."

"Is there anything else that was fishy? Anything odd or strange that you might remember? Maybe something from the police investigation into the crash?"

"Since the wreck happened outside of the city limits, the Sheriff's department took the lead in the investigation. When I joined the Lost Valley police force last year, I tried contacting the county sheriff's office to look into the matter, but there wasn't much to find. Frank Evans, the driver that hit your brother, had been drinking. He had some deep cuts and broken bones, but his injuries were relatively minor considering the severity of the wreck. That old Nova he was driving was a pretty heavy steel boat and that probably saved his life. He was kept in the hospital over the weekend and then released into the sheriff's custody where he was fingerprinted, cited for driving under the influence, then released. A few days later, a couple of deputies came right down the hallway of the high school, burst into our classroom, cuffed him and hauled him away. None of us ever saw him again. *Deputy* Andrew Smith had run Frank's fingerprints and discovered he was a fugitive. The Lake City police department had issued warrants for his arrest in connection with another alcohol related incident that resulted in the death of a teenage girl named Lindsey Cobble. The old county prosecutor was more than willing to turn him over for extradition out of state and wash his hands of the situation. Less work for him, I suppose. The investigation ended after that. Your mom and dad pushed for it to continue, but some of the church deacons urged them to put the matter behind them for the good of the church, so they stopped. Frank is now serving time over in the Lake City State Penitentiary."

Benny was silent for a few minutes. He watched his bobber, hoping for a fish to give him a nibble and break the tension. Then he found his courage. Slowly, he pulled Daniel's diary out of his jacket pocket and read the entries about the girls who had been so upset at school and about the revealing game of 21 questions and the boys looking for the so-called aphrodisiacs.

Nick was saddened, but did not seem shocked by the information. He explained "There were a lot of nefarious things going on back then. I remember girls sobbing at school from time to time. I don't quite know what to tell you. I don't know what was going on, but if you find any more clues in that journal, let me know."

As twilight fell, the two said their goodbyes and Benny headed home. Something struck him strangely about Nick's story. How could those boys have been so sure that help was on the way at 11:15 if there were no phones out there? He went straight back to the shed, flipping the light switch as he entered. The bulb hummed as it slowly woke up, the sodium light casting its dim, yellow glow over the room.

Benny grabbed a flashlight off the workbench and walked over to the storage boxes. In addition to Daniel's belongings, his father's records were here as well. Throughout his years of ministry, Mark Shepherd diligently kept track of his evangelistic contacts with a log book and retained itemized copies of his phone bills to document follow up calls. He also kept receipts of all work-related expenses. Back then, the church's old computer wasn't very reliable and the Shepherds didn't own one, so he kept backup hard copies of important documents. Benny had been pretty young at the time of the wreck and he had never thought about the car phone until his talk with Nick. He remembered how his dad had purchased the car phone at his own expense. As a good and loving pastor, he always wanted to be available to his flock if an emergency arose when he was out of the office. When the church finally purchased him a little sedan for making house calls and hospital visits or preaching funerals, they installed a car phone in it, so Mr. Shepherd had left his old phone in the truck, just like Nick reminded him. While his former church maintained their own financial records, Mark Shepherd had kept copies of all of his personal ministry-related expenses and evangelistic communications. Those boxes had been sitting here, stacked, since the Shepherds moved in. Benny had noticed them while he was searching for Daniel's jacket and it wasn't difficult for him to find what he was looking for now. It was a banker's box, clearly marked on the end *1997*. He removed the boxes stacked on top of it, carefully setting them aside and then opened up the container. Inside he found color coded file folders sorted and marked by month. He pulled the records for October of 1997. Thumbing through the papers, he found the car phone bill from that month. His parents had been so distraught after Daniel's death that they probably just paid the bill, stuck it in the folder and never even looked over it. The first part of the month contained a list of various phone numbers from ministry-related calls his father had made. The phone had barely been used the second half of the month after Daniel got the truck. Two entries stood out above all others. There were two phone calls made on the night of his brother's death. The first was made at 11:15 and the second at 11:45, October 31, 1997. He immediately texted the numbers to Nick to ask for a favor. Shocked and numb, he restacked the boxes and went inside to clean up for dinner. He was surprised at how hungry he was. The sandwich had been a nice after school snack, but somehow all that fishing had really worked up an appetite.

After dinner, exhausted from the revelations of the day, Benny decided to call it an early night and head up to bed. He threw on some sweatpants and a t-shirt and turned out the lights, but curiosity got the better of him. He switched on the lamp and pulled out Daniel's diary to read a few more entries before falling asleep. One stood out.

Thursday, October 23, 1997

Today after lunch as Freddy and I we were standing around in the courtyard, some guys next to us were talking about making punch for a party using powdered fruit punch packets and how to get the ingredients to dissolve. One of them asked what the clear stuff was that you put in punch. He said he couldn't remember what it was called, but it was something clear. I told them you are supposed to add clear, lemon-lime soda and sherbet to make punch for a party. They laughed at me like I was an idiot. I wish Nick had the same lunch shift as us. I don't think they were talking about making regular punch. They may have been talking about spiking it.

This reminded me of a conversation I heard last spring when some guys were talking about buying wine coolers and dumping them half out to poor something clear in there. When I questioned them, they told me they were watering them down for their girlfriends, now I think they were lying. But I don't know what they were mixing them with.

"I have got to talk to Freddy," Benny muttered. "Maybe he knows something about this."

Haunted Homecoming

School let out early on Friday for the Lost Valley High School Homecoming parade. It was pretty late in the year to be hosting a Homecoming football game, but the November 2 contest against the perennially hapless Ridgeview Wildcats afforded the best opportunity in the second half of the season for the mediocre Lost Valley Coyotes to get a win on their big night.

Making the best of the late date, the student council went all in by choosing the theme "Haunted Homecoming." With Halloween earlier in the week and Día de los Muertos continuing through Friday, the student body had taken the idea and run with it. Each class spent their free evenings that week constructing spooktacular floats for the parade. The weather cooperated nicely, providing a sunless afternoon with dark, ominous clouds looming overhead, spreading a ghastly gloom over the town.

Benny's stomach lurched as he, Coop and Mason walked down the lane in between the school and the football field, looking over the trailers before the parade began while nonchalantly kicking a hacky sack back and forth as they went.

The Freshmen had built a cemetery on the back of a trailer out of gray-painted plywood with creepy tombstones bearing the names of the mascots from each team the Coyotes had defeated that season. Herbie the Howler, Edgar the Elk, Billy the Bullfrog, and Marty the Mountain Goat all had grave markers with their names and pictures drawn on them. Clyde the Coyote, the Lost Valley mascot, was dressed as an undertaker and triumphantly waving a large shovel in the air. He was leading a group of freshmen gravediggers, all of whom were holding shovels while standing around a black tarp, signifying a freshly dug grave laid out in front of the marker for the Ridgeview mascot, Wally the Wildcat. They had cut dead branches out of trees and placed them upright around the trailer by using Christmas tree stands and duct tape, then covered them over with black cloth tree skirts. Fake cobwebs were hung in the limbs for effect. The float was surrounded by a skirt of black butcher paper, bearing the name "Freshmen," and highlighted with more fake cobwebs.

The Senior class float featured an odd combination of the traditional homecoming décor and dark Halloweeny touches. The deck of the trailer was covered with green miniature golf grass, painted with white stripes and some yard line markers that looked suspiciously familiar...since they had been stolen from the marching band's practice field. Goal posts were constructed at each end of the trailer out of white PVC pipe with spider web netting spread between them.

One of their classmates was dressed in a long, black, hooded Grim Reaper robe with a rubber coyote mask. He looked like a serial killer, brandishing a very large and very real scythe while chasing a pair of tabby cats around the trailer. One of them was orange and the other gray and they were both going berserk, darting back and forth and trying to climb the goal posts, which apparently, someone had laced with catnip. Several Seniors, dressed in traditional Día de los Muertos costumes, were arguing with the eccentric Mrs. Cartwright who kept trying to tell them they could not have live animals on their float.

The trio laughed as Mason whispered, "Isn't that lady ever going to retire?"

"Better question," Coop replied, "What is the point of that float? Everything is so random."

Benny was too focused on one of the students doing the arguing to laugh or answer. Hanging out the window of the truck that was pulling the trailer was his attacker, Riley Jones, the youngest of the Jones brothers, whose suspension was over today. "What's his problem now?" Benny asked.

"He wrecked the fancy pickup he got for his 16th birthday and now his dad is *punishing* him by making him drive the old family work truck," Coop answered.

"He's been in a bad mood ever since, not that he was ever in a particularly good mood to begin with," Mason commented.

"I don't know why. It ain't too bad of a truck," Coop continued, "except that if you look up close, the paintjob on the grille has drips in it, like its been touched up with black, glossy spray paint."

As they talked, Riley had climbed down out of the cab and stalked over to Mrs. Cartwright.

"Jones, take a step back," Benny said.

"Shut-up Shepherd. Mind your own business."

"No man," Coop added, "You need to back off."

"Show some respect," chimed in Mason.

After a tense moment, sensing the eyes watching him and knowing there was no way to win, Riley threw his hands up and said "whatever," kicking the massive grille of his jacked up 4x4 before climbing back into the truck. A row of off-road lights mounted on a sport bar rocked back and forth as he slammed the door shut. Benny noticed that some of the black paint had flaked off where Riley kicked the grille revealing a streak of indigo blue paint underneath.

For their entry, the Junior class constructed a funeral complete with bench style church pews. Their class sponsor was the theater teacher, Miss Soubrette. She had allowed her star pupils, Maven Lister and Michelle Tucker, both talented seamstresses and make-up artists, to fill the pews with mourners costumed and face-painted as a variety of frightened felines, reminiscent of a certain Broadway musical. Facing the grieving chorus was a black pulpit bedecked with a large, medieval cross. Its occupant was attired in gothic black priestly robes with a quaker hat and buckled shoes reading a highly sarcastic funeral sermon for a wildcat. In between the pulpit and the mourners was a cat in a casket. This classmate was wearing the most elaborate of the cat costumes, covered in fake blood and splayed out inside a black, plywood coffin with an arm and a leg draped over either side for effect. Each time the cat tried to rise out of the coffin, it was fake knocked out by a theatrically make-upped coyote wielding a plastic pick axe which he then brandished toward the scaredy cat mourners causing them to gasp, shriek, reel back, meow and hold up their claws in a useless defense against the coyote.

The sophomore class had obtained a semi-sized flatbed trailer and gone full zombie. Their football field was gray instead of green. The goalposts were fallen over and they were attired in grayed, washed out colored, heavily soiled, old-fashioned versions of the two team's uniforms complete with numbers-only jerseys and open-faced leather helmets dug out of the school basement. There were zombie cheerleaders in letter sweaters and long skirts, as well as zombie band members with marshmallow hats and old lacquer-less instruments, also from the school basement. Their clothing was torn, ragged and full of holes. They wore various shades of graying and black wigs with some intense zombie face make-up. The trailer was skirted with ragged black cloth bearing the name "Sophomores," in shaky letters and decorated with the now-familiar fake cobwebs. Their float was equipped with a wicked sound system and when the music started, the zombies ceased roaming and broke into a complex dance sequence led by a tall, moonwalking zombie with a coyote face and a drum major's mace.

The entire scene along the lane was morbid. Benny felt sick. This time of year used to be celebratory and somewhat innocent with fall festivals, the Harvest Carnival at the church and costume parades at the schools. Now it felt like a twisted pagan ritual. It had been a fun time to bake or buy special treats for the neighborhood kids and provide a nice atmosphere for family memories, but over the past ten years, the annual festival had gotten progressively darker, just like everything else in Lost Valley. This obsession with the macabre was enough to turn anyone's stomach sour, and after another run in with Riley, it was all just too much for Benny.

And then he saw it—a trailer decorated with a large banner that read *1997 State Champions*. For Homecoming this year, the class of 1997-1998, Daniel's Senior class, was being honored. They were holding their ten-year reunion a bit early and in conjunction with Homecoming because the football team was being recognized at half time on the ten-year anniversary of their state championship. Their class president, Tripp Barber, would be the Grand Marshall and the football players and cheerleaders would ride on special floats in the parade.

"The whole class is invited to a cake and punch reception after the parade in the brand-new atrium of our church," Coop explained. The Riverside Community Church had just completed a multi-million-dollar expansion by building a state-of-the-art auditorium and connecting it to the rest of the church building with an elaborate two-story atrium which was large enough to double as an event center for wedding receptions, anniversary celebrations, or in this case, to host a class reunion in style. The new worship center was built on top of the site where Benny and Daniel had lived in the parsonage with their parents.

"Too bad they took away the old lot we used to play baseball in," Mason added. The church had purchased five additional houses from that neighborhood and combined them with the vacant lot to make room for the massive new building project. Watching the church that betrayed his family seem to prosper like this made Benny queasy.

As they passed the reunion float they saw the young new county prosecutor, Stanley Marshall, running for re-election. He was sitting with his family on beige metal folding chairs in the back of a pick-up decorated with red, white and blue campaign signs that read *Straight-Shootin' Stan*. "Someone's a fan of the alliteration," Benny remarked. Coop and Mason were too busy trying to catch gumballs being thrown by the attorney's children to notice the pun.

Next in line, they saw silvery haired J.C. Jones, the fit-looking patriarch of the Jones family, sitting atop the back seat of a shiny, black Corvette Stingray. "You've got to be kidding me. *He's* running for mayor?" Benny retorted.

"He's sure getting a jump on things. The municipal election isn't until next April," Coop commented.

"I hear they're hosting the big reunion dance out at his fancy country club," Mason reported.

"Have you ever been out there? It's amazing. They have a championship golf course, a five-star restaurant, a lavish banquet hall and an extravagant, nature themed swimming cove with faux stone waterfalls and lush greenery, all within a ten-minute drive from town," Coop explained.

"What are you, an infomercial?" Benny quipped rhetorically.

"Of course, nobody from Lost Valley can afford to live out there. Most of the residents are wealthy retirees from Ridgeview," Mason complained.

"But it's fun to visit," Coop added in his defense. "It'll be a cool place to have a reunion."

Suddenly, Benny had a thought. Maybe he could ask some of Daniel's former classmates for information while they were in town. But for now, it was all much too triggering. "I gotta get outta here," he sighed.

"You're coming to the game tonight, aren't you?" Mason asked.

"Nah man. It's just too much."

"You alright?" asked Coop.

"I'm fine," Benny lied. "I'm out."

"See ya," Coop and Mason responded in unison as they exchanged looks of concern and disappointment.

As he made his way back up the lane toward the parking lot, Benny noticed two familiar faces, the girls from Lucy's picture, coming toward him. They were decked out in jeans with fashionable boots and embroidered peasant tunics, one sewn from plum colored fabric and the other from persimmon. Gabby's glossy dark brown hair was freshly cut and styled and Hannah's once-wild blonde mane of poofed, permed locks was now tamed, straightened and fashionably coiffed as well. *They were some of the last people to see Daniel on the night that he was killed, maybe they saw something...or know something*, Benny thought. When Gabby saw him, she leaned over and whispered into Hannah's ear.

"Benny? Is that little Benny Shepherd?" Hannah asked.

"Yeah, that's me," Benny said, offering a weak smile.

"How *are* you? I know this time of year is tough...on all of us."

"I'm fine."

"I'm so glad we bumped into you. I have something for you. We were going through some old photo albums, looking for pictures to put on display at our reunion reception this afternoon and I found this," Hannah said as she dug in her purse, pulling out an old polaroid which she handed to him. It was a picture of two small children, a boy and a girl, sitting on a bench eating suckers. The boy was holding his candy out toward the girl while wrinkling up his nose and she was smiling contentedly with her lollipop.

Gabby explained "This is a picture of your brother and Annie Wheeler enjoying lollipops at church camp. Annie had just dropped hers on the ground and Daniel was offering to give her his as a replacement when Annie picked that candy right up, licked off the dirt, spit it out and went right back to eating. She said "Can't let a little dirt ruin a perfectly good sucker.""

"It was so sweet...and hilarious. I want you to have this," added Hannah.

"Thanks. That was very thoughtful," Benny said. Then, recognizing the opportunity before him, he asked "Was there anything strange or out of the ordinary that happened at the party? You know...*that* night?"

"I'm not sure what you mean," Hannah said as she and Gabby glanced at each other with that weird thing girls do with their eyes.

"Was anyone acting suspiciously? Did you notice anyone that seemed a little off or creepy?"

"Well, there was Charles Carpenter," offered Gabby. "He kept trying to hang around Annie all night."

"That guy was definitely a creeper," added Hannah.

"Did you see my brother, or Annie drinking?"

"NO!" I didn't have any alcohol at my party, despite what everyone says!" Hannah protested.

"The only thing I saw them drinking was soda," Gabby contributed.

"And Annie spilled some punch on the floor of the trailer," Hannah added. "My dad griped about the stain on the floor boards, but I was like, seriously? You haul cattle in this."

"Anything else?" Benny persisted.

"Those were the beginnings of some really bad times," said Hannah.

"For all of us," added Gabby.

"After your dad left Riverside," started Hannah.

"Was fired," Benny interrupted.

"Yes. After your dad was fired, J.C. Jones and Lester Crow went on a rampage. My whole family was basically run out of the church because of the rumors about my party. They even convinced the Sheriff's department to investigate us, but there was nothing to find. They just grilled my parents with a bunch of questions. The newspaper ran an article about the so-called investigation. It was humiliating," Hannah explained.

"And so unfair," Gabby added. "I was formally kicked out of the church...when people found out I was pregnant our Senior year. You know what those men are like. Remember a few years ago when the city wanted to build the new Riverwalk area to increase revenue from the tourists who come in to float and fish and vacation on the river? Mayor Fuller required construction companies to submit sealed bids for the job so the city would get the best price and value for their investment. J.C. Jones was livid when his company didn't get the contract. His son Rhett has been going door to door with handouts stirring up the whole town against the mayor in preparation for the next election."

"There's a third Jones brother?" Benny asked.

"Yes. Rhett is the middle brother. He works for Jones, LLC as well," Hannah answered.

"Rhett does the dirty work. Reed is the poster boy," commented Gabby.

"Good grief," Benny responded.

"Anyway," Gabby continued, "J.C. Jones has chosen *this* week to launch what *could* turn out to be the most polarizing mayoral campaign in the history of Lost Valley trying to unseat Mayor Fuller. I heard an attack ad on the radio this morning and there are negative fliers posted all over town."

"It's just horrendous," agreed Hannah. "I hope he doesn't win. J.C. Jones made our families' lives a nightmare. My parents haven't set foot in a church in nearly ten years. And you *know* what they did to you and your parents. That is one man you do not want to cross. You probably shouldn't ask too many questions."

"Maybe it *is* best to just leave it alone, Benny," warned Gabby. You might not like what you find if you go digging around in the past."

"Yeah, that's probably true. Thank-you for the picture. I really appreciate it. Have a nice time at your reunion."

"Bye Benny," the girls said in unison as they exchanged concerned looks and walked away. He didn't notice as one of his attackers, Riley Jones's pal Jason Simmons, walked behind him in the middle of their conversation...slowly. Benny looked down at the picture of young Daniel and Annie and gave a little grin. Daniel, always thoughtful. Always others-centered. Always the gentle, man.

Riverview Lanes

By nightfall, a wind kicked up and blew the darkened clouds away, but Benny decided to skip the football game and head down to the bowling alley instead. He bowled frequently enough, but on this night, he had another agenda. His brother's old friend Freddy Fisher managed the place and he always let him bowl for free as long as there were lanes available. Benny had never paid for any of his favorite snacks there either. He could have anything he wanted from popcorn to funnel cake or a barbecue sandwich to chicken strips and whatever he ordered, Freddy would hook him up. Tonight, he was really hungry so he pushed his luck a bit and ordered the chicken strip basket with gravy fries and a funnel cake. As always, he pulled out his wallet and offered money, but as usual, Freddy refused to let him pay a penny.

Riverview lanes was originally a classic old-fashioned bowling alley. The lanes were all constructed with real wooden floors. The narrow planks were waxed so shiny and slick you could just put on your bowling shoes and slide around as if they were ice skates. By day the place was lit up brightly, but on Friday nights Freddy hosted Glow-Bowl. There were special balls treated with glow in the dark paint and running lights between the lanes. The pins glowed purplish-white under the black lights and the walls were covered with black light artwork and neon advertisements. The arrows on the lanes were treated to make them glow in the dark and a giant disco ball completed the look. Freddy cranked up a variety of fun tunes ranging from oldies to hair metal. In addition to bowling there were a couple of air hockey tables, a row of pinball machines and a dozen pool tables. A trip to Riverview lanes was always a fabulous time.

On this particular night, business was super slow due to the Homecoming game. Benny was just starting on his third game after breaking one-hundred twice in a row and was feeling pretty proud of himself when Freddy came over for a little hang out time.

"How ya doin' Benny? You look kinda down."

"Not great Freddy. Lots of heavy stuff to deal with this week."

"Yeah. I heard about the fight."

"It wasn't a fight. They jumped me in the parking lot."

"Sorry to hear that. Any clue why?"

"It was about Daniel. The things they say about him are so awful."

Freddy bowled a game with him and they kept the conversation light, discussing school and family and the Coyote's miniscule chances of winning. And then, as they were finishing up the last frame, Benny seized his opportunity. "Is there anything you can tell me about *that* night, Freddy? Anything unusual that you can remember that happened before the crash?"

"Something funny did happen. It started raining really hard and Mrs. Farmer made everyone take their shoes off before going in the house if they had to use the bathroom to keep them from tracking mud inside. I was sneaking around the side of the house, doing a bit of shoe-pirating, tying everyone's laces together and hiding their shoes. She had left the kitchen window open to air out after all of the goodies she cooked up and I heard her catch Aden Crow in there trying to use her phone. Mrs. Farmer was all riled up and hollering, 'What's all this talk about wizards and dragons? You better not be playing that satanic role-playing game all the kids are getting into nowadays. And what are you doing with your shoes on in my house? Git outta my kitchen.' Then she whacked at him with her broom and chased him out the back door. It was hilarious."

"Do you know who Aden called?"

"I have no idea."

"Or why he was talking about dragons and wizards?"

"No clue."

"What about the crash? Was there anything that struck you as odd or out of place about the accident?" Benny persisted.

Freddy paused and wrinkled his brow to think before offering "I have always felt like one thing was pretty weird. People kept saying that there was toilet paper and eggs smashed all over the road at the scene of the wreck and that they must have been thrown out of the back of Daniel's truck. They said it was further proof that he was up to no good, but I rode with him up there and I know he didn't have any of that stuff."

"Is there anything else you can think of?"

"Nothing else comes to mind," Freddy replied.

"I read an entry in my brother's diary. He wrote that you and he overheard some guys talking about mixing up some sort of punch, possibly spiking it with something. Do you recall who it was?"

"No. I can't remember anything about that. Ten years was a long time ago. You need to let this go. Some stones are best left unturned Benny. You may not like what you find underneath."

"I need to know."

"I think it's best just to leave it alone. Sorry I couldn't be of more help. I need to go check the paper towel dispensers in the bathroom and tie bowling shoes to put them away. I enjoyed our game." And with that, Freddy was off, just as Coop and Mason walked in, which was quite a surprise.

"Hey, I thought you guys were going to the game."

"We were there," answered Coop, "but Riley and Jason were looking for you and we were worried about you being alone. We thought you might be here."

"That, and we decided our best friend shouldn't be hanging out all by himself, anyway," Mason added while tearing off a big chunk of Benny's funnel cake. Coop finished off the fries as they filled him in on the other happenings of the evening. Benny didn't mind at all. He was glad for the company. They had watched the game until halftime, long enough to see Susan Glover crowned Homecoming Queen. Then they headed over to the lanes. The sophomores had won the class float contest with their stupid zombie apocalypse trailer. All three boys agreed that the juniors got ripped off, their cat costumes were way better.

They bowled one more round, which Benny narrowly won, and then headed over to the table games. Coop and Mason got into an intense air hockey battle and Benny had to step in and referee before it came to fisticuffs. He took the puck and wouldn't give it back until they agreed to stop arguing. Everyone had a good laugh afterward. Benny had the highest score at pinball and they declared him to be a wizard. They played a couple games of cut-throat pool, a contest that allows three people to play against each other, and then they finished off the night with red-flavored slushies from the snack bar.

After the homecoming game ended, people began slowly trickling in. Riley Jones and Jason Simmons were among the first to arrive. Coop and Mason crossed their arms and flanked Benny on either side as their nemeses walked right up to him.

Riley gave him a shove as he said "Just wait until I get you away from your friends you little commie. You're gonna pay for making me look bad today."

"Keep your hands off of him," Coop said as he placed a firm hand on Riley's shoulder to hold him back, which Riley angrily swatted away.

"What were you talking about with those women at the Homecoming parade today?" Jason demanded as he encroached upon Benny. Mason extended an arm across the aggressor's chest, blocking his advance. "I heard you mention Riley's brothers and his father," Jason continued, straining against Mason. "What did you tell them? What did they say?"

"None of your business," Benny replied.

Jason grabbed Mason's arm to throw it off just as Freddy stepped into the fray.

"You two get out of here! Right now, before I call the police!"

"I'm not done with you," Riley glowered as he and Jason retreated toward the doors.

"See you *soon* Shepherd," Jason added.

"Thanks Freddy," Benny said after they left.

"No problem," Freddy replied before heading back behind the shoe counter.

"You ok?" Coop asked.

"I'm fine. Thanks," Benny replied.

He knew his buddies wanted to go to the Homecoming dance, but there was no way they were going to leave him unguarded after what just happened. Neither of them had girlfriends, but there were plenty of nice girls without dates and they would have a good time dancing with as many of them as possible, so Benny took that as his cue to leave. Faking a yawn, he thanked his pals for hanging out with him and said goodnight.

Flooded with adrenaline from the confrontation and still riding a sugar high from the funnel cake and slushies, when Benny got home he settled in to read some more of his brother's journal. What he found was the most upsetting entry yet.

Monday, October 27, 1997

I heard a very disturbing conversation after PE today. I was the last one out of the showers and while I was changing clothes, I overheard two guys talking. They couldn't see me on the other side of the lockers. I couldn't quite tell who it was because they were talking softly and their voices were masked by some music that had been left playing in the weight room. I really had to strain to hear them.

The first one told the second one "I need you to get me some more APHRODISIACS."

The second guy said. "No way. People are starting to ask questions and I'm tired of always being the one to take the risk. You can go buy them yourself."

"Where did you even get them?"

"Up at Gordo's Beer-Mart. He'll sell you anything you want...for a price. Just say 'Uncle Robert sent me,' and he won't card you. If he asks you where your uncle is at, be sure to answer "He's resting in Lexington""

"What kind should I get EASY-F or AROUSAL?"

"Get Easy-F, but just call it EASY. You know why we call it that don't you?"

"Because it makes girls easy?"

"Exactly."

"Why not Arousal?"

"Because it's not powerful enough and it makes girls too hyper. Easy works better. Girls are powerless and can't resist when you give them Easy."

"Should I get anything to go with it?"

"Obviously moron. Buy a six pack of wine coolers. I'll take care of the other 'groceries' we need."

"What flavor?"

"I don't care. Just make sure you get them so we can mix them up before this weekend, ok?"

I don't know what any of those words mean, but from the way they were talking, it sounds like they found what they have been looking for. This sounds like some sort of drug that makes girls want to have sex. I tried to hurry so I could confront them, but by the time I got my clothes on, they were gone. This is getting really scary.

EASY and AROUSAL. Benny had seen these words mentioned in his brother's diary before. Daniel had heard whisperings, but this was the first time he had identified where these things were coming from, though he still didn't know what they were. It was a good thing Benny came home early. He needed to call Nick again and to use that number Lucy had put in his phone just a few short days ago.

Before he went to bed that night, he said a prayer for Freddy. He wasn't sure what was going on with his brother's friend, but something seemed a bit off.

Sting

On Saturday morning, Benny, Lucy and Nick met up out at the old mill and Nick was fully prepared. Benny had briefed him over the phone, but Lucy needed filled in.

Benny pulled Daniel's diary out of his jacket pocket and read the entries he had shared with Nick by the pond about the weeping girls and the revealing game of 21 questions. He also read the entry about making punch and both passages about the so-called aphrodisiacs, Easy and Arousal.

Benny continued "Boys from Daniel's class were mixing something they called Easy into wine cooler bottles to disguise it. I think they were making punch with this Easy and covering the taste with sugar and powdered drink mix. People had no idea what they were drinking. I believe this might be what happened to your sister and maybe to Daniel as well. Daniel didn't identify anyone by name in his diary, but he did note that whatever they were buying, they were getting it at Gordo's Beer-Mart out on state line road."

"That store is notorious for selling alcohol to minors, but we've never been able to prove it," Nick agreed. "Old Joe Gordon has owned that store since I was a kid and he's clever, tough to catch."

Benny continued, "Daniel's diary said that if you say *Uncle Robert sent me*, it's like a passcode and the old man will sell you anything you want and not ask for identification. You just have to remember that if he asks you where your uncle is, say

153

He's resting in Lexington. Nick and I thought you might like to help with a little sting operation we have planned for today."

"Absolutely I would," affirmed Lucy. "Let's take this scumbag down."

Nick fitted Benny with a wire, clipping it to the inside of his leather jacket and instructing him to zip the coat and conceal the transmitter in the inside pocket.

"Why can't I just call you and leave the phone on in my purse? Wouldn't that be easier?" Lucy suggested.

"The phone transmits both ways and we can't risk old Joe hearing something and getting spooked. We're only going to get one shot at this, so we have to get it right," Nick explained as he handed Lucy a digital recording device to put in her purse as a backup. "I'll be listening in from just around the bend," he assured them. "If anything goes wrong just get out of there and drive to safety. Now, we need to have a safe phrase in case you need assistance. If you get into any trouble, one of you ask the other *Do you have any leftover Halloween candy?* As soon as I hear those words, I'll come rushing to your side. Do you think you can handle it?"

"Yes," the undercover gumshoes replied in unison.

They drove out to state line road with Nick following at an inconspicuous distance in his Mustang so as not to raise suspicion with a patrol car. As Nick pulled off onto a dirt side road where his car was hidden behind a grove of cedar trees, Benny and Lucy continued on, pulling into old man Gordon's seedy liquor store. Old Joe had deviously positioned his store close to the border because he could sell beer with a higher percentage of alcohol than was legal for stores on the other side of the state line. He sold snacks and called it Gordo's Beer-Mart to make it sound innocuous, but everyone in town knew this was the place to come for hard liquor and serious alcohol. Fortunately, the store was on the Lost Valley side of the road and technically within city limits, so Nick had jurisdiction as an officer of the law.

Benny nervously held the door for Lucy as they entered the old building. It smelled faintly of beer and sweet pipe smoke. Joe Gordon eyed them warily, but turned his attention back to the program he was watching on a little television set he kept behind the counter. The pair of newly minted spies made their way past the beer coolers and the wine bottles and into the hard alcohol section, then Lucy spotted something "Could this be EASY?" she whispered. Benny looked down at a bottle filled with clear liquid labeled:

EDWIN CULPEPPER'S

FINEST

GRAIN ALCOHOL
190 PROOF

E-C, Benny sounded out as his eyes got big and he started to reach for the bottle, but Lucy took his hand in her own and said "Here's what we're looking for." She led him over to the refrigerator units in the back, opened the door and handed him a six-pack of watermelon wine coolers while she picked up a sixer of strawberry ones herself. "These look delicious," she added," giving him a *don't you dare say anything* look.

They made their way to the register and placed the illicit beverages on the counter as Benny said "My *Uncle Robert sent me here. You really do have the best selection."*

Grumpy old Gordo looked up over his glasses at the pair and asked. "Where is your uncle?"

Lucy replied *He's resting in Lexington.*

Gordo then proceeded to ring them up, hitting an extra button at the end that added a 20% upcharge to their bill. Benny handed him the money. Joe didn't offer change or a receipt, so they just left.

"What was that all about," Benny asked when they made it to the safety of the car. "Why didn't you let me buy the Edwin Culpepper's?"

"Isn't it obvious? A teenage couple buying hard alcohol. Old Joe would've seen right through it. Wine Coolers were much more believable. The goal wasn't to *buy* E C. The goals were to *find* E C *and* to prove he would sell alcohol to minors, and he just did! We accomplished both."

"You're brilliant Lucy."

She just smiled. As they drove past Nick's car, he pulled out behind them and followed them back to the bridge by the old mill.

"That was excellent work you two. Now hand over the alcohol. It's evidence."

They coughed up the booze and returned Nick's wire and recording device. They told him about finding the Easy, or E C, Edwin Culpepper's Finest.

"I'm going to go have a little talk with Mr. Gordon. Meet me at Burger Barn tonight at 5:00 and I'll buy you a burger basket after my shift is over.

As Nick walked toward his car, Benny took Lucy over to sit down at a picnic table facing the bluffs across the creek and he explained everything he and Nick had learned thus far in their investigation until she was completely caught up.

Then Benny asked a strange question. "Hey Lucy, do you have a library card?"

"Yes, why?"

"The town library gives free internet access to anyone with a library card. I want to research Edwin Culpepper's. You game?"

"Definitely," Lucy replied as she hopped in the car with Benny and they rode away together.

The Library

The Lost Valley Library was a charming small-town amenity offering free library cards for residents. They boasted a carefully curated selection of classic and quality books, a modest periodical section and half a dozen computers with internet access. There were a few tables overlooking the river with a small counter offering free coffee with sodas, cookies and sandwiches available for purchase.

After a few minutes of searching, they found Edwin Culpepper's Finest 190 Proof grain alcohol.

"It says here that 190 proof means it contains 95% alcohol by volume, compared to beer which is 5% alcohol. E C is known for having a neutral flavor and for not having a strong smell like other types of hard liquor. It takes on the taste of whatever it is mixed with which is why it is popular with bar tenders who pour tiny amounts as an ingredient in cocktails. However, it is frequently stirred in with drink powders and other ingredients to make a hard-hitting party punch or mixed with wine coolers because it assimilates the flavor of the wine," Benny explained. "If a person used a larger amount of this stuff..."

"Someone could drink E C and not even know it. It would hit them like a ton of bricks. They could think they were drinking a wine cooler or some simple fruit punch and be downing a massive amount of 95% pure alcohol," Lucy exclaimed, holding her stomach. Here, trade me places."

"Be my guest," Benny offered with a sweeping hand gesture as he relinquished the computer and took Lucy's seat. "What are you thinking?"

"Let's call it, playing a hunch. I noticed that sleezy old Joe Gordon had some pills on the counter called Arouse-All," she explained while typing away, "When you showed me your brother's diary earlier, the word Arousal stuck out to me. Sounds about the same, doesn't it?"

"Yes, it does."

"Here it is," Lucy continued: "Arouse-All. Factory workers take this drug to stay awake when they have to work the overnight shift. It is a powerful stimulant with a mega-dose of caffeine which also makes it a metabolic enhancer." Lucy typed away some more, modifying her search parameters. "Oh my gosh," she gasped, "People take overdoses of Arouse-All to get high. There is even a theory that if you dissolve Arouse-All into liquor it will cause you to metabolize the alcohol very quickly. That is to say, your body would absorb it and you would feel its full effects within minutes. There is speculation that a woman who drinks such a mixture could get very drunk really quickly on a relatively small amount of alcohol."

"I'm not sure it could work quite like that," Benny commented.

"Me neither, which explains why they moved on to Edwin Culpepper's, which is much more powerful and far more dangerous. But if a girl *was* given Arouse-All, she would still have seriously impaired judgement from the alcohol, but remain highly active because of the stimulant and be more likely to make bad decisions. These maniacs were treating girls like guinea pigs, trying their concoctions out on them."

"Mixing stimulants into alcohol is hazardous enough, but pouring 190 proof into drinks could knock a person out. E C is why those girls were blacking out and unable to remember their first-time having sex. They *didn't* consent to having sex. They were sexually assaulted by these criminal psychopaths. These boys were monsters who created their own date rape drug to deliberately poison girls with a substance they knew would cause brain damage in the form of short-term memory loss," Benny ranted.

"They wouldn't be able to identify their attacker," added Lucy. "And a lot of them probably blamed themselves, but let's not call it a *date* rape drug. Let's just call it a rape drug, or a sexual assault potion. This is straight up witchcraft. Those deviants were brewing up wicked libations. They're lucky no one died from alcohol poisoning after consuming their knock out potions. Those boys are vile, sociopathic, serial rapist fiends. This is sick, twisted, perverted..."

"It is Pure Evil," finished Benny. "Yesterday, before the Homecoming parade, I ran into Hannah Farmer. She told me that Annie had spilled some punch all over the floor of the trailer the night of her party. What if it had E C in it?" Benny inquired.

"That would explain why Annie appeared so drunk," Lucy replied. "She didn't know what she was consuming. Edwin Culpepper's is odorless and practically tasteless. Even if her sense of smell and taste had been working properly, there's almost no way she could have detected it," Lucy offered.

"Those poor girls never had a chance, Benny concluded."

After some additional research, Benny bought them sodas and croissant sandwiches with kettle chips and chunky chocolaty cookies. He had turkey and cheese. Lucy had chicken salad. As they sat down, Benny admired the view of Gabby's flower shop across the water. The steep river bank had been reinforced with a retaining wall that served as the foundation of the old building.

"That's the same type of stonework as out at the mill," he noticed. "Check out that cornerstone."

"Impressive. No wonder it's lasted so long and stayed so strong. In fact, all of these main street shops are historical," Lucy observed. "Someone really built this town to last and they chose a great location. The valley is breathtaking this time of year."

"It really is a beautiful place. I don't always take the time to appreciate it, but there also seems to be this darkness hovering over us, lurking around every corner," Benny replied.

"What do you mean?"

"I just don't understand what would possess my brother to get into his truck and drive drunk."

"That could be a rumor like everything else, Benny. Or maybe he had some punch with Annie and didn't realize how much it was affecting him. He could have seemed ok to drive one moment and fallen heavily under the influence just a few minutes later. The point is we don't know everything yet. We need to keep investigating."

"And I think I know just where to go next," Benny suggested.

The Sticks and The Flats

The road along the hillside East of town was sparsely populated and surrounded by woods, but that afternoon, Benny Shepherd and Lucy Wheeler knocked on each door, seeking to find out if the residents had witnessed any suspicious behavior or if anyone had stopped in to ask for help on that fateful night, a decade ago.

They visited half a dozen houses in the sticks and most hadn't seen much of anything out of the ordinary. The door of a kit log home got slammed in their faces by a man who accused them of being with a political campaign.

One woman in a small A-frame house did recall that her colicky baby had been woken up by roaring car engines and when she looked outside the next morning, someone had decorated the oak trees in her front yard with toilet paper at some point during the night. "Probably teenagers getting up to no good," she guessed. "I remember, because I had just gotten this little guy off to sleep and had a fit trying to get him back down," she said as she looked fondly over at her son who was happily zooming his toy trucks around in the background.

As Benny and Lucy approached a little rock house nestled into a clearing in the trees, two Blue Tick hounds came rushing toward them, barking madly like they just treed a raccoon. Benny quick-stepped in front of Lucy, using his body as a blockade, while she dove back into the truck. He flinched and winced, holding his hands up in front of his face as the dogs leaped upon him. Striking a blow to his chest with their front paws, they nearly knocked him over as they began licking his palms and whining with a high-pitched whistle. Barking was just their way of saying hello. They were actually pretty friendly, so he scratched them behind the ears and rubbed their bellies.

Lucy laughed, "Their bark really is worse than their bite."

The owner, a pot-bellied older gentleman, who had come out onto the porch in his overalls with bare feet and a green trucker hat, set his shotgun down on a chair and whistled to call the dogs, "Blue and Shadow, you git yourselves back here."

Apologizing for his pets, he explained, "I call this one Shadow, 'cause she's always underfoot like a shadow. She follows Blue around everywhere he goes, when she's not trippin' *me* up. "How can I help ya?"

"Sir, do you remember the night of the crash, ten years ago, when Annie Wheeler and Daniel Shepherd were killed?" Lucy inquired as she and Benny cautiously approached the porch.

"Yes, that was awful, just awful. Cryin' shame."

"Well, we were wondering...if you saw or heard anything strange that evening?" Benny asked.

"Come to think of it, old Blue here was just a pup back then, but he went plumb crazy that night, just a barkin' and a yelpin' at the woods, like someone musta been out there. He ain't one to go a howlin' for no reason, so I grabbed my shotgun and went to check it out. I heard a twig crack, like somethin' stepped on it, then some rustlin' through the leaves, but when I called out nobody answered. After a few minutes Blue went quiet and I figured it must have been some kind of critter or maybe a lone coyote I'd heard howling earlier that night, but the next mornin' when I went for a walk out there to check things out, I found a plastic sword in the woods. No idea how it got there."

They thanked him for his time and headed up the road, out of the sticks and up onto the flats.

Hannah Farmer's parents place, the site of the infamous party, was the last house down a country lane before the blacktop ended. The remaining half mile only served a couple of hayfield gates at the back entrance to somebody else's pastures. There weren't a whole lot of folks living out there and it was highly unlikely anyone would have seen anything, or been driving by at just the right moment to witness something, but they had to try. Houses were few and far between out on the dirt roads of the flats, but Benny and Lucy set about to canvass the area. They visited a couple of new double-wides and three old country cottages with no luck.

The last house they visited was a little two-story white farmhouse, the kind with one bedroom, a kitchen and a living room downstairs and one attic bedroom upstairs with windows looking out in each direction. Out in back there was an abandoned rock dairy barn and a stone grain silo with a leafy treetop poking out where the roof used to be.

As they entered the driveway and got out of the car, they noticed an older woman trying to coax a cat down out of a tree in the front yard. They introduced themselves and learned that her name was Bertha May Cartwright, and she liked to be called May. She was proud to say her daughter teaches Spanish down at the high school. Benny climbed the tree and rescued the cat which thanked him by scratching up his arms. As they went inside to wash and doctor his cuts, they noticed a handful of cats roaming about, making themselves at home.

Benny winced as Lucy cleaned his battle wounds with hydrogen peroxide and then took a deep, relaxing breath as she applied some antibiotic ointment. Then he asked May

Cartwright if there was anything strange or out of the ordinary that she could remember from the night of the crash, a decade ago.

"I'll never forget that night," she replied. "What a horrible tragedy, those young people getting killed like that. My daughter was beside herself with grief, losing two of her students.

I did have some ruffians about the place causing trouble that night. I still operated the dairy back then. My husband had just passed and I was getting used to living by myself, so it startled me to hear an engine idling and see lights outside my bedroom window. There was a big white truck with one of those rows of lights across the top. They cut the engine and shut the lights off, but the moon was really bright that night after the rain let up and I could see their shadows sneaking across the pasture, stalking toward my cows. It looked like they were trying to push Flossie, my best milker, right over. I could tell it was her, 'cause if you approach her too quick, she'll kick. She must've gotten at least one of 'em because I heard a yippin' and a yelpin' as they limped back to the truck. Serves 'em right for puttin' their filthy paws on my cattle. Only a real ignoramus would think you could tip a cow over. Probly a couple of city slickers."

Continuing on, May Cartwright explained. "There's this dumb rumor city folk believe that cows sleep standing up and will fall over if you push on 'em. Who'd be that mean to a cow anyhow? Anybody who knows anything about cows knows they lie down when they really want to sleep, just like people do. If you push 'em, they might butt or toss at you with their head, sling slobber on you, step on your foot as they walk away, kick at you, or just moo in annoyance, but they sure ain't gonna fall down. Anyway, once they were on the other side of the fence, they howled at the moon like a couple of coyotes, then hopped into the truck and took off. One of 'em left a bloody fringe of gray fiber behind on the barbed wire."

They thanked May Cartwright for her time and she insisted they take a piece of hard candy and a handful of quarters for rescuing her cat. Benny tried to refuse the money, saying it was no problem, but she insisted and wouldn't take no for an answer, so he relented and accepted the gift.

After they got into the car, Benny said "That truck with the offroad lights sounds like the one Riley Jones has been driving around town. It used to belong to his brother Reed. I don't know why he put that enormous cattleman's grille with the bull bar on it. He probably thought it looked tough and intimidating, but they don't have any cattle. I bet Reed was out there with his pal Aden Crow trying to tip Flossie the cow."

"They definitely aren't real country boys," Lucy added. "I bet the only barn they've ever been inside of is the Burger Barn."

"Speaking of which, it's about time for us to meet Nick."

Burger Barn

Benny and Lucy arrived at Burger Barn about a half an hour before Nick got off work. "Well, we've got these quarters," Benny said.

"Might was well put them to good use," Lucy replied.

They took advantage of the time to play some video games in the backroom arcade. They sat down and took turns racing each other at a cross country car game with a steering wheel and pedals that vibrated when they went off-road or crashed. Benny dominated the race cars, but Lucy easily bested him in a motorbike race. They teamed up to save a princess from a fireball breathing dragon and then punched out mobster crime bosses in partner mode. It was oddly therapeutic after the day they'd had. By the time Nick pulled in, they had found a corner booth, their burger patties were sizzling on the flattop and strawberry shakes were on the way. For Nick, they ordered everyone's favorite chubby-dubby with cheese and a side of Burger Barn's famous hand-battered onion rings. Benny thought better of the onions, though he loved them, and went with the tater tots instead. Lucy decided on the curly-q fries. When Nick slid into the booth, they already had a fresh cola waiting for him. He took a long drink and then smiled, really big.

"First of all, you two were awesome today. I made a little deal with Mr. Gordon. An audio recording of a man allegedly selling a few wine coolers to a couple of teenagers isn't going to warrant the kind of punishment that man deserves, especially without a receipt. But I played the tape of your conversation back to him and he was scared enough that I was able to shake him down for information. I know the names of some of the boys who bought E C that school year. The ones he could remember were Reed Jones and Aden Crow, two deacon's kids, plus another student named Charles Carpenter. I'm sure he conveniently forget to mention Frank Evans. He was probably too scared to admit that one."

"Carpenter," gasped Benny. "Gabby Shoemaker told me that Charles Carpenter was creeping on Annie at the party. What if he's the one who spiked the punch?"

"I don't know Benny," answered Nick, but there's something else. The week of the crash another student old man Gordon had never seen in his store before came in to purchase a bottle of Edwin Culpepper's. Benny...it was Freddy Fisher. Back then, when I asked him about that night, he couldn't look me in the eye. He told me he didn't see, or know anything. I knew that he was lying to me or keeping a secret about something. It's the reason we drifted apart and stopped being friends."

Nick let the shock of the revelation settle for a minute as Benny reeled from the stunning information, his jaw and eyes wide open.

"And there's more. I ran a check on one of those phone numbers you gave me. Benny, Lucy, this might be very upsetting for you to hear."

"Go on," they both insisted.

"I knew it looked familiar for some reason. It was easy to find because it is a public entity. It is the phone number for Ridgeview Regional Hospital. Back in the day, most of our classmates would have known it by heart because our Health and First Aid teacher, Mrs. Boatwright made us memorize it. When the nearest emergency room is fifteen miles away in another town, every minute counts, so calling directly was the quickest way to get help. Plus, if they would have dialed 9-1-1, there would have been a record of the caller's voice and the number they called from and the caller wished to remain anonymous."

Benny thought he might wretch. Lucy asked, "What does that mean?"

Nick explained how he was re-routed away from the wreck at 11:15, forty-five minutes before the time the news reported that the crash happened. "If the phone was still operational after the crash and the call was made at 11:45, that means that Reed Jones and Aden Crow lied about the phone being destroyed in the wreck and they lied about being the ones who called for help. I've looked into it and only one emergency call came in to the hospital that night. This means that they lied about going door to door until they found someone to let them in to use the phone because the call was made from the car phone."

"We went to every house on that road this afternoon and no one reported anyone asking for help that night." Benny added.

"You did what?" Nick asked with a look of stern disapproval on his face.

"We did some investigating on our own this afternoon," Benny said matter-of-factly. "Anyway, what were you saying?"

"Well," Nick continued, "This means, as I've always known, that Daniel and Annie were never missing for an hour and all of the rumors and speculation about what happened during that time are malicious lies and ridiculous nonsense. It means that they were involved in the wreck just a few minutes after they left the party and someone lied to the news media about the time of the crash. It also means that someone reached over Daniel and Annie's bodies to make a phone call at 11:15 and then just left them there in the car for at least half an hour before anyone called for help and it was another fifteen minutes before assistance finally arrived. It took a total of forty-five minutes for an ambulance to reach them. The questions are: Who made the first call and where was it to? Why was there such a long delay before the second call? And what was being covered up by lying to the media? Daniel and Annie might have been saved if help had gotten to them sooner."

Lucy gasped and burst into tears. Benny had anticipated this was coming, but his eyes still filled with moisture. He put an arm around Lucy like he had when they were little. She softly sobbed into his shoulder, but quickly gathered herself and wiped away the tears to avoid making a scene.

"There is more to this story and we are going to find out ALL that went on that night. That is my promise to you," pledged Nick.

Benny nodded somberly before saying in a shaky voice, "Yes we will."

"And this also means that Daniel did not hurt Annie the way some people say he did," Lucy declared, steeling herself. "Every rumor has a source, and trust me, there is always a reason for it. We know *what* they were doing with the E C. Now we need to find out *who* was doing it. We got some good leads today and they *could* all be guilty. We are going to figure out why they lied, and who was really hurting girls back then."

"And now we have four serious suspects," Nick added. "That will certainly help guide our investigation."

"Lucy and I already discovered some things this afternoon," Benny offered.

Lucy explained all they learned about E C at the library while Benny recounted their door-to-door search for information.

171

"We spent all afternoon interviewing people from the flats and the sticks, but all we came up with was loudly revving car engines, a bit of toilet paper thrown into some trees, a varmint running through the forest, a plastic sword found in the woods..."

"And a couple of nincompoops, Reed Jones and Aden Crow, trying to tip over Flossie the cow," Lucy finished.

With Nick's back turned and Benny focused on Lucy, no one noticed Jason Simmons lingering outside at the open pick-up window, trying to read lips.

After he took a moment to let it all sink in, Nick expressed his displeasure with the risky house searches, but noted his admiration of their tenacity and courage. Then he said "It's interesting that Jones and Crow were hanging around the area and I would be very curious to know who lost their sword in the woods. Tonight is our big class reunion dinner and dance out at the country club. I'll do some snooping, under the guise of remembering old times, to see what I can find out."

"If they are serving food there, didn't you just spoil your dinner?" Lucy asked.

"They're serving finger foods and fancy hors d'oeuvres. This was my only chance for a decent meal. And I really need to get going before I'm late. One other thing. I think it's time to bring Hannah and Gabby into our investigation."

"I agree," said Lucy.

"Definitely," agreed Benny.

"Be careful," warned Lucy, "Once we kick this hornet's nest, there's no telling who'll get stung."

Benny took Lucy back to the mill and waited to make sure her car started up before departing for home.

Stung

They didn't have to wait long to find out who would get stung. As soon as Benny walked through the door at home, he knew something was wrong. Both parents were sitting in the living room, awaiting his arrival. "Come sit down son," his father softly demanded.

"What's going on? Is something wrong?" Benny didn't like the looks of this.

"You better believe something is wrong," his father replied.

"We received a phone call this afternoon that you and Lucy Wheeler were seen purchasing alcohol from Gordo's Beer-Mart," his mother stated somberly.

"Don't even try to deny it. They saw you with the alcohol," added his father.

"It's not what you think," Benny insisted.

"No excuses. I don't want to hear a word of it," his father said curtly. "We have spoken to the Wheeler's and agreed that you two are not to see each other again. Now go to your room."

"No."

"Go."

"NO. LISTEN TO ME," Benny bellowed. Lowering his voice, he explained. "We were working with Officer Nick Baker, Daniel's friend. We were helping the police. Thanks to Lucy and I, he caught old man Gordon red-handed, selling alcohol to minors."

"Why on earth would you be involved in such a thing?" his mother asked.

Benny hesitated for a moment.

"Well?" his father sounded off impatiently.

"We have been investigating Daniel and Annie's crash. I found Daniel's diary and I've been reading it. Today we just uncovered some really disturbing new information."

Benny showed them some of the diary entries and what Daniel had been concerned about. He shared what he, Nick and Lucy had learned so far.

After he finished, Benny declared decisively "I need to go over to the Wheelers and get Lucy out of trouble. Are you coming?"

The whole Shepherd family loaded into the car and began the drive over to the Wheelers. Prior to that day they hadn't spoken since Annie's funeral when Mr. Wheeler blamed Daniel for his daughter's death and held Mr. Shepherd responsible.

John Wheeler had moved his family out north of town to a place that backed up to the river, down the hill from the Shepherd's home. He met them before they ever made it to the front steps. His piercing blue eyes blazed with anger as he warned "You're not welcome here. You've caused enough damage to this family. Now my daughter won't even speak to me. Get off my property."

Mark Shepherd spoke up first. "We're sorry to intrude, but our children have discovered some things that you really need to know. They've been investigating the night of the accident. Today was part of their investigation. They were working with Nick Baker from the police department to prove that Mr. Gordon has been selling alcohol to minors, as he was ten years ago."

Mr. Wheeler, visibly shaken, lowered his voice. "Well, I reckon you best come inside."

Mr. Wheeler was a stout man of shorter than average height. His thinning once-blonde hair was neatly combed and he wore round spectacles that gave him the look of a dignified country gentleman. Mrs. Wheeler was just a bit taller than her husband. She was an elegant woman with light blue eyes and fiery red hair that matched her wits and strength of personality. She greeted the Shepherd's at the door as her husband walked down the hallway of the ranch style house. He gently knocked on Lucy's door and asked her to please come into the living room, letting her know the Shepherds were here. Benny had been seated on the couch by his family, but rose when Lucy came into the room. She had obviously been crying and her eyes were red and puffy. Benny gave her a big hug and she took his hand, leading him over to the love seat where they sat down together, their fingers interlocked. Mrs. Wheeler offered them some lemonade and sweet tea she had brought in from the kitchen.

Benny read to them from Daniel's diary and he and Lucy took turns explaining everything they had learned about the code phrase and E C and all of it. Benny then concluded by reading one of the journal entries from the last day of Daniel Shepherd's life.

Today Annie wheeler asked me to take a class with her next year. I think she might like me. And then Benny and I ran into her and her sister trick or treating. She is so cute. I was invited to a party tonight. Hopefully she will be there. I know mom and dad won't be happy, but I feel like I NEED to be there, to make sure those creepy guys don't try anything and to be a protector, to make sure no more girls get hurt until I can figure out what is going on and put a stop to it.

Then Benny added "Daniel went to the party that night to protect Annie. We don't know all of the details of what happened yet. But we know his intentions were pure."

Mr. Wheeler spoke first. "I can see that now. We have been so angry toward your family. We have harbored hatred in our hearts and it was unwarranted. Can you please forgive us?"

"Of course, we can," Mr. Shepherd answered for the family as his wife and son nodded in agreement and said "Yes."

The families exchanged hugs and handshakes. "This is not over yet. Nick is doing his detective thing tonight at the class reunion and I've got to have a conversation with Freddy Fisher," Benny announced.

"And I'm coming with you," added his dad.

"As am I," resolved Mr. Wheeler.

"Won't he be at the reunion?" Mrs. Wheeler asked.

"He told me he isn't going," Benny replied.

"Wait," Mrs. Shepherd said firmly. "I don't want you men running down to the bowling alley and accosting the poor boy."

"He's hardly a boy..."

"Mark."

"Let's wait and see what Nick finds out at the reunion tonight. Then we can come up with a plan for how best to approach Freddy," Lucy offered.

"I agree," said her mother.

Everyone conceded that waiting another day or two was in their best interests.

"Wait. Dad, who was it that called you and told you about us being out at Gordo's Beer-Mart today?"

"The caller didn't identify himself," said Mr. Wheeler, "But he sounded like...Reed Jones," both men said at the same time.

"Jinx," Lucy instinctively whispered to Benny and they both laughed.

"Jinx for Reed Jones when we get to the bottom of this," Benny whispered back.

"Would you like some apple pie?" Mrs. Wheeler offered. "I've got one baking in the oven."

"YES," was the unanimous reply. Karen Wheeler could really bake a pie. The delightful smell filled the house. Mrs. Wheeler asked Benny's dad if he would like to bless the food before they ate. He blessed the food and thanked God for it. He prayed for wisdom, for the truth to come out, and for protection over their families. Everyone agreed with a hearty Amen.

Benny savored every delectable bite of dessert, "Whoever thought of combining cinnamon with nutmeg and a hint of cardamum was a genius."

"Touched off with a sprinkling of cinnamon sugar on top," finished Lucy.

"Would you like some pie with that plate of whipped cream you've got there?" Benny teased.

He felt a warmth spreading throughout his body and an almost supernatural sense of calm. He thought back to that Halloween night all those years ago, trick or treating with the Lucy and Annie and Daniel. There was something so healing about sitting down to eat with the Wheelers.

After the pie, while the parents sat down for coffee, Lucy and Benny sat out on the back porch swing watching the final embers of sunset shimmer across the river before disappearing into the night sky. The peaceful sounds of the water bubbling across the rocks granted them a welcome moment of repose. As the stars slowly began to appear, Lucy took Benny by the hand.

"There's something I have to tell you. Tonight, on my way home, Riley Jones was following me. He was tailgating me on the curves, I thought he was going to smash into me. Once we hit a straightaway, he floored it past me, nearly hitting my bumper and then swerved back in front of me so close I had to slam on the brakes and slide off onto a dirt road to keep from hitting him. He might have just been being 'Riley,' reckless and angry, but it felt like more."

"Are you ok?"

"I'm fine."

"Lucy."

"I'm scared."

"Was there anyone else in the truck with him?"

"Some guy, I couldn't see his face."

"Jason Simmons, I guarantee that's who it was. We've got to tell your parents Lucy."

"NO," she said firmly. "I don't want them to worry."

Benny's parents slid open the door before he could reply and stepped out onto the patio. "Ready to go?" they asked.

"Sure. Goodnight Lucy. We'll talk soon."

"Goodnight Benny," she said, as she gave him a lingering hug. Benny held on too, with his eyes closed.

"Tell your parents what Riley did," he whispered into her ear. "I want you to be safe."

"Ok," she whispered back. As they entered the house, she took a deep breath and then said "Wait. There's one more thing I need to tell you. This afternoon I saw Riley Jones drive by in that old white 4x4 as we walked out of Beer-Mart. I bet he was the one who called to try to get us in trouble, not his older brother Reed. Their voices probably sound similar. Later, as I was driving home, he started following me, then tailgating and then he ran me off the road."

"I'll be giving his father a phone call," announced Mr. Wheeler.

"This has gone too far," agreed Mr. Shepherd.

"Are you alright?" asked Mrs. Wheeler.

"Mom, I'm fine," answered Lucy.

"You said you used a secret code phrase to get Mr. Gordon to sell you the wine coolers. What was it?" Mr. Shepherd inquired.

"We said *Uncle Robert sent us*," Benny replied.

"And then when he asked us where our uncle was, we answered *He's resting in Lexington*"

"My word," Mrs. Shepherd gasped.

"What?" Lucy and Benny responded in unison.

Their parents exchanged a knowing and concerned glance. Mrs. Shepherd explained "Robert E. Lee is buried in Lexington, Virginia. You could say he was *laid to rest* there. I remember because Mr. Webster, our History teacher, was quite the Civil War buff."

"Yes, Mr. Webster moved up to this area to attend college over in Lake City. He was *very* proud of his southern heritage. He talked about General Lee all the time," added Mrs. Wheeler.

"We haven't studied the Civil War yet in his class this year," said Benny.

"Robert E. Lee is revered in *certain* circles," Mr. Wheeler commented.

"There may very well be a racial component to all of this,
Mr. Shepherd added.

"Code words and phrases like this have been commonly
used by certain *affinity* groups for over a century," Mrs. Shepherd
added.

"Somehow, somewhere, these teenagers learned to use
that phrase, maybe from a parent, possibly without fully
understanding the meaning behind it," Mr. Shepherd
commented.

Mr. Wheeler spoke next. "I think we need to impose a sort
of safety lockdown. We don't want either of you going anyplace
by yourselves."

"I agree. We were talking about this while you were out
on the porch and now it seems obvious that we need to do it,"
Mrs. Wheeler added.

"That's not fair," Benny protested.

"We haven't done anything wrong," Lucy agreed.

"This isn't a punishment," Mrs. Shepherd insisted.

"Not at all," agreed Mrs. Wheeler.

"It's just, after what happened today, we want to keep you
safe," Mrs. Shepherd explained.

Lucy gave Benny's fingers a little squeeze and put her
hand on top of his. They exchanged a nod that communicated
what they both understood. After what happened to Annie and
Daniel, their parents were terrified of losing them.

"There is obviously something nefarious going on here
and we don't want to give anyone an opportunity to hurt you,"
Mr. Wheeler pleaded.

"And we think it would be best if you stayed home as much as possible and let things cool off," Mr. Shepherd continued. "And no more risky endeavors."

"Tomorrow's Sunday, and I was hoping to go to church at Hilltop," Benny requested hopefully.

"We'd be happy to pick him up and bring him back home afterward," offered Mr. Wheeler, "For safety."

"I don't see any problem with that," agreed Mr. Shepherd.

"These precautions aren't forever kids. We just need a few days to figure out what to do next," encouraged Mrs. Wheeler.

"We're not kids," Lucy lightly protested, but her smile betrayed the truth that she was looking forward to riding to church with Benny tomorrow.

"You're still *our* kids no matter how old you get," her mother added with a smile.

"And then you'll stay for lunch, when you bring Benny home," stated Mrs. Shepherd. "I mean, please stay for lunch tomorrow, we'd love to have you."

"That sounds delightful," accepted Mrs. Wheeler. "Should I bring anything?"

"Bring more of that pie," said Benny before his mom elbowed him in the side.

"No thank-you. You have been gracious hosts to us this evening and we would be honored to return the favor tomorrow."

"We should invite Nick to come too. He could fill us in on what he finds out tonight at the reunion," Benny suggested.

"I think that's an excellent idea," his father concurred.

"We should invite the Bakers to stay after home group then. It would be pretty awkward for their son to be walking in to a dinner they weren't invited to," his mother insisted.

"Yes, we should definitely invite them," Mr. Shepherd agreed.

"I'll call them when we get home tonight," Mrs. Shepherd replied.

"And Benny and I can invite Nick at church tomorrow," offered Lucy, "We don't want to interrupt his investigation tonight, but he'll be at church in the morning. I saw his name on the greeter's list."

"It sounds like we've got a plan," Mr. Wheeler concluded.

"It sounds like we do." Mr. Shepherd concurred.

While everyone said their goodbyes, Benny gave Lucy one more goodnight hug and she held on with her eyes closed. As he let go, Benny trailed his fingers down the back of her forearm and gave her hand the slightest squeeze before their fingertips slowly slid apart and the Shepherds took their cue to depart.

November 4, 2007

Sunday Dinner

After they left the Wheeler's, Mrs. Shepherd insisted they make a *quick* run into town for groceries. It's a good thing Mr. Shepherd always finished his teaching preparations early...

Full of anxious energy and anticipation, Mrs. Shepherd spent hours that night making ready. It had been many years since they had company other than family or the small group that met in their home for worship each Sunday and she wanted everything to be just right. Benny helped dust and sweep the living room while his mom and dad busied themselves in the kitchen.

Even in the wake of losing Daniel, Sarah Shepherd had tried her best to make this a happy home. They had little time and money when they first moved in, but she had been determined to paint the old kitchen cabinets. Benny helped her pick out the color, a cheery cornflower blue. She adorned the windows with yellow gingham curtains and hung lemon yellow tea towels decoratively on the cabinet doors. The bright colors contrasted perfectly against the butcher block counter-tops and beautiful dark wood floors. When she saw the kitchen, Rebecca Thatcher, or Grandma Becky as Benny called her, had sewn them a yellow gingham table cloth to match as well as light blue napkins adorned with tiny yellow flowers. Benny smiled as he heard his parents singing away and whistling while they worked in the kitchen. He hadn't heard his father whistle in years.

The next day after church, Sarah Shepherd laid out an impressive feast. She had slow cooked a large rump roast in the oven, allowing the drippings to fall down onto peeled potatoes and chopped carrots. She made savory beef gravy from the broth and baked fresh hot rolls as the meat rested under tin foil to allow all the juices to gather inside. Mr. Shepherd helped too. He mashed those potatoes—with the drippings they didn't need milk or butter added—and then placed them in a large bowl which he covered with a towel to keep them warm. He also cooked up some home canned green beans while she prepared a salad with fresh garden lettuce, spinach, home grown heirloom tomatoes and cucumbers, then mixed up some ranch dressing to go with it. Benny even pitched in, making a large batch of banana pudding from scratch. He chopped up bananas, mixed them into the pudding and poured it into a dish, layering it with vanilla wafers and covering it with whipped cream before putting it in the fridge overnight to chill.

When Benny and the Wheelers arrived after church, they could see Mr. and Mrs. Baker through the windows, relaxing in the living room while his parents put the finishing touches on lunch. Nick was the youngest of three children and the Bakers were somewhat older than Benny's parents. Josh Baker's hair was a distinguished gray, but Donna Baker's hair was still black like her son's and her eyes were the same honey-brown color.

The Baker's smiled and waved to the Wheeler's through the window as Sarah Shepherd came out to greet her guests. Lucy's mom, Karen, complimented Mrs. Shepherd on the lovely fall display she had put together. On either side of the steps was an attractive presentation of orange and yellow fall mums, offset by cornstalks and surrounded by a variety of heirloom pumpkins. Sarah thanked her for the compliment and offered them coffee as she invited them to join the Bakers in the living room. Benny went into the kitchen to put the finishing touches on dessert. He lined the outside of the banana pudding dish with vanilla wafers and sprinkled crumbs of crunchy cookies over the top of it. Lucy started setting the table. As Mrs. Wheeler returned to the kitchen, Benny sheepishly said "Mom, we're gonna need to set two extra places for dinner. When I invited Nick, he had already made lunch plans with Hannah and Gabby, *Annie's friends*, so I asked them all to come."

"The more the merrier," his mom replied with a smile, "We've got plenty of food. Go fetch the card table and chairs out of the shed."

"What about Maggie?" Lucy asked.

"She went home from church with her grandparents," Benny replied. "They're taking her for ice cream and to feed the ducks down by the river this afternoon."

As Benny was heading to the shed, he heard the distinctive purr of Nick's Fastback pull into the drive. He walked around front and greeted the trio. They helped him retrieve the chairs and table, and brought them inside, setting it up in the space between the kitchen and the dining room.

Benny sat down at the end of the card table with Lucy and Hannah to his left and Nick and Gabby to his right. Mr. and Mrs. Shepherd sat at either of the rounded edges opposite Benny with the Wheeler's to his left and the Baker's to his right.

The table was trimmed with a tasteful centerpiece created by placing a vibrant yellow mum in a blue ceramic pot in the center of a piece of burlap and surrounding the flowers with colorful dried maize and small gourds. They had a good laugh when John Wheeler reached for an ear of maize, thinking it was there to eat. He chuckled good naturedly as his wife gently pulled his hand back. Everyone knew why they were gathered, but the dinner conversation was casual. The pain of the past formed a sort of glue that bound them all together, but the meal itself was celebratory. There was a certain feeling of relief in the room as a group of people who had all been maligned or ostracized in one way or another simply enjoyed a meal at a table where they were accepted and not judged. Grace is a beautiful thing.

"So, how was the class reunion last night?" Mrs. Baker asked.

"It was...interesting," Hannah answered.

"Everyone's dresses were so pretty," Gabby said, skillfully steering the conversation. "Hannah lent me the most beautiful vintage gown from her shop."

"And you looked stunning in it," Nick added.

"Thank-you," Gabby said, blushing. "And the food was...unique, mostly hors d'oeuvres and finger foods."

"Told ya," Nick whispered in Benny's direction. "I'm not really into snails and fish eggs myself," he snarked.

"They did have these delicious cinnamon glazed pecans," Hannah reminded, as Benny and Lucy exchanged a grinning look.

"They were amazing and the artisan pizza bites weren't half bad," Gabby offered.

"They weren't half good either," Nick teased, cackling at his own joke.

"But the dancing was nice," Gabby said smiling over at him.

"The dancing was...*very* nice," Nick agreed.

"And the venue was just beautiful," Gabby added.

"Oh, my goodness," Hannah exclaimed. "The banquet room at the country club is like a ski lodge with a gigantic fireplace in the corner. It has a vaulted wooden ceiling with round timber support beams reinforced by smooth tree trunks spaced along the walls of thickly varnished logs."

"It was very rustic-chic," Gabby commented.

"Exactly," continued Hannah. "And the decorations were lovely. They had beautiful ice sculptures of ducks and furry woodland creatures."

"And little white twinkly lights wrapped around the trees and spread across the ceiling like stars. They were all reflected in the water from this gorgeous stone fountain in the corner opposite the fireplace. It spilled out over a waterfall and flowed along a stone stream bed right through the middle of the room," Gabby gushed. "It was really beautiful, like the prom I never had."

Lucy started to ask, but Hannah caught her eye and gave her an almost imperceptible shake of the head.

"And the centerpieces on the tables were especially nice," said Hannah.

"Thank-you," replied Gabby.

"She made fall wreaths out of tiny vines twisted with little red honeysuckle berries and lilac colored buckbrush and set them on a bed of glitter painted maple leaves, then placed locally made, pumpkin spice scented candles into glass vases in the center. Simple, yet elegant," Hannah finished.

"That sounds just lovely," Mrs. Baker replied.

"How was church this morning?" Mr. Shepherd asked. "It must have been a fairly lengthy service."

"It was longer than usual," Mr. Wheeler replied.

"There was a baptism after the invitation," Lucy added.

"Wonderful! Who was baptized?" Mrs. Shepherd asked.

"Freddy Fisher," answered Benny.

Eyes got big all around the room.

"Well good," suggested Hannah.

"How was your Bible study?" Lucy inquired hopefully.

"It was excellent," offered Mrs. Baker. "We studied Colossians chapter three. We learned about the change that happens when we are saved, how we put off our old selves and are made new through Jesus."

"And we discussed equality among the people of God, how all sorts of class and racial barriers are meant to disappear as Christ works in our lives," Mr. Baker added.

"And we talked about how love binds us all together and how we are supposed to be kind, compassionate, humble, gentle, patient and especially forgiving toward each other," Mrs. Shepherd concluded.

At the end of the meal, Benny and Lucy dished out banana pudding to everyone and they took their bowls into the living room where a warm, crackling fire awaited them in the old, stacked stone fireplace. Nick, Gabby and Hannah carried their folding chairs with them so there would be enough seating for everyone.

Swapping stories on a Sunday afternoon is a favorite pastime in the Ozark hills. It's how folks used to entertain company in the days before television sets, radio and modern distractions made everyone so busy. Family, friends and neighbors would spend hours catching up on the news, sharing true histories, listening to funny anecdotes, telling tall tales, embellishing fish stories and spinning yarns about ghostly adventures. This time-honored tradition is how people learned about their kinfolk and got acquainted with newcomers. A talented storyteller could transport the listeners to a different time and place, help them picture events in their heads and make them feel just like they were there themselves. On this particular Sunday afternoon, the stories that were shared had a deeper purpose. They were darker. They were foreboding. And they were all one-hundred percent true.

The Secret

As the guests finished their dessert and settled into their coffee, Benny stood up, moved to the front of the room, and began to speak. Lucy came up to stand beside him. Since Josh and Donna Baker had not yet been informed about what was going on, they gave a brief summary of what they had discovered.

"As some of you know, last week I found my brother Daniel's diary and started reading it. Daniel was upset about some things he had been seeing and hearing at school and he wrote them down. Girls had been coming to school devastated. They were often crying, sobbing and utterly despondent. Daniel began to overhear disturbing conversations. The boys at school were obsessed with finding substances they thought would make girls want to have sex with them. He heard them talking about buying something they called Easy from Gordo's Beer-Mart and mixing it into wine coolers and punch."

Lucy then added "Benny and I did some investigating at Gordo's and at the library. We discovered that Easy was their nickname for E C, Edwin Culpepper's Finest, a 190-proof grain alcohol. It is 95% alcohol by volume. E C is odorless and has no flavor which makes it almost impossible to detect and would have hit anyone who drank it like a freight train. Daniel went to the Halloween party that night because he wanted to make sure no more girls got hurt...and because he wanted to see Annie."

"That's right," Benny added. "There were girls who reported blacking out and not being able to remember their first *time*, often after only drinking a wine cooler, a beer, or even just some punch. We have come to understand that these delinquents were tricking girls into drinking the equivalent of 4 to 6 shots of

THE DIARY OF DANIEL SHEPHERD

190 proof alcohol. That's more alcohol content than you would get from 10 shots of whiskey. They were overdosing girls in order to render them defenseless and rape them. Daniel recorded the names of specific girls he believed had been assaulted."

"Was my name in that diary?" asked Gabby.

The room went dead silent.

"Yes," answered Benny.

The ladies in the room covered their mouths, the men intook air quickly.

"That happened to me. No one believed me except for Hannah, my parents, and apparently Daniel."

"We knew Gabby was pregnant at my Halloween party and we wanted it to be a safe place for everyone, that's why we were so careful not to allow any alcohol that night," added Hannah. "I'm still not sure what happened...at either party."

Benny and Lucy exchanged glances, but allowed Gabby to continue. She had waited a decade to tell her story.

"I was put under church discipline and kicked out of Riverside Community Church when it was discovered that I was pregnant out of wedlock. They didn't even ask what happened. They just assumed I had sinned. All I did was drink a glass of punch at a back-to-school party and I woke up the next morning, unable to remember anything."

Hannah interjected "I was outside swimming with Annie, so I don't know what happened. We got worried when we hadn't seen Gabby for a while, so we came inside and started looking around and found her unconscious...and unclothed in a bedroom. We didn't want anyone to see her like that so we put her clothes back on and carried her out to the car. We should have taken her to the hospital, but we were just kids. We didn't know what to do."

Gabby continued "I woke up the next morning with no memory of how I got home and almost no recollection of the night before. I could only remember going to the party. I was self-conscious and didn't want boys ogling me in a swimsuit, so I didn't bring one. When Annie and Hannah jumped in the pool, I went inside the house to get a snack and someone, I don't know who, handed me a glass of punch. I can't recall anything after that. Hannah and Annie spent the night to be there for me the next morning. I didn't have any memory of it, but when I woke up, I knew I had been raped. They helped me to the shower, holding up a towel to respect my modesty as I undressed, then they stood close at hand, averting their eyes in case I needed them and handed me the towel, then a bathrobe when I was finished. I had bruises all over my body. We cried for hours. My daughter's birth certificate doesn't even list a father.

A few months later, on the night of the Halloween party, as we were leaving the Spooklight, walking up the hill back to the trailer, some girls confronted me. One of them had seen me at the pregnancy center over in Ridgeview and they wanted to know what was going on. I was so humiliated and so upset. Hannah was trying to comfort me and we didn't notice what was going on with Annie and Daniel. We didn't see them leave."

Hannah put her right arm around Gabby's shoulder and held on to her friend's hand with her left as the other ladies in the room comforted her. A hush remained over the men.

Mr. Baker was the first to break the silence "I'm so sorry for what happened to you...and for what was done afterward. I begged them not to put you out of the church. That is one of the reasons I resigned from being a deacon," he admitted, "I'm sorry I didn't do more to stand up for you, for any of you," he confessed.

"What could you have done against those men anyway?" his wife asked.

"Very little," Mr. Shepherd consoled. "Those were stubborn men with hardened hearts."

Reunion

Benny couldn't wait any longer. The question practically burst out of him "What did you find out at the reunion last night, Nick?"

"We learned a great deal, from each other and from our classmates," Nick replied as he, Hannah and Gabby exchanged looks.

"Reed Jones insisted on hosting the main event out at River Glenn Country Club," Hannah commented with annoyance in her voice.

"To show off the new bar he just put in," added Gabby grimly.

"And so that he could pocket all the profits," Hannah finished.

"Of course," contributed Nick.

"We caught the bartender with a bottle of Edwin Culpepper's behind the counter," continued Gabby. "So, while Hannah distracted him with her witty repartee, I swiped the bottle and dumped it out in the bathroom."

"Reed gets obnoxiously braggadocious when he gets a few drinks in him," Nick added.

"Even more than usual," Hannah retorted.

"True. He was boasting about how much money his real estate company, Jones Properties, LLC made on the recent expansion at Riverside Community Church. He mocked Mr. Shepherd, calling him short-sighted and stingy. Sorry, Mark," he added, glancing over apologetically.

"Oh, that's fine. That was a major point of contention between myself and most of the deacons. They wanted to shell out big money to develop an extravagant long-term expansion plan that was well beyond our means. I felt that we could accommodate our growing church's needs by building more modestly and within our resources. I wanted to use the lot next to the church, which we already owned, to save real estate costs and preserve quality, affordable housing for the community by not tearing any homes down. I suggested that we save up money and remain debt free, paying for the new construction in phases such as building a simple square fellowship hall with a well-equipped kitchen as phase one. For phase two, I planned to hold two separate worship services in the new fellowship hall for a period of time while using the space from the old fellowship hall to expand the worship center and add a balcony. It would have been attractive, but reasonably designed. They wanted to take on millions of dollars in debt to do it the way they did," responded Mr. Shepherd.

"Yes, as soon as they voted to dismiss Pastor Shepherd, J.C. Jones and Lester Crow immediately began lobbying the rest of the deacon body to put their plan into place," Mr. Baker explained.

"They kept throwing around words like 'dream big' and 'trust God to do big things.' They sounded like an infomercial on one of those religious television networks," Mrs. Baker continued.

"They used the tragedy of Daniel's accident as an opportunity to make a power grab," her husband replied.

"They really took advantage of the situation," she agreed.

"Which is another reason why we left," Josh Baker admitted.

"In the wake of the wreck, J.C. Jones and Lester Crow began loudly bemoaning the moral decay of the town, constantly complaining about out-of-control teenagers and warning about the consequences of sin," Donna Baker continued.

"Touting the need for better leadership and running on a platform of righteousness, they lobbied the church to modify their bylaws to create new positions as elders to watch over the church's business," Mr. Baker explained.

"And *humbly* accepted when they were asked to fill the new roles themselves," Mrs. Baker added.

"Then a few years ago they were both named as Consulting Elders for the church, positions for which they receive generous financial compensation, though neither of them keeps any office hours," concluded Mr. Baker.

Nick continued "Wow. So yes, Reed was bragging and bragging about how he went to work for the family business straight out of High School, helping to manage Jones Properties, LLC while he earned a degree in Entrepreneurship. He continued what his father had started by purchasing a total of five additional properties near the church. They used them as rental properties until the church got ready to build and then exploited legal loopholes to evict any tenants who were reluctant to move out so he could sell the properties to the church for use with his master plan. With the huge profit he made from selling those properties to the church, plus all of the demolition costs, and then the construction itself, Reed has turned that church into his own personal cash cow."

"Wait, didn't one of those families move out after people kept putting "For Sale" signs in their front yard?" Benny asked.

"Oh my goodness, yes," Lucy added. "It was the Blumenthal family. I used to play with their daughter Esther before we moved. I was at their house when they discovered that a glass jar of pickled pig's feet and a copy of *Mein Kampf* had been placed in their mailbox. They moved to Ridgeview after someone spray painted a swastika on their tool shed."

"Her father Jonah is such a kind man and an absolutely brilliant doctor, a brain trauma specialist. He helped one of our classmates, Cindy Spicer, when she suffered...a brain injury," Hannah commented, with a quick sideways glance toward Gabby, who continued "Back then he was just a young resident, but now he is the director of the brain trauma recovery unit at Ridgeview Regional Hospital."

"It's such a shame they were treated that way," Lucy said.

"It really is a disgrace," Mr. Shepherd added. "I was friends with Jonah Blumenthal."

"His wife, Leah, was really nice as well," Mrs. Shepherd added. "We used to take walks around the neighborhood and stop to visit with them in the front yard from time to time."

"They are, of course, devout Jews," Mr. Shepherd explained. "Jonah and I had friendly, and quite frankly, fascinating discussions regarding his beliefs about the Messiah. I explained why I believe Jesus fulfills every prophecy of such a Savior in Scripture."

"I had similar conversations with him," Mr. Wheeler interjected. "He seemed open and genuinely interested, until the harassment began, then he sort of shrunk back into his protective shell."

"Those boys were doing the devil's handiwork by harassing that lovely family," Mrs. Wheeler observed.

"We used to get a lot of noise complaints from that neighborhood, engines revving in the middle of the night, tires squealing in the wee hours of the morning," Nick confirmed, "but anytime we sent a patrol car to sit on that block, it remained quiet. Then if we left to go on patrol elsewhere, the activity would start back up."

"That's why *we* moved out north of town," Mrs. Wheeler added. "And Jones Properties purchased the house."

"Do you think they were *trying* to intimidate you and your neighbors into moving out?" Benny asked.

"Yes, I do." Mr. Wheeler replied.

"I think so too, but we could never prove it," Nick agreed. "And it isn't just the real estate business they are profiting from. Have you seen the fleet of cars that church owns now?"

"Aden Crow was bragging at the reunion about how the lot of them were purchased from Crow's Car Palace," Gabby answered. "All those fancy SUVs were paid for with church money, directly into the Crow's pockets."

"Sounds like they've got quite the racket going on," Hannah commented.

"Oh, it is," Nick agreed. "Aden manages the car dealership while Reed runs the day-to-day operations of Jones Properties, LLC. Meanwhile J.C. Jones and Lester Crow both sit on the JP board of directors."

"It sounds like they have reaped a lot of benefit since getting out from under Pastor Shepherd's watchful eye," Lucy added.

"Indeed, they have," agreed Nick.

"It's easy to see they had motivation to perpetuate damaging rumors about the accident, which is precisely what their sons Reed and Aden were doing again last night," Hannah added.

"Ten years later, and they're still repeating the same old lies about Daniel that so many people believed back in the day," Gabby continued.

"Gabby and I spoke with some of our classmates, without the guys around," Hannah stated. "We told them what Nick shared with us about Daniel's true intentions. Some of them confessed that they had believed the rumors about Daniel back then because so many girls had been hurt, but agreed that it never fit his character to do such a thing."

"Right, Gabby agreed. "He wasn't even around when the incidents occurred. About half a dozen ladies told us that it was either Aden or Reed whom they first heard the rumors from. What if it was them hurting girls all along and Daniel was just a convenient scapegoat who couldn't speak up for himself?"

"That would make a lot of sense," Lucy suggested. "We learned that Reed Jones, Aden Crow, Charles Carpenter...and Freddy Fisher were among the boys buying Edwin Culpepper's back then."

"We know Freddy and Charles were at the party and Charles was hanging around Annie," said Benny.

Hannah jumped back in, saying "I spoke to Charles at the reunion last night while Nick and Gabby were dancing. I was kind of surprised he came, but he seems like a decent guy if you actually take the time to talk to him. His wife is so cute and they have two darling kids. They showed me pictures. While his wife went to the bathroom, I confronted him and he admitted to buying a bottle of Edwin Culpepper's back then, but it wasn't to drink. Charles and his mother are very sensitive to smell. They had just moved into a rental property owned by J.C. Jones and it needed some serious cleaning and attention. There was mold in the tub and around the edges of the linoleum in the kitchen. Bleach, vinegar and ammonia-based cleaners were making them nauseous. Some people use E C as a sort of country remedy cleaning agent because it has such a high alcohol content without any scent. It makes a potent additive to normal household cleaners without the severe smell. He heard some guys at school talking about using a passcode to buy alcohol over at Gordo's, so that's why he went there and bought the stuff."

"No one would ever think up a story that bizarre as an alibi. We can take him off our suspect list," Nick added.

Hannah continued "Reed and Aden tried to crash the party...that Halloween night."

"We certainly didn't invite them," Gabby explained.

"But we didn't let them go on the hayride with us," Hannah continued. "Reed kept staring at Daniel and Annie talking together and got really, really angry. I told them to get out of my yard. They hung around for a while, but eventually, they left."

"They were both furious," added Gabby. "I thought maybe Reed was jealous, that he liked Annie or something, but that doesn't explain why both of them were so mad."

"Did you say the Crow boy was one of them?" inquired Mrs. Baker.

"Yes. Aden Crow," Hannah responded.

"We had an illuminating encounter with that family a few years back," Mrs. Baker continued. "We were having a new, larger septic tank dug and the workers came across an unmarked grave, right there in the back yard. On the lid of the coffin, the name *H. Crowe* was carved. That's Crow, with an *E*. We tried to find out if there were any living descendants who might know who this person was, in case they were interested in giving the body a proper burial in a graveyard."

"We learned that there were two Crowe brothers, Hiram and Harold, though it wasn't clear whose coffin this was," Mr. Baker contributed. "Aden Crow and his father Lester are descendants of that family. They claimed the body and had it buried in Shady Hill Cemetery."

"We were curious to know why the name was spelled differently, but that family was so unpleasant, we were hesitant to ask, so I did some research," explained Mrs. Baker. "It seems there had been some kind of trouble down south and the family was running from the law when they came to reside in Lost Valley. It appears that they may have changed the spelling of their family name to evade detection."

"We also learned that the Crowe family was part of the landed gentry of the south," added Mr. Baker. "They were ardent supporters of the Confederacy."

"That *was* a very long time ago," Mrs. Baker reminded.

"But racism dies hard," Mr. Baker asserted.

"I hoped all of that was far in the past, but with what we've been learning of their behavior and the Confederate code words for buying alcohol, it's looking more and more like race was a factor in all of this," Mrs. Wheeler chimed in.

Mrs. Shepherd spoke, "About a year after we moved here, Daniel played the role of young Jesus in the temple for the church Christmas pageant. We received some horrible anonymous letters, enraged that we had a black boy portraying Jesus. They demanded that only whites play Jesus. Apparently, they didn't know our Lord was Jewish. The letters were shockingly hateful and bigoted. I always suspected they came from those families."

"I will never forget the looks on J.C. Jones' and Lester Crow's faces our first Sunday at Riverside," Mr. Shepherd added. "They knew we had children, but I had come by myself to preach in view of a call. They didn't see our family until we arrived in town. It was clear they were...*displeased*."

"After the Christmas play, they were always out to get rid of us," Mrs. Shepherd added, "but I'm not sure how racism plays into the events of that evening."

"I know," announced Benny.

The Missing Entry

"Speaking of these racial issues, now that we know Reed Jones and Aden Crow were stalking the party that night, there's something else I need to tell you, all of you," Benny said. "There was an entry in the diary that was stuck to the back of another page. It had gotten wet. I just found it last night. Two days before he died, Daniel had a major run in with Reed and Aden. He heard them talking in the locker room while he was concealed by a row of lockers."

Wednesday, October 29

Today I overheard voices talking in the locker room while I was dropping my clothes off before school. It was Reed Jones and Aden Crow. Aden had managed to purchase a cache of EASY and AROUSAL. Reed told Aden not to use the Arousal because it makes girls too hyper and they're likely to bolt. He asked "Didn't Frank tell you not to waste your money on the Arousal? Easy is a guarantee." He told him to only use the Easy and was explaining how to mix 1/3 of a glass of punch with Easy. He told him to only dump out 1/3 of a bottle of wine cooler and replace it with Easy to make it more potent. He said don't dump out half the bottle like you did before...you remember what happened. This time, I had courage. I confronted them face to face. I asked them point blank what they were doing and demanded to know what Easy and Arousal were. I accused them of conspiring to hurt girls. Reed got up in my face and told me to shut my stupid "N-word" mouth and back off, using a lot of profanity. Spewing out every cuss word he knows, Aden told me I better mind my own business or he would lynch me. I told them NO and stood toe to toe. I called them liars and I told them I was going to figure out what they were up to and report it. I told them I would never back down.

Coach Cook heard our raised voices and came down into the locker room, yelling "What's all the commotion?" He ordered us to break it up and they left. He asked what happened and if I was alright. I should have told him.

"And there's more," Benny continued as tears filled his eyes, "When Daniel came to school on Thursday, the day after the confrontation, an ugly racial slur had been written in black marker on notebook paper and taped to his gym locker with a picture of a rodent, dangling from a gallows and the word R A T written out like a game of hangman. I'm pretty sure it was his tears that caused the pages of the diary to stick together. Between that and the creepy white ghost faces, he had every right to leave school early. The next day, on Halloween, Reed nearly ran into him in his truck."

"And then that buddy of theirs, Frank Evans, nearly ran us over on Halloween night," Lucy added.

"It must have taken incredible courage and moral resolve to venture out to the party after all of that," Benny concluded.

There were many tears shed over what Benny had read. His mother doubled over in sobs, while Mrs. Baker and Mrs. Wheeler comforted her and his father stood up and went to look out the front door for a moment, just in time to see Pastor Dave's car coming up the drive, and Freddy Fisher was with him.

The Confession

Mark Shepherd wiped a tear from his eye and walked down the front steps to meet them. Holding up his left hand firmly, he said "Stop. Now is not a good time for you to be here Freddy."

"Actually Mark, what Freddy needs to say is long past overdue. Trust me?" appealed Pastor Dave.

"What is *he* doing here?" Benny asked, stepping outside behind his father.

"Trust me, you are all going to want to hear what he has to say. You *need* to hear it," Pastor Dave pleaded.

Benny held open the door as the dinner party spilled over the front steps and onto the lawn, drawn outside by the sound of raised voices. As they stood there, staring angrily, men with crossed arms, ladies with arms interlocked, Pastor Dave stood alongside Freddy with his arm around him. Mr. Shepherd put his hand on his son's shoulder and gave him a nod to steady him. Freddy was trembling and had obviously been crying. The guests reacted with shock when they saw him. What part had he played in all of this?

Pastor Dave spoke first. "I think most of you know Freddy Fisher here." Freddy looked up at Nick. If he was looking for a sign of approval, he certainly did not get one. "As some of you know, Freddy was baptized this morning. He came by the church yesterday, overwhelmed with guilt and despairing over sins in his past. I truly believe that he has repented and turned away from his sins and turned toward Christ. He expressed his genuine belief that Jesus died for his sins on the cross and rose from the grave. He has placed his faith in Jesus as his Lord, his trust in

Christ as his Savior and he has prayed to invite Jesus into his heart and life. He is a new creation in Christ. He has asked the Lord for forgiveness, but he wanted to come here to ask you for forgiveness as well. We had planned on driving from house to house today, but providentially, most of the people with whom Freddy needs to make amends are gathered here at this home. I can see that there are strong emotions right now, but I would ask that you listen to what Freddy has to say."

Freddy began to speak, his voice shaking, "I am so sorry. Sorry to all of you. There are things, things about the night that Daniel and Annie died, that you need to know. I have been so afraid and so ashamed for so long. I was afraid to admit what I did."

"Freddy, I am a police officer. Anything you confess in front of me will not be kept a secret and I will arrest you if I have to."

"I understand that Nick. Please stay. You need to hear this and I will face whatever consequences are necessary for my actions...and inactions. On the night of the crash, I was the one who put alcohol in the punch that Annie drank. I didn't mean for anyone to get hurt. Daniel and I heard some guys at school talking about making punch for a party and while he was in the bathroom, I overheard them talking about it making people relax and enjoy themselves, and how to get Mr. Gordon to sell alcohol to you, so I bought a bottle of Edwin Culpepper's. I had no idea how powerful it was. I was carrying around a white Rum bottle as part of my Pirate costume and everybody thought it was a joke. I told them I just had water in it, but that was a lie. It was full of odorless E C.

While everyone else was at the Spooklight, I stayed behind at the trailer. It was so dark, no one noticed. I dumped out half of two jugs of punch and filled them back up with as much E C as I had. Everyone had gotten so mad at me about my little shoe pirate joke, I just thought it would help them loosen up a bit and enjoy the party. I truly did not understand how dangerous that substance is. When I heard Daniel and Annie coming back to the trailer, I hid in the woods. Annie drank a full glass of the tainted punch. It has no scent and almost no flavor, so she couldn't detect the difference, but as soon as Daniel, the terrific taster, sipped the potent punch, he immediately knew something was wrong and spit it out. He was never drunk. Annie was very upset as she began to feel the effects of the alcohol. When I realized how badly it was affecting her, I immediately regretted what I had done. I am so, so, sorry. I had never drank before and did not understand the dangers. I just thought it would give people a little bit of a party buzz. I had no idea what would happen. I felt horrible, so I acted like I was the first one back to the trailer and helped Daniel dump out the punch so no one else would drink any.

When we got back to the house, we helped Annie get into the truck and I thought Daniel would be able to get her home safely. If they wouldn't have left the party early, they would never have been in the crash. It's all my fault."

As the families started to respond, Freddy begged, "Please stop. Wait. It gets worse. Since I had ridden to the party with Daniel, I got a ride home with Charles Carpenter.

Charles and I left the party just a few moments behind Daniel and Annie. Reed Jones had been waiting in his truck on one of the side roads and when Daniel drove past, he flashed on his brights and his blazing off-road lights and pulled out behind them. He started tailgating, or more like bulldozing, Daniel. Reed kept revving his engine and trying to force Daniel to go faster. He was chasing Daniel down the hillside and around the curves, going faster and faster until Daniel blew right past the turn-off onto Bethel Road, which was the way he drove us *to* the party because it was safer. I'm not sure if he was too scared to slow down or what was wrong. Then it happened, two old muscle cars came around Hell's Half-Moon racing, one of them was a green Oldsmobile Cutlass and the other, a brown Chevy Nova, was in the chicken lane, in Daniel's lane. Daniel swerved as hard as he could to the right to try to miss it, but it smashed into him anyway. That's why his injuries were even worse...he tried to save Annie by taking the full impact on his side of the vehicle. Even in a split second, Daniel was self-less. Reed was following so closely that he bashed into Daniel and knocked his little truck off the road, causing it to roll over and over down the hill.

Charles and I were the first to arrive on the scene. Reed appeared to be uninjured. His solid steel ranch grille with the push bumper and the wing extensions was strong enough to absorb most of the impact, limiting the damage to one wheel. Aden Crow was with him. Aden kept saying, "It was an accident. It was just an accident." He told us that he knew First Aid and would help Daniel and Annie but that we needed to watch for traffic to make sure no one crashed into them. He said to turn our headlights into oncoming traffic and wave people around the crash on the side we came from. The driver of the Cutlass pulled around—I assumed to do the same on the other side. I told them to use the phone in Daniel's truck to call for help and he said 'good thinking,' promising that he would. I watched as he made a call. There isn't a whole lot of traffic out that way and the party wasn't ending for forty-five minutes, so we only had to wave a few cars around. They probably couldn't see much besides us waving because of Charles' headlights in their faces. I remember thinking how strange it was that a tow truck arrived before the ambulance, but you know they have to come all the way from the hospital in Ridgeview.

The tow truck showed up and hooked up to the 4x4, then a Jaguar pulled in. Aden got into the tow truck and Reed got into the Jag. They all left and the Cutlass just drove away.

Charles and I waited for the ambulance but it never arrived. So, about half an hour after the crash, I called the hospital from the car phone. Aden had never called them like he said he would. Charles got scared and left.

It was horrible. Daniel and Annie were both unconscious and covered in blood. I was wearing a red bandana underneath my hat as part of my pirate costume, so I took it off and tied it around her head to try and stop the bleeding until the ambulance could get there. I waited with them, until I saw lights coming and heard sirens, then I panicked and ran away into the woods like a coward. I left my best friend, assuming he was dead, and fled. I walked about five miles through the woods and backroads by moonlight to get back to town. Some old man's dog went crazy barking as I passed through the trees by his house and I thought he was gonna shoot me or sic the dog on me. My only defense was my plastic scimitar sword but I was so scared and my hands were shaking so badly that I dropped it and lost it in the dark."

Benny and Lucy exchanged a look, but did not interrupt him.

"That next week, when Reed found out that an anonymous phone call had been made to the hospital, he took credit. It gave him an excuse for leaving the scene if anyone had seen his truck there. He said he had driven upon the wreck and went door to door to call for help. He and Aden were the ones that lied about the timing of the wreck, claiming it happened at midnight, to cover themselves and act like the heroes of the story. Plenty of people saw the flashing lights and diverted around the wreck about that time, so no one questioned their report."

Then Nick interrupted "Frank Evans was an easy scapegoat. They told all the newspapers that his vehicle was the only one involved in the crash and he was extradited before even being interviewed by the local sheriff's department."

Lucy deduced "Reed and Aden were the ones that started the rumor about Daniel dosing Annie with something. They knew people were starting to talk and wonder who was hurting all those girls. It was convenient for them to pin it on a boy who was dead and couldn't speak up for himself."

Mr. Baker added "And their fathers were more than happy to use the rumors to oust Pastor Mark. It covered their own son's indiscretions and furthered their own selfish ambitions."

Benny continued "Lester Crow owns a tow truck. Was he driving it himself?"

Yes, Freddy continued. "They must have towed the truck to the car lot to get it fixed because Reed drove it to school on Monday with a freshly painted black grill. And there's more. They pulled up next to us before they fled the scene. Reed and his father stepped out of the Jag and Aden and his dad climbed down out of the tow truck. They threatened Charles and I. They told us that they owned this town and influenced everyone who mattered. They told us they would tell everyone that Charles and I had been involved in a race that caused the accident. Aden pulled a sawed-off shotgun from the tow truck on us and Reed grabbed a forty-five out of the glovebox of his dad's Jag. They said they would kill us and bury our bodies under a slab of concrete in the Jones' new housing division if we ever spoke about that night again. And we never did. I know that I don't deserve it and I have no right to ask, but could you ever find it in your hearts to forgive me?"

Freddy finally broke down. Nick was already next to him. He hugged his friend. Benny was next. He just cried and hugged his brother's two friends. Lucy was sobbing and Gabby and Hannah, who were closest had their arms around her.

Mrs. Baker was knelt down with her arms around Mrs. Shepherd and Mrs. Wheeler. Mrs. Shepherd had collapsed to her knees with her face in her hands and was crying so hard she was hyperventilating. Mrs. Wheeler had knelt around her and was holding her while sobbing uncontrollably herself. The two mothers were inconsolable in that moment. They just kept saying "They murdered our babies. They killed them."

Mr. Baker put his arms around Mr. Wheeler and Mr. Shepherd to steady them as the tears started to flow and then walked them over to their wives. Tears streamed down their faces and dripped onto the floor as they knelt down next to the women. Mrs. Baker rubbed her hands on their backs as their husbands collapsed down and held them in their arms. The horror of what had been done to their children, the utter disregard for human life, the horrifying depravity of those boy's actions was just too much to cope with in that moment.

Benny walked over to Lucy and they sobbed into each other's shaking shoulders while Gabby and Hannah went over to Freddy and Nick, offering long hugs and empathy.

After her breathing regulated and she gathered herself a little bit, Mrs. Shepherd went to Benny and wrapped him up as tight as she could, while Mr. Shepherd put his arms around both. Mr. and Mrs. Wheeler did the same with Lucy as she gently released Benny's hand.

As the Bakers made their way over to check on Freddy, Pastor Dave made the rounds, praying with each family and group.

One by one each person eventually approached Freddy, to thank him for telling the truth and to offer their heartfelt forgiveness, the type of forgiveness that is only possible when the Spirit of God is at work in the midst of a group of people.

Everyone could see that Freddy was a changed man. They knew that he loved Daniel and Annie, that he attempted to fix his mistake, that he had genuinely done everything he could to help them and that he had been tormented by this for a decade. Nick discreetly assured him there was nothing more he could have done.

The Wheeler and Shepherd families verbally forgave Freddy, hugged him, thanked him for his honesty, thanked him for trying to help their children and then insisted that he and Pastor Dave come inside for some heated up leftovers.

There were a great many tears shed that day, but after the initial wave of horror as they came to grips with the reality of what had been done, the tears turned into something different. They were different than the tears that had been shed ten years earlier. After all these years of not knowing, yes, these were tears of deeply felt grief, but they were also tears of long-delayed relief in finally knowing the truth, at least more of it. They were tears of healing.

The revelations of that Sunday afternoon were the turning point in the investigation. Most people would have simply been satisfied to know part of the truth and move on with life, but Benny Shepherd wasn't most people, neither were Lucy Wheeler or Nick Baker. The knowledge they acquired that day served as a catalyst, like dynamite blowing the case wide open and propelling their quest forward. As hard is it may be to believe, some of the biggest bombshells were yet to be dropped. But first, Benny had to deal with school.

PART THREE

THE NEXT WEEK

2007

Monday, November 5

Showdown

On Monday morning, Mrs. Shepherd insisted on driving Benny to school, despite his protestations. She didn't want any more encounters with Riley Jones on the road after what happened with Lucy that weekend. Benny didn't see Riley for most of the day, but they had American History together last period, due to the fact that Riley had previously failed the course. With Riley's suspension over, this would be the first time they were in class together since the assault and the encounter at the bowling alley.

Anger had been simmering within Benny since Saturday night when he learned that Riley ran Lucy off the road. That Monday afternoon as he walked into class Riley smirked at him and said "How's your little girlfriend Shepherd? I heard she had some car trouble over the weekend," he taunted. Then he asked if Lucy was as much of a whore as her N-word loving sister.

Benny dropped his books and rushed across the room to Riley's desk. He grabbed the front of Riley's jean jacket and pulled him out of his seat, dragging him to the front of the room where he picked him up and put his back against the chalkboard.

"Don't you EVER speak that way about Lucy, OR her sister, OR my brother. Don't you dare EVER come near Lucy Wheeler again." Riley opened his mouth to speak and Benny ordered him to "SHUT UP! You caught me off guard last week when your friend jumped me from behind like a coward, but that will NEVER happen again. I *chose* not to retaliate after you assaulted me, but I WILL NOT tolerate you threatening, harassing or bullying my friends or putting their lives in danger." Riley opened his mouth again. "NOT A WORD!" Benny roared fiercely. "I am imposing a one-hundred yard restraining order around Lucy Wheeler. If you see her driving, you turn around and go the other direction. Do you understand me? You don't speak to her. You don't look at her. And if you ever try to intimidate her or put her life in danger again, YOU-WILL-ANSWER-TO-ME."

Mr. Webster, the History teacher, had been using the restroom and as he arrived back in the classroom, he attempted to intervene. "Let's calm down here boys. Now Benny, you put him down."

"He tried to run Lucy Wheeler off the road Saturday. The dirty coward waited until she was alone and chased her down with his truck. He scared her half to death and almost caused her to get in a wreck. I will NOT calm down and do not interfere with me. Now listen here Riley. You WILL Back off and you WILL stay away from Lucy. Is that understood?"

Riley remained silent.

"Have I made myself clear?" Benny asked as he gave Riley a shake with both hands.

"Yes."

"Yes, what?"

"Yes sir."

"Say it. I will leave Lucy Wheeler alone...NOW.

"I'll leave her alone. I'll leave her alone." Riley was broken. He sniveled and shook like the yellow-belly he was.

"And you tell your little minion Jason Simmons that goes for him too," Benny added.

Mr. Webster interrupted, "Benny, I need you to put him down and go to the office."

"Fine," he replied. But before he complied, Benny looked Riley Jones straight in the eye and said "You, and your family are DONE bullying this town. No one is afraid of you anymore. You. Are. Finished."

Benny set Riley's feet on the ground and Jones flopped to the floor like his legs were made of gelatin. He curled up in the fetal position as the class clapped and cheered. Coyotes are predators, but they are cowards at heart. When you confront them, they will cower or flee, but don't turn your back on them.

Then Benny walked over beside Mr. Webster's desk where a small collection of replica flags hung on the wall. He reached up and ripped the Confederate Battle Flag down. The St. Andrew's cross, a blue "X" adorned with thirteen white stars, disappeared into a ball of red as he wadded it up and slammed it into the trash can. Rounding on Mr. Webster, he said "It is one thing to show a picture or have an object lesson, but to display that insidious rag in your classroom is inappropriate. That symbol of racism and hate has no more place hanging in a classroom than a Nazi flag does. Do not let me see it in this room again."

Benny had never looked closely at the pictures behind his history teacher's desk before. That day was the first time he noticed that a young J.C. Jones and Lester Crow were both pictured in Mr. Webster's Whitfield College fraternity photograph. *It figures he would be friends with those two scumbags. Gamma Omicron Sigma needs to pick classier pledges,* he thought to himself as he wheeled and left the room.

Principal Potter threatened to suspend Benny for fighting. Benny pointed out that no punches were thrown and he did not cause any physical harm to Riley whatsoever.

"Are you going to kick me out of school for having a conversation, for standing up to a bully that you have been too cowardly to confront because you're afraid of his father? You haven't protected the kids of this school from their family. You didn't protect my brother who was bullied in this school. If you won't stand up for what is right, then I WILL. Are you ready to face a lawsuit for slandering my name with false accusations? Because that is exactly what's going to happen if you accuse me of fighting. Trust me, if I wanted to fight, you'd be calling an ambulance for Riley Jones right now. I showed restraint. There are laws that allow students to defend themselves against bullies and you better believe my lawyer will know that. You failed to administer the appropriate punishment or to take steps for my protection when you witnessed me being assaulted on school grounds. He should have been expelled, not given a measly, slap-on-the-wrist, three-day suspension. The first thing he did when he came back was to get up in Mrs. Cartwright's face trying to bully her at the homecoming parade. Do I need to press formal charges for what happened to me on school grounds last week? I bet *that* would look great in the newspapers. Should we call the police right now? I've got Officer Nick Baker on speed dial."

"No, No, that won't be necessary," was Principal Potter's reply. "Let's just have you wait in the library until the final bell rings and I will speak with Mr. Webster to straighten everything out."

"I don't want to be in the same class with Riley Jones anymore. I want him transferred to another room. Should we get my parents down here?"

"No, no that will be fine. I will instruct the counselors to have Mr. Jones complete the rest of his coursework for that class as, uh, an independent study course. He can sit in the in-school suspension room to do his assignments each day. Would that be alright with you?"

"That sounds fine."

"You can go to the library now, if that's ok."

"Yes, Mr. Potter, that is ok."

After school, Coop and Mason flanked Benny as they walked out the doors and onto the sidewalk.

"What's gotten in to you?" asked Mason. "Are you trying to get kicked out of school?"

"No, I'm trying to stand up for what's right and I will not allow my friends to be terrorized or victimized anymore."

"I thought you were awesome," admired Coop. "That was the greatest thing I've ever seen."

"Did you see Riley's face?" Mason asked. He's gonna want revenge."

"No way," replied, Coop. "He knew he was beaten. He won't dare bully anyone at this school again."

"I *am* starting to think it was Riley the officer saved when he stepped in between you two after the attack last week," Mason admitted. "Seriously, when did you get so strong, Benny?"

"It's all those shifts I picked up at the lumber yard this summer working with my dad to put away money for college."

"Well, it paid off. That was the best moment of our high school careers," Coop concluded.

Benny, on the other hand, was already beginning to have doubts about the way he handled the situation. Had it been wise to humiliate Riley like that? Yes, the guy deserved it. And yes, he had to stand up for Lucy. But was there a better way to have done so?

Hunch

Fortunately, Nick was posted in a patrol car by the school parking lot, casually keeping an eye on things or the situation could have gotten out of control. Benny saw him having a word with Riley Jones as he made his way to his car.

"Have you heard?" Benny asked Nick after Riley left.

"Yeah, I heard. You alright?"

"I'm fine."

"Good. Your mom gave me permission to pick you up after school. Let's go get Lucy."

"Where are we going?"

"To the salvage yard outside of town. There's something we need to look into."

Nick took them to one of the older sections of the junkyard where a dust-covered, indigo blue pick-up truck sat up on cinder blocks with all of the windows missing. Most of the parts under the hood had been removed, as had the steering wheel, gauges, glovebox, gas cap and anything else that could be re-used.

"Why are we here?" Lucy asked.

"This was my brother's truck," Benny answered softly as he opened up the center console, pulling out a green glob of something wrapped in cellophane. "I think this used to be a popcorn ball," he chuckled. "Daniel knew how much I loved them. I bet he was bringing it home for me."

He reached underneath the seat and pulled out a hand-sewn blanket, protected from the elements in a heavy plastic zipper bag. "Dad's rules," he commented. "If it's cold enough to wear a coat outside, carry a blanket, gloves and a stocking cap in your vehicle. That way if a sudden cold snap occurs and you have car trouble, you won't freeze."

"Country common sense 101," Nick replied. "Daniel was always prepared."

Peering inside, Lucy could see that the car phone was still sitting there, an unbroken relic of days gone by and a reminder of lies. "I wonder why no one ever took the phone?"

"My dad," Benny replied. "He bolted it in place with thread-locking fluid. It's this special type of superglue that permanently seals bolts in place. He wanted to make sure no one could steal the phone. He let me help him and I got some on my hands so he had to whisk me over to the garden hose to rinse it off before my fingers stuck together. Daniel brought out some dish soap and helped me lather up and scrub it off. They were both always so patient with me. Everything was an adventure. They acted like it was just a normal part of learning how to do manly stuff."

Nick laid down on a mechanics dolly he had borrowed from his uncle and rolled underneath the truck. He took a couple of flash pictures and then dusted the brake lines with a little brush before rolling back out with four sealed plastic bags in his hand. "Something in Freddy's story caught my attention. He said that Daniel blew by Bethel Road which was the safer way home and trust me, your brother always took the safe way. Freddy said it seemed like he was afraid to slow down. I thought, what if he *couldn't* slow down." Holding up the bags, Nick showed them the brake lines. "These were cut. Your brother's car was sabotaged. This just became a murder investigation."

"Annie and Daniel would have wrecked going around Hell's Half Moon whether they ran into that Nova or not," Benny observed.

"They killed them because they didn't like a white girl spending time with a black boy," Lucy said.

Benny and Lucy turned to each other with tears in their eyes and hugged for a long minute. This was all just too much to bear.

"What were you doing with that brush?" Lucy asked.

"Dusting for fingerprints."

"Why didn't you dust the rest of the vehicle?" Benny asked.

"For one thing, this truck has been picked apart by scavengers and their hands have been all over it. For another, dashboards are notoriously difficult to get prints from because of the pebbled surface. Any prints Reed or Aden left on the phone or other plastic surfaces inside the truck would be gone after this many years and we don't yet have the capability of getting prints from fabric. Fingerprints only last about two and a half years on metal, so dusting the exterior of the vehicle won't do us any good at all. Since we already know they were at the scene, simply finding fingerprints on the vehicle wouldn't be enough evidence to prove they sabotaged the truck anyway, but I thought I might have some luck trying underneath the chassis. A fingerprint can last over ten years on a rubber surface such as a brake line and I found one. I'll take these back to the station, recover as many prints as I can and see if we get a match. That would be strong evidence of malicious endangerment."

"What do we do now?" Benny asked.

"Now you let the law finally do its job and you stay away from Riley Jones."

Lucy looked at Nick suspiciously. "What?"

"Your boy here had a little run in with Mr. Jones at school today."

"It was just a conversation, Lucy."

"A conversation with you holding him by his shirt up against the chalkboard in the middle of class," Nick added.

"I told him to leave you alone. I told him to leave all my friends alone."

Lucy stood on her tip toes and kissed Benny high on the cheek. He kissed her on the forehead as she took his hand in hers.

"Ugh, you two. Does anyone feel like bowling?" Nick asked as he jokingly rolled his eyes.

"Seriously?" Benny and Lucy exclaimed.

"*Very* seriously," Nick replied. "Give me a quick moment, I need to make a phone call."

As they pulled into Riverview Lanes, Benny was surprised to see Hannah pull up and park next to Nick's Mustang.

"I thought you would be back at your shop in Lake City by now," Lucy remarked as she gave Hannah a hug.

"I gave myself today off work. Benefits of being self-employed. Gabby and I had some planning to do. We met up with Nick for lunch and he asked me for one more favor before I go home. Gabby is picking Maggie up from school and I've just come from talking with my parents. On the night of my Halloween party, Reed Jones and Aden Crow were being obnoxious jerks, walking around in their gray Confederate soldier uniforms saying stupid stuff and answering each other with rhymes, like *One, two, three...Robert E. Lee* and *Three, two, one...The South should have won.*

After I told them to get lost, I just assumed they left while we were loading up the trailer to go on the hayride, but today I asked my mom and dad if they saw anyone hanging around while we were gone. When my dad went to take the trash out from the party, he caught Reed and Aden hiding out near where the cars were parked. The back of Reed's truck was filled with toilet paper, shaving cream and cartons of eggs, so dad just figured they were up to the typical Halloween mischief and ran them off."

"The T P and eggs must have flown out of Reed's truck when he smashed into Daniel, that's why they were all over the road," Benny observed.

"So, what's going on Nick?" Hannah asked.

"We've just been out to the salvage yard. I inspected Daniel's truck and found that the brake lines had been cut. You just confirmed that it could have been Reed and Aden who did it."

Hannah was speechless. Nick gave her a hug and then they all walked inside. Monday afternoon was typically slow at the bowling alley and Nick asked Freddy to come bowl a game with them.

Freddy brought them over some funnel cakes and they bowled, filling him in on the results of the investigation. As they finished the last frame, Freddy asked, "Is this some sort of last supper. Have you come to arrest me?"

"No Freddy, why would I arrest you? You stopped to help at a traffic accident, which you were under no legal obligation to do. You instructed others to call for help and had the presence of mind to tell them about the car phone. You were informed that First Aid was being administered. I was finally able to trace the first call made from Daniel's car phone that night," he said as he looked over at Benny and Lucy. "It was to Lester Crow. Freddy, when you thought Aden was calling for help, he was actually calling his father to bring the tow truck, but you had no way of knowing that. You put yourself at risk directing traffic around the wreck and in so doing, you saved lives, including my own. I didn't see you because I drove up on the opposite side, but your actions kept the road safe for the rest of us. You called for help immediately upon learning that others had failed to do so and waited until you saw help arriving. There is nothing you could have done to help the EMTs.

The only things you did wrong were to run away and to buy alcohol and mix it into some punch, which you dumped out upon learning of its dangerous effects and you made sure the person affected was on her way safely home.

We just learned that the brake lines to Daniel's truck were cut and Hannah's dad caught Reed Jones and Aden Crow sneaking around near the vehicle while everyone was gone on the hayride. No matter what time Daniel left the party, Reed and Aden would have been hiding in wait for him and he and Annie would have been headed down the hill and around the perilous curves in a rolling death trap. They will be dealt with, and I will need your help."

Tuesday, November 6

Sleuthing

On Tuesday, Benny and Lucy were allowed to miss school (and homeschool) to help Nick track down the driver of the green Oldsmobile Cutlass that had been involved in the race that doomful October night. After school started, when they were unlikely to encounter Riley Jones or any other trouble makers, Benny was allowed to pick Lucy up and drive her down to the police station where they spent a couple of hours that morning sifting through DMV records. Neither minded the work as they were engaged in delightful banter. They took a break for lunch to enjoy a quality cheeseburger pizza from Mr. P's. The combination must be good for the mind because Benny suddenly had an idea, which he quickly shared with Nick. Lucy also had a brainstorm.

"Why are we looking to see who owned the car back then? Let's find out who owns it now."

"That's good thinking," Benny agreed, "Most of the vintage cars around here are old vehicles that people couldn't bear to part with, or didn't think they could get enough money for. They've been stored out in a barn or found under a tarp in a granny's garage. Folks either fix them up or run an ad in the paper to sell them locally."

Nick chimed in, "That's how we got my 1965 Mustang Fastback. The owner passed away and it was just sitting in the garage, hadn't been driven in years. Dad bought it at an estate sale for cheap and my uncle got it running again."

"That Cutlass is a classic, maybe it's still with the same owner, or the same family, or at least in the area." Lucy suggested.

"And you should narrow your vehicle description and widen the area of your search parameters," Nick suggested.

Searching based on Freddy's description of the vehicle, they were able to determine that the Cutlass was a mountain green, 1967 model coupe. Then, they expanded their hunt throughout the entire county for current owners and found the information. The owner turned out to be Sam Weaver. The previous owner was a George Weaver of nearby Grainfield, probably his father. A targeted internet search found Sam, who turned out to be a new car salesman at Crow's Car Palace, living in a suspiciously large house out in River Glenn with a four-car garage where the Cutlass currently resided.

Since Benny and Lucy were still technically under safety lockdown by their parents and Nick was leaving the station, they said their goodbyes and made him promise to call or text periodically with updates.

Following a tip from Benny, Nick got a warrant for a sample of the indigo blue paint smears from the grill of the Jones's 4x4 which he retrieved from the school parking lot without Riley even knowing. It was a perfect match to the paint on Daniel's pickup. Luckily, at the time of the accident, the fresh paintjob on Daniel's little truck wasn't cured yet so it had transferred quite easily when Reed Jones smashed into him. The height of his truck allowed the grill to clear Daniel's tires and bumpers and contact directly with the fresh paint. They had obviously spray-painted the grill glossy black to cover up the paint transfer and when Riley threw a tantrum and kicked the grill at the homecoming parade, the hastily applied, ten-year old paint job had cracked and flaked off, revealing smears of metallic indigo blue paint underneath. Now, in addition to eye witness testimony that Reed Jones and Aden Crow were involved in the crash, they had physical evidence of Reed's guilt.

That afternoon, Sam Weaver cut a deal in exchange for his testimony. The prosecuting attorney agreed not to press charges for leaving the scene of an accident if Sam would write out a deposition and testify to seeing Reed Jones and Aden Crow involved in the wreck and then fleeing the scene.

The paint match and cut brake lines combined with the testimonies of Sam Weaver, Mr. Farmer (Hannah's father), Charles Carpenter, and Freddy Fisher gave the County Prosecuting Attorney enough ammunition to work with and he got busy obtaining written statements from the witnesses and gathering the information he needed to present to the judge to get warrants.

Into the Woods

Having done all they could to help Nick, Benny and Lucy busied themselves that afternoon as well. Since Riley Jones and his henchman Jason Simmons would be getting out of school soon and they wished to avoid further confrontation, they went back to Lucy's house to work on a special project. Lucy had taken detailed notes from their research at the library. Now they set about to write an article, revealing the full truth to the town. It was time to clear Daniel and Annie's good names and to blow the lid off the conspiracy that besmirched them. Working from Lucy's notes, Daniel's diary and the information they had learned throughout their inquest, the dynamic duo graduated from amateur detectives to investigative reporters. They spent a couple of intense hours carefully weighing what information to share. They were diligent to avoid unwarranted accusations, meticulously wording the article in such a way as to allow the facts of the case to guide the audience to draw the proper conclusions.

When they finished, Lucy placed a call to T.S. Clemons, editor of the Lost River Gazette, giving him a tip to keep an eye on Reed Jones and Aden Crow the following day as arrests were likely to happen. The erstwhile newspaper man assured her that he would send his best reporters out in disguise, cameras at the ready, to capture the moment. She also informed Mr. Clemons about their in-depth inquiry and guaranteed him an exclusive on the story of the decade if he kept it under wraps until Thursday morning when the weekly paper was released. She gave him an approximate word and character count, as well as the title to the piece so he could prepare adequate space and promised to deliver the article by Wednesday afternoon, so that no one would have time to pressure him into not printing it. He told her that as long as he received copy by 5:00 pm, it would be printed.

As they wrote, Nick had updated them with all the events of the afternoon. With their article complete, now they would pray and wait. Benny began "Lord, thank-you for helping us find the truth."

Lucy continued "Help the judge to be fair and impartial and to grant the prosecutor warrants for the arrest of Reed Jones and Aden Crow."

Benny added "Please protect our families from harm."

"And keep the officers who will be arresting them tomorrow safe."

"We pray that all of the evil schemes of the lawyers will be thwarted."

"And we pray that you would give comfort to all of the women who were victimized back then as this situation could stir up painful memories. Help them find peace and comfort in the truth that is revealed and in you."

"We pray for things to finally be put right for our families and in our town."

"In Jesus' name we pray,"

"AMEN," they both finished together.

"And Amen," Mrs. Wheeler added as she brought them in a tray of warm snickerdoodle cookies and ice-cold milk.

"Thanks Mom," Lucy said.

"It's my pleasure. So nice to have you over Benny."

"Thanks Mrs. Wheeler."

"Call me Karen."

"Thanks Karen."

"You are most welcome. I am so very proud of the two of you."

After they finished their cookies, Lucy suggested they take a walk down to the riverbank. She fetched a pair of bright pink galoshes from the mud closet and handed Benny a pair of her dad's rubber boots to borrow. He pulled on Daniel's leather jacket while Lucy bundled up in a light blue coat and then they trekked out the back door, across the yard and through the gate. Benny caught a whiff of dried grass smell drifting down from the hayloft as they passed the old barn. Its red paint was streaked with gray from decades of weather revealing the wooden planks underneath, but the silvery metal roof was a fairly new addition. A donkey's head emerged from the barn and he let out a loud bray. Lucy walked over and ran her fingers up and down his forehead between his eyes. "Come meet Otis," she invited. "He's new around here," Lucy explained, "but he's really friendly."

"I think he likes me," Benny observed as he smoothed his hand along the donkey's neck.

"Yes, this one loves attention," Lucy commented.

As they continued down the sloping pasture Lucy counted out twelve head of cattle. They were all polled, dark red or black and some had white faces or markings. There were half a dozen cows, all but one with a spring calf still on them and one large, well-muscled bull, who Lucy assured Benny was harmless and nothing to worry about as long as you didn't get between him and his hay, the feed trough, or a cow in season. One little black baldy was without a calf.

"What happened to her calf?" Benny inquired.

"Coyotes got him when he was just a newborn. He had nursed and fallen asleep and she was grazing. Dad looked out the kitchen window as the sun disappeared behind the hills and there they were, sneaking in. He was too late. He said they seemed unusually aggressive. That's why he bought Otis. He's our new guard donkey."

"Donkey's fight coyotes?"

"They sure do," Lucy answered as she led Benny over to a stream.

From underneath the roots of a large oak tree, a fresh water spring seeped out of the ground, forming a tiny pool before trickling away. Lucy removed a long-handled dipper hanging from a nail in the tree and scooped up some of the clean, clear water, insisting that Benny take a drink. It was the purest, most delicious water he had ever tasted in his life. Lucy waded ankle deep into the current, reached upstream and overturned a rock. A crawdad came swimming out from underneath and she grabbed down and picked it up by the tail. She held its wriggling body up for Benny to see before softly placing it back into the water and flipping the rock back into its place. The crawdad quickly hid under a new rock. Laughing, they walked along the spring as it bubbled and gurgled its way down to join the river. As they reached the edge of the bank, they could see schools of minnows darting back and forth among the rocks in the crystal-clear water.

"It's beautiful here," Benny said.

"I really love it. I'm so glad we moved out here when our old neighborhood in town got...noisy."

They turned right to walk upstream, out of the pasture and into a wooded area. Up here, north of the old ford, the river was more like a large, gently moving creek. At a spot where a small island of rocks with a few scraggly trees split the current, they found a beaver's dam which had created a nice little pond. "This is a great swimming hole," Lucy said. "You'll have to come back this summer and we can go swimming."

"I'd love that," Benny replied.

"Really?"

"Really."

"You're not going to disappear on me after this is all over?"

"Not a chance," Benny assured her.

Benny picked up five smooth stones from the bank and skipped three of them across the beaver pond in a competition with Lucy to see who could get the most skips or reach the bank of the island. Benny slipped the remaining two stones into his pocket, saving them to skip later as they continued walking. The couple circled the pond, wading across the side stream at its narrowest point above the pond, right where the flow of water splits. Then they traveled back toward the beaver dam along the island.

As they walked, Benny said "You were pretty amazing this afternoon. Your notes. Your writing. The way you handled the newspaper editor. Do you think that's what you might want to do for a living?"

"Thank-you. But no. I enjoy writing and I think I might like to freelance as a reporter or even write a book one day. But what I really want to do is lead the music at a church, or work in student ministry. I've never told anyone that before," Lucy confided.

"Wow. You would be incredible at it, that's for sure."

"Thanks. What about you, Benny?"

"I honestly don't know. Everything has always been such a struggle...since Daniel died. I've been so focused on just making it through each day that I feel like I haven't had time to dream about the future or make plans."

"That's understandable."

"When I was little, I always wanted to be a preacher like my dad, but seeing what he's been put through, I just don't know if I can take it."

"You could. I've seen strength and resilience in you these past few weeks. Don't sell yourself short."

"It's just hard," Benny replied. And then he asked the question that had been burning in his heart, the question that haunted him. "Do you think it was God's will for our families to be put through this?"

"No Benny, I don't. It is never God's will for people to sin and do evil things. But it *is* his will for us to be faithful and trust in Him to get us through when they do. What was done to our families was evil accomplished by lies. The Bible says that it is impossible for God to lie. People bore false witness against our families, breaking the ninth commandment. They sabotaged Daniel's truck putting his and Annie's lives in danger which broke the sixth commandment not to murder. It is never God's will for people to break his commandments. Habakkuk 1:3 teaches that God is so holy and pure, He cannot look upon evil approvingly and that he cannot tolerate wrongdoing. The prophet then asks why God seems to put up with that kind of stuff. Why doesn't he bring it to a quick and decisive end? The answer is Love, Benny. God desires people to repent of their sins and be saved. It isn't his will for us to be the victims of evildoers, but it *is* his will for us to trust in him, faithfully endure and be good witnesses when it happens. Ultimately, there will come a day of judgement, but until then Luke 6:27-28 tells us that it is God's will for us to love our enemies, to do good to those who hate us, to bless those who curse us and to pray for those who mistreat us. But his word also tells us in Psalm 31:9 and many other places to speak up for the poor and needy and judge fairly."

"So, it's a sort of balancing act between standing up for others who are being mistreated and praying earnestly for bad people God wants to save and change?"

"Exactly."

"So do you think it was right for us to go after Reed Jones and Aden Crow?" Benny asked.

"Yes. Absolutely, I do. They have done a lot of harm to so many people and had to be stopped. Their families have made a mockery of the church and used it for their own personal gain," Lucy answered.

"And God is not mocked," Benny responded. "They did all of this from inside the church."

"Right. Remember when Paul told the church to remove the evil people from among them?"

"Yes, to put them out of the church. This was never about vengeance for me. It was about justice. God loves justice and righteousness and we are called to respect the civil authorities and Peter wrote that it is the government's responsibility to punish evil and reward the good."

"Exactly right. And that is the point that we're at. Like you said. It's a balancing act between offering grace and forgiveness, and protecting vulnerable people from evil men," Lucy concluded.

"Wow. I feel so much better. I've never spoken like this with anyone in my life," Benny confessed.

"Me neither," Lucy replied. "It's nice to have someone to talk to about the serious stuff."

"Most people aren't interested in diving into deep conversation."

"They're content to just dip a toe in the shallows."

"You're pretty amazing."

"You're kind of wonderful yourself."

They both smiled and then hugged in the warm glow of sunset before wading back across the river just below the beaver dam to complete their circle of the pond. As they walked over to take a closer look at the beaver's handiwork, Lucy noticed fresh paw prints in the damp mud near the bank. "Do those look like coyote tracks to you?" she asked.

Squatting down to take a look, while remaining alert, Benny replied "No. See how rounded these toes are? Canine prints are elongated. Feline prints are rounded. These are definitely cat tracks."

"That must be a pretty big cat."

"A bobcat, I'd say."

Just then, they heard a rustling and as Benny turned his head up to look for the source, his gaze was met by a pair of eyes so piercing they nearly glowed, peering at him through the brush at the edge of the beaver dam. Attached to the eyes was a fuzzy, mottled yellowish cat with tufted ears and a bobbed tail. Benny kept his crouch and maintained his gaze whispering "Lucy, look there."

"Wow, cool. I've never seen a bobcat before."

"Hey there fella, are you a friendly wildcat?" Benny asked.

"We're not going to hurt you," Lucy promised.

As Benny slowly stood up, the cat took off, almost silently, in the direction of upstream. The intrigued teens watched as its dappled yellow form gradually melted into the fall palette of the trees and disappeared into the woods.

"That was cool," Lucy said.

"Yes! That was awesome," Benny agreed "Do you think anyone will believe us?"

"Maybe, if the tracks are still here. It's so rare to see a bobcat I wasn't sure they really lived in this area."

"Me neither. Now we know."

The ground was blanketed with leaves and the trees were half bare as the pair walked back the way they came, so they swished leaves with their feet and kicked up the leaf-drifts at the edge of the forest, whooshing along as they crunched through, making as much noise as possible. Lucy grabbed a handful of fall color and threw it high in the air. Benny watched as a leaf caught the breeze and floated away while others see-sawed to the ground. He playfully threw a few leaves her direction and she retaliated in kind. They played a game of chase around, tagging each other with handfuls of soft leaves for a minute before Lucy allowed herself to be caught in a long, lingering, snuggly hug in the cool evening air. She looked up into Benny's eyes and ran her fingers through his hair, resting her hand on his cheek. And then he kissed her, softly, sweetly, gently. For a moment the whole world disappeared and it was just the two of them, everything else swirling like the leaves. Benny slowly separated his lips from hers...and Lucy put her hand behind his neck, gently pulled him close and kissed him right back. After another moment of head spinning ecstasy, they stood there, forehead to forehead, wrinkling nose tip to wrinkling nose tip as their smiles burst into giggles of pure joy.

With the final embers of sunset beginning to extinguish behind the hills, Benny and Lucy continued walking back toward the house with their arms around each other. As twilight faded and darkness quickly snuck up on them, they neared the edge of the forest. Lucy said, "Come look over here. There's one last thing I want to show you."

As the pair peered up an incline into the trees, Benny saw a cluster of stacked stone pillars in the waning light. Crossing into the woods to get a closer look, he noticed the darkened side of the stones was covered in moss. Clumps of dying grasses spilled out over the tops of the pylons. On the higher side, the pillars were about two feet tall. On the lower side, they were about three and a half feet high.

"Isn't this neat?" Lucy asked. "Someone must have lived in a little cabin here by the river a long time ago."

"This is really interesting," agreed Benny. "They must have built the house on these risers to keep their home from flooding when the river overflows its banks."

The rotting remnants of the collapsed cabin formed a knee-high wall across the back of the structure. The couple heard a twig snap followed by a swishing sound moving through the leaves. Standing still, they heard the stalking of soft footfalls approaching from behind the barrier. Straining to see into the darkened woods, they caught the faintest shadowy glimpse of pointy ears moving behind the wall.

"Do you think that's the bobcat?" Benny whispered.

"It might be," Lucy softly answered as she pulled a small flashlight out of her parka pocket. "Is that you little buddy," she said as she turned her light toward the direction of the sound. Slinking around the right corner of the wall, Benny saw a pair of glowing white eyes reflecting back at them. Another pair of eerie eyes appeared from around the logs on the left. Expanding his range of view, he noticed the bodies attached to those eyes. A coyote's eyes are yellow in the daylight, but their eyeshine at night reflects bright white. Normally, coyotes will shy away from humans, but these began creeping closer, growling and huffing.

"Git," Benny shouted. They continued to advance.

"Go on," Lucy hollered, but they kept coming.

"I think they might be rabid," Benny observed as he stepped between Lucy and the carnivorous canines. "Keep your light on them." Taking the two remaining smooth stones out of his pocket, Benny wound his right arm and pitched, eyes fixed on his target, carefully following through just like his dad taught him. There was a loud yelp as he nailed the first coyote right between the eyes. In one smooth motion, Benny pivoted, swept the second rock out of his left hand into his right and launched it directly between the glowing eyes of the other coyote.

"Quick," Lucy shouted as she grabbed Benny's arm pulling him into a run, heading out of the woods. "To the water!"

They could hear the sound of chasing pawsteps getting ever closer, pursuing them through the leaves as they fled. Benny glanced over his shoulder, but couldn't see anything as darkness had overtaken light under the canopy of trees. As they crashed through the leaves at edge of the forest and splashed into the river, Benny could see the menacing shadows of the coyotes in the pale light of the crescent moon. They growled ferociously where they had stopped, several feet away at the lip of the bank. They howled and then slowly slunk away, disappearing into the black of night as the clouds shrouded the moon from view.

Panting for oxygen with his hands on his knees, Benny asked "How did you know that would work?"

Wheezing in the cold night air with her hands on her hips, Lucy replied, "You said that you thought those coyotes were rabid. Do you know what they used to call rabies?"

"Hydrophobia," Benny answered.

"Exactly, because it makes the animals afraid of water," Lucy explained.

"That's brilliant Lucy." Benny was grateful for the rubber boots as they waded along the shallow edge of the riverbank. Using the flashlight to navigate as the stars began to appear in the nighttime sky, they turned left into the spring to cross the pasture. Lucy shone her light out across the field and they caught a chilling glimpse of the intense white eyes of the two coyotes, hungrily hunting them from a distance. When they reached the mouth of the spring, they paused for a moment to gather themselves, and then sprinted as fast as they could across the short distance past the barn from the spring to the house. As the adventurers ran hand in hand, they heard the sound of galloping hooves and Otis braying loudly hee-haw, hee-haw, followed by yips and yelps, then the sound of shuffling through leaves as the coyotes retreated into the woods.

"Good donkey," Lucy said.

"It seems like no matter where I go, I can't escape predatory coyotes of *some* kind," Benny mumbled. "It's a good thing you thought so quickly or we would be goners."

"It's a good thing you had such great aim with those stones," Lucy replied. "I'll tell my parents about the coyotes later," she added as they entered the house and removed the muddy boots. "Dad will be glad to hear that he's been getting his money's worth out of Otis."

As he opened the front door to leave, Mrs. Wheeler told Benny, "Be extra careful driving home."

"I will," he promised, "it's only a few miles."

Out on the front porch, as they got ready to say their goodbyes for the evening, Benny had a thought. "I think we should go talk to Frank Evans at the prison."

"Why?"

"He was there that night. Reed and Aden just abandoned him, they might have even threatened him like they did Freddy and Charles. Maybe there's something he can tell us."

"Ok, but we're under lockdown, there's no way our parents will let us drive seventy miles to Lake City State Penitentiary."

"Maybe your mom can drive us?"

"I'll ask, but don't hold your breath. I'll call or text you later and let you know what she decides."

They said their goodbyes for the evening, snuck one more kiss on the front porch, and then Benny went home.

Wednesday, November 7

Behind Bars

After much discussion, the Shepherd family decided that Benny was better off not being at school near Riley Jones with what was going to be happening the next day and they agreed to allow he and Lucy to try to see Frank Evans in prison as long as Mrs. Wheeler would drive. However, Mark Shepherd warned his son "Several years ago I went to see Frank Evans. He was angry, vile and utterly unrepentant. You might not get what you're looking for."

"I have to try."

"Maybe you could take him a gift," his mom suggested.

"That's a great idea," his dad agreed, "but when we started our prison ministry from the church, I learned that most penitentiaries will not accept walk-in gifts, you must have them delivered."

"Maybe I could call the prison and put $50 on his account at the prison commissary," Sarah Shepherd replied.

"That's a brilliant idea," Benny agreed.

He called Lucy to let her know the good news, just as she was about to pick up the phone to call him. Her parents had acquiesced as well. Her mom would drive and they could go. He also told her about the gift idea.

Mrs. Wheeler and Lucy picked Benny up early Wednesday morning for the drive to Lake City and he brought his cell phone to receive updates from Nick.

As soon as the decision was made the night before, Karen Wheeler had cleverly logged onto the internet and purchased a mystery book and a devotional for which she paid extra for overnight delivery to the prison.

Sarah Shepherd called ahead to the prison and used her motherly powers of persuasion and the tragic story of their family's past to prevail upon them to issue visitor's passes to Benny, Lucy and Mrs. Wheeler. Her pastor's wife superpowers, while often under-appreciated by those outside her family, remained fully intact.

Benny's stomach turned flip flops as the prison doors slammed closed behind them with a metallic echo. Karen Wheeler sat in the waiting room while Lucy and Benny were taken back to meet with Frank Evans. Lucy said "I think I might throw up."

As they sat down, Frank came limping in. He had a deep scar across his eyebrow and his nose looked like it had been badly broken a long time ago, but otherwise, he appeared peaceful. His hands were shaking a little bit as he sat down. "Thank-you for the gifts. That was very kind."

"You are most welcome," Lucy replied.

"Thank-you for agreeing to meet with us," Benny added.

"It was the least that I could do."

"Do you remember us?"

"I remember nearly running you over when you were just little kids."

"Yes."

"I am so very sorry. I was really messed up back then, not to make excuses, but I've had a lot of time to think about things."

"How are you doing?" Lucy asked.

"Much better and it is incredibly kind of you to ask, much more than I deserve."

"Can you tell us what happened that night?" Benny asked.

"What really happened?" Lucy inquired.

"Reed Jones, Aden Crow and myself were really angry that we didn't get invited to that stupid Halloween party. I can't say that I blame them, I was a monster back then. I hung out with those guys because our parents knew each other. Our fathers were in the same fraternity together here in Lake City at Whitfield College, *Gamma Omicron Sigma,* or GOS. They called themselves *Gentlemen of the South* and idolized the confederate general Robert E. Lee. After graduation, they held networking events once a year at private country clubs, secluded resorts or out-of-the-way restaurants. They did it to form business contacts, *white* business contacts, and there were others there besides the fraternity members, influential people who didn't go to college, but were, nonetheless, part of the GOS. Tokens and Secret passwords were used to gain entrance to the meetings. When the man guarding the door asked for the password you had to say *1-2-3*, to which he would reply *Robert E. Lee.* Then he would count down *3-2-1* and you were expected to answer back with *The South Should Have Won* while showing them your token which was a button printed with the letters *SYM* and *WAO* superimposed onto the red field above and below the Bonnie Blue bars of the Confederate battle flag. Those letters are an acronym that stands for Spend Your Money (in) White America Only.

I met Reed and Aden when our fathers took us to one of those events. I am very ashamed to admit that is where we learned about using Edwin Culpepper's Finest to dose girls so we could have sex with them. It was an old fraternity trick. As I said, I was a monster back then.

When I got in trouble and was running from the law, I went to hide out in Lost Valley. My dad called up his fraternity brother, J.C. Jones, who let me live in one of his rental properties. You see, they had a rule in their order. They called it a circle of brothers. At induction, every member of the order is given a special coin depicting Robert E. Lee and Stonewall Jackson on horseback. They are 1925 Stone Mountain half dollars. The reverse side reads *Memorial to the valor of the soldier of the South.* In the blank space, they engrave the letters Gamma Omicron Sigma. These are like currency to them, exchangeable for help when you are in trouble or need really big favors. The leadership can also award a coin to people who do extraordinary things for the order. If a brother asks you to do something and uses the phrase *The wizard sent me,* you must ask them *Which wizard?* If they reply *The Wizard of the Saddle,* you must grant their request, whatever it is, or be exiled from the order. The phrase refers to Nathan Bedford Forrest, the first Grand Wizard of the Ku Klux Klan. He won the nickname *the wizard of the saddle* because of his calvary expertise during the Civil War. Once the code phrase has been invoked, it is like giving them your marker, after the favor has been completed, you have to give them your coin. My dad cashed in his coin to J.C. Jones to *persuade* him to let me live in that rental house and to hide me from the authorities.

When I moved here, Reed and Aden began to take things even further than our fathers had. They got really into learning about their family history. Aden discovered that his family is descended from James Crowe, one of six former Confederate soldiers who were the founding members of the Ku Klux Klan. The family eventually fled north to escape trouble and changed the spelling of their name to conceal their ancestry, but Aden was proud of it. He and Reed wanted to start their own local chapter of the KKK like their forefathers had done. I am ashamed to say that I was drawn in. We started calling each other the Gentlemen of the South, like it was our own high school chapter of the fraternity. Reed appointed himself as our leader and called himself the Grand Dragon."

Up to this point, Benny and Lucy had just let Frank ramble on. While they were learning a lot about the Jones and Crow families, he had hardly said a word about the night of the crash, but they had allowed him keep on talking to see what secrets he might reveal.

"You mentioned the code phrase *the wizard sent me*. Did you ever hear the phrase *Uncle Robert sent me*?" Benny asked.

"Yes. *The Wizard* was the codeword if you were cashing in a coin for a major abetment of some kind. *Uncle Robert* was used when one simply wanted to identify themselves as a member of the order and ask for a favor. They traded in favors like currency. Any time you obliged a brother by helping them out, you gained an invisible bargaining chip for future use. J.C. Jones cashed in chips like those to secure financing for his first housing division and to launch Jones Properties, LLC. Lester Crow collected on favors to purchase his car lot. But the Stone Mountain coins with General Lee on them were reserved for the most serious and sometimes illegal stuff. In order to keep his son out of trouble, J.C. Jones utilized a coin with the former prosecuting attorney to have me extradited and to put a stop to the investigation into the crash in Lost Valley before Reed was implicated. My sentence might have been much longer otherwise."

Lucy asked "Is there anything else you can tell us about that night?"

"Well, Reed was infatuated with your sister Annie and when he asked her to the Homecoming dance that year, she turned him down. It made him really angry. When he saw her paying special attentions to Daniel, a black boy, he was furious. Reed thought that he was superior to Daniel and could not tolerate being rejected for someone he viewed as inferior to himself. And I am sorry to say, Aden and myself got caught up in the madness with him. When he saw them together at the party that night, he lost it and flew into a rage. I was hanging out down in town at Riverview Lanes, hustling pool. When Hannah kicked them out of her party, Aden snuck into the house through the back door and called me at the bowling alley. They knew the party was ending at midnight and told me to come up that way so we could ambush Daniel on his way home. I figured they wanted to throw him a beating or something. I didn't want to go, but he said *The Grand Dragon commands it.* I said I wasn't in the mood to take orders from Reed, so Aden called in a favor, saying *Uncle Robert sent me.* His dad had fixed up an old beat up, burnished brown 1969 Chevy Nova that he'd gotten as a trade-in and gave it to me to drive, so Aden figured I owed him. Like I said, favors are currency in their world. I asked him to cash it in for something else, but then he said *The wizard sent me.* I asked which wizard and he said *The wizard of the saddle.* I didn't know how he could have gotten his hands on one of those coins, but I didn't question it. I thought it might be a chance to earn back the coin my father lost because of me and to get back in his good graces, so I agreed to meet them up there about a quarter 'til midnight before the party ended."

"Did he say anything to you about cutting the brake lines to Daniel's truck?" Benny asked.

"No, he didn't say anything like that. My word. I had no idea. Mrs. Farmer caught him on the phone while we were talking and I could hear her hollering 'Git outta my kitchen! Shoo! Go on. Git out!' So, he hung up. I had time to grab a bite to eat and was hoping to get in several more games of pool before I left, but the men I was playing against got really irate when they realized I was hustling them and I had to leave early and in a hurry, so I headed up to where my buddies were at in case them guys tried to follow me and take their money back. I'd had a little to drink that night and wasn't thinkin' real clear so when I saw Sam, I tried to pass him, but he floored it in that old Cutlass coupe of his and wouldn't let me around, so I started racing him up the hillside and forgot where I was at. I came around Hell's Half-Moon and I hit your brother, almost square on. I am so, so sorry.

I was in bad shape and my buddies took off and left me before the law showed up. A young deputy named Smith was the first on the scene. He must have heard the ambulance coming on his radio and was close by so he beat them there. He threw up when he saw your brother and Annie. He was real upset, but he pulled himself together and took charge. He put a tourniquet on my leg until the paramedics arrived, probably saved my life. I figure you know the rest."

Benny spoke up first "You seem...different than I expected." Lucy kicked him in the shin.

"I figured your dad might've told you how rude I was when he came to visit. I'm sorry about that. You'll tell him I said I was sorry?"

"Yes, of course."

"What changed?" Lucy inquired.

"There's this church that comes in here to give us a service. I went, just because it's an excuse to get out of my cell, and because they play music, but they're so nice, so friendly. I eventually realized that my anger and hatred was eating me alive. I admitted that I had done horrible things and confessed them to God. I asked for forgiveness and asked him to save me. I've been learning about Jesus."

"That's really good," Lucy responded.

"I'm very glad," Benny replied.

"There's one more thing. You've been very polite not to ask what I'm in here for. There is something you have to know about the story that Reed Jones and Aden Crow made up about your brother. That story...is what I did, when I lived here in Lake City. That is the reason I was hiding out in Lost Valley and it is why I am still in prison. I gave a girl named Lindsey Cobble fruit punch mixed with Edwin Culpepper's. I drank a little bit myself. I drove her away from a party to a secluded place and had my way with her when she was too weak to fight me and had no idea what was going on. I got in a wreck on the way back to the party and she was killed. I am imprisoned for her rape and for the drunk driving that caused her death. As I said before, I was a monster. Reed and Aden knew all about it and used to hold it over my head. After the crash, they got the idea to begin spreading *that story* around about your brother to cover up their own activities. They made an innocent man into their scapegoat.

I know that I have no right to ask forgiveness, but I want you to know how sorry I am about your brother and your sister. Daniel and Annie never did anything wrong and it's my fault they're dead."

"Frank, Thank-you for being so honest with us today," Benny said softly.

"It really means a lot," Lucy whispered.

And then, choking back tears with a bit of a shake in his voice, Benny said "I forgive you."

And Lucy whispered, "I forgive you too," as the tears ran down her face.

And the guard said "Time is up."

Frank was speechless, but he mouthed the words "Thank-you," through the tears as the guard took him away.

As they were escorted back to the waiting room, Benny said "It's too bad Aden Crow didn't brag to him about cutting the brake lines."

"But we did get a lot more of the truth," Lucy encouraged. "And as sad as it is, we now have a second witness that they were lying in wait and testimony that the attack was motivated by racial hatred."

"And we know why the crash was never properly investigated," Benny added.

"Because of corruption in the former prosecutor's office," Lucy asserted.

"And because J.C. Jones was the corruptor," Benny concluded.

It had been a long morning and Benny and Lucy were practically starving by the time they left the prison. Lucy's mom suggested that they stop off at Chicken Betty's for lunch. "It's the finest fried chicken you will ever eat," she guaranteed. It was close by so they enthusiastically agreed. And boy was she right. As an appetizer, each of them was served a pair of the most incredible smelling little hot rolls and the taste was even better than the scent. When the waitress brought them out, Benny noticed a tear in her eye.

He asked, "Are you alright?"

"Oh, it's fine," she replied.

"What's wrong?" Lucy asked.

"It's my son, she replied. He's really sick with a high fever. My sister is watching him while I work my shift and she just called to let me know the medicine doesn't seem to be working."

"What's his name?" Mrs. Wheeler asked.

"Matthew," the woman replied.

"Would it be ok if we prayed for him with you?" Mrs. Wheeler asked.

She agreed and the four of them held hands right there at the table and prayed for Matthew. The waitress, Angie, thanked them and smiled as she continued working.

She served up everything family style to the table. They had as much fried chicken as they wanted along with real mashed potatoes and skillet cream gravy, black-eyed peas and corn. The chicken was the best Benny had ever tasted.

For dessert, there was a chilling case with the tallest slices of pie Benny and Lucy had ever seen. He chose French silk chocolate. Lucy had banana cream and Mrs. Wheeler ate lemon meringue.

By the time they finished their pie and Angie came back by the table to bring them the check, she informed them that her sister had phoned and Matthew's fever had broken. He was sleeping peacefully and appeared to be on the mend. They praised God and offered a prayer of thanksgiving right there on the spot.

As they were climbing back into the car, Nick finally called with an update that was well worth the wait.

While Benny and Lucy traveled to the prison that morning, Nick led a team of local police who marched into the offices of Jones Properties, LLC and arrested Reed Jones in the glass-walled board room. They pulled him up out of his leather chair, bent him over the long, glass table, cuffed him and mirandized him right there in front of the board members as their employees watched through the glass. He was charged with obstruction of justice, leaving the scene of an accident, witness intimidation, unlawful use of a weapon and for his role in chasing Daniel and Annie down and crashing into them, he was served up with two counts of first-degree vehicular manslaughter.

Simultaneously, a team from Sheriff Smith's office apprehended Aden Crow in the parking lot of Crow's Car Palace. The arresting officers approached him as he was showing a high-dollar luxury SUV to a customer. When he tried to bolt, they slammed him down over the hood, cuffed him and read him his rights as potential buyers scurried to their cars to take their business elsewhere. He was booked and charged with obstruction of justice, witness intimidation, unlawful use of a weapon and since he had knowledge of cars from his family's business and was seen lurking near the vehicle on the night of the accident, they charged him with voluntary manslaughter for cutting the brake lines to Daniel's truck.

Exposé

When Lucy and Benny arrived back in town from the prison, they swung by the Wheeler's house to make a few last-minute additions to the article and print it out. They convinced Mrs. Wheeler it would be safe enough for Benny to drive them down to the offices of the Lost River Gazette as long as they went straight there, directly to church after their meeting and then came right back home when they were finished.

They met with T.S. Clemons, the editor himself. He was an older man with a thick white mustache and a mane of wild white hair. Dressed in a seersucker suit with thick horn rim glasses and oxfords on his feet, he looked like a turn of the century author who had just stepped out of the past. Mr. Clemons was so impressed with the article and its flawless composition that he sent it straight to the presses without any edits.

Thanking the pair robustly with enthusiastic handshakes, as his cheeks flushed with excitement, he explained how his reporters had posed as car shoppers, dressed as delivery men and carted around janitorial supplies to capture the day's arrests on camera. They had even overheard a few juicy quotes for the paper as Reed Jones and Aden Crow were hauled away. He presented each of them with a check for the article and welcomed them to submit any future writings for consideration. "My door...and phone...and e-mail...are always open...to you."

"Thanks," Benny replied as they stepped out of Clemon's office.

"We may have something in the works already," Lucy hinted.

"We'll just have to see how it GOS," Benny finished as they shared a laugh before exiting the building.

They made it to church just in time for youth group to begin. After the day they had, it was nice to hang out and chill for a while after the service. Roger beat Benny in a very aggressive game of foosball, but after the game Roger was a bit more friendly than before, much less sulky staring from him this week. Benny figured he was an alright guy, probably just jealous that he was the one who caught Lucy's eye.

As Benny and Lucy sat down with hot chocolates and caramel lattes, Tony and Bella were shocked to learn they had been inside an actual prison and Lucy relished telling the tale to the sound of Roger and Kent overzealously battling it out at the foosball table in the background.

Before they left, Pastor Dave took Lucy and Benny to the side. "Since we spoke last Wednesday, and especially after what we learned Sunday, I've been thinking. I would like to do something to memorialize your brother and sister, to show proper respect as we are so close to the ten-year anniversary of...their passing. Would you be interested in sharing a few words about them, maybe at youth group next week? You could talk about the type of brother and sister they were, what they meant to you, anything you'd like to share would be welcome."

"I would love that," Benny said as he nodded in agreement.

"Yes, I would like that very much," agreed Lucy.

By the time Benny made it home, his mom had his homework for the week waiting for him. She had called Principal Potter and reminded him of the assault her son had endured. She explained the situation, that with the hostility between Benny and Riley and the arrest of Riley's brother, it was in everyone's best interests for Benny to complete the week's work at home to let things cool off. She insisted that it not count against his attendance and that Benny receive extra credit in his English class for the news article...Mom superpowers at work again. Having received phone calls from Nick, who updated them on the case, Mrs. Shepherd and Mrs. Wheeler agreed to permit Benny and Lucy to go down to the police station Thursday, where they would be allowed to watch the wheels of justice in action...as long as their homework was done.

Thursday, November 8, 2007

The next morning pictures of Reed Jones and Aden Crow being handcuffed and led away appeared on the front page of the Lost River Gazette. There was a news story with a complete list of all the charges below the fold, but the headline of the day belonged to Benny Shepherd and Lucy Wheeler. Near the ten-year anniversary of the crash, an article co-authored by the siblings of the victims was featured in what became the highest selling issue in the history of the Gazette.

What Really Happened on Halloween 1997?
by Benny Shepherd and Lucy Wheeler

The tragedy that struck our town on October 31, 1997 was not an accident. On the previous day, Daniel Shepherd found a crude drawing of a hangman on his locker along with the word RAT and various racial expletives directed toward him. This death threat appears to be retaliatory in nature. Daniel had grown suspicious that several of his classmates were dosing and sexually assaulting girls and he had confronted Reed Jones and Aden Crow about their suspected involvement.

They began by dissolving a powerful stimulant, Arouse-All, into alcohol in an attempt to make girls experience a euphoric high. Just one tablet contains the same amount of caffeine as a 12-ounce energy drink. Mixing stimulants with alcohol causes the drinker to remain more active while having the same diminished decision-making capacity. Studies have shown that consuming a mixture of alcohol and stimulants makes the drinker more likely to engage in risky sexual behavior and more likely to need medical intervention for injuries. When they didn't get the results they wanted, they turned to a much stronger and more dangerous substance.

Through our investigation, we learned that underage teens were using a code phrase with ties to a white supremacist organization known as the Gentlemen of the South, to buy alcohol from Gordo's Beer-Mart. They were purchasing the brand of alcohol known as Edwin Culpepper's Finest or E C for short. This potent product is 190 proof grain alcohol, 95% alcohol by volume. It is known for being odorless and tasteless which makes it impossible to detect. They were mixing this alcohol into punch and with wine coolers or other beverages to concoct a highly intoxicating rape drug.

This toxic concoction is incredibly powerful and harmful. It is the most intoxicating beverage in the world, so strong that it is used to remove varnish from violins. Drinking just one 12-ounce red plastic cup of punch mixed with 1/3 E C would be the equivalent of 4 shots of 190 proof grain alcohol. That is more alcohol than is contained in 9 shots of vodka. Consuming only one 8.5-ounce wine cooler mixed with ½ E C would be the equivalent of 4.5 shots of 95% grain alcohol. Combined with the alcohol from the wine, that is more alcohol than would be found in 11 shots of tequila. That is enough to cause alcohol poisoning which can lead to brain damage or even death. Edwin Culpepper's Finest should be outlawed in this state as it already has been in 14 others due to its frequent use to facilitate sexual assault and increased instances of alcohol poisoning.

The dangerous potions they were brewing with this lethal liquid were designed to render the drinker incapacitated, causing them to black out and incur short term memory loss. Multiple young women were raped and then slut-shamed when they could not remember enough details about their assault to press charges. Many blamed themselves. Daniel believed these rapes occurred during a relatively short time frame, but were never reported or prosecuted due to lack of evidence and the inability of the victims to be able to identify their attackers. He recorded multiple conversations and observations in his diary which spurred us to investigate further.

Through an undercover sting operation, we were able to verify that Reed Jones and Aden Crow were among those who purchased E C during that period of time, and Daniel overheard them discussing their intentions for using it on girls and documented the conversation in his journal. This had been going on for several months and others were involved including someone who snuck E C into the infamous party that Halloween night without the knowledge of the hosts, Hannah Farmer and Gabby Shoemaker, who had made diligent efforts to prevent the presence of alcohol.

That night, Annie Wheeler unknowingly ingested this deadly brew. Daniel Shepherd realized what had happened and dumped the remaining mixture out before anyone else drank it. Daniel was absolutely sober when he attempted to drive Annie home to the safety of her parent's house.

The claims that a wild party took place that evening with multiple teens consuming alcohol are patently false. Hannah Farmer and her family made every effort to provide a safe environment free of alcohol and drugs and were wrongfully accused. The investigation into the Farmers was a clever ruse, instigated by J.C. Jones and Lester Crow, to distract from the true criminals, their sons.

Further investigation on our part uncovered the fact that while Daniel and Annie were gone on a hayride, someone cut the brake lines of his truck. Knowing the winding road he would have to travel to get home, someone tried to kill Daniel Shepherd. Annie Wheeler was either collateral damage, or a target herself. Because another vehicle crashed into Daniel before he ran off the road, his truck was never investigated for signs of foul play and the would-be murderers got away. The investigation was halted after the former prosecuting attorney was bribed by J.C. Jones to extradite Frank Evans and end the probe into the accident before his son could be implicated for his role in the crash.

Prior to the hayride, eye witnesses report that driver Reed Jones and passenger Aden Crow appeared demonstrably furious that Daniel and Annie were together due to the interracial nature of their relationship. They were seen lurking around the Farmer homestead near the vehicles while the others were gone on the hayride. After the young people returned, as Daniel attempted to drive Annie to safety, they chased them down the hill in Reed's truck and around the tight curves with their bright headlamps shining and off-road spotlights blazing in Daniel's eyes in an apparent attempt to intimidate and/or run them off the road. Daniel was unable to stop the vehicle due to the disfunction of his sabotaged brakes and missed his turn off.

As Daniel was being chased down the hill by Reed Jones and Aden Crow, Frank Evans was simultaneously driving his brown Chevy Nova out to meet them to lie in wait for Daniel, unaware that he had left the party before the scheduled end time of Midnight and was already headed down the mountain. Frank was in the process of racing Sam Weaver in his vintage green Oldsmobile Cutlass when he rounded Hell's Half-Moon in Daniel's lane and struck him head on, just before 11:15 pm. The white 4x4 driven by Reed Crow smashed into Daniel Shepherd's truck, knocking it over the embankment and causing it to overturn.

Daniel's brakes were sabotaged and vengeful young men with secrets to conceal and racist hatred in their hearts devised a scheme to lay in wait to chase him down the hill to his death. This was no accident. This was a lynching. It was a lynching in progress that was both interrupted and aided by a fatal car crash which helped to obscure the facts and conceal the tracks of the murderous perpetrators of this heinous hate crime which was subsequently covered up by the white supremacist fraternal organization known as the Gentlemen of the South.

Aden Crow pretended to use the car phone in Daniel's truck to call for help, but he did not. Phone records prove that he called his father, Lester Crow, instead, who brought a tow truck to the scene of the crash and proceeded to remove Reed Jones's vehicle. Aden Crow left the scene of the accident with his dad while Reed Jones fled the scene with his father in the family Jaguar. Sam Green, who had been directing traffic to turn around, got into his Cutlass and drove away when he saw the others departing. Freddy Fisher and Charles Carpenter witnessed the collision from behind and directed traffic around the crash to safety until the others left. Freddy called for help using the phone in Daniel's truck when he realized none was coming. This is the reason people saw flashing lights as they were leaving the party and assumed the reports that the crash occurred around midnight were correct. Freddy and Charles remained silent under duress after Reed Jones and Aden Crow threatened their lives with firearms. They recently provided depositions to the county prosecuting attorney detailing these events.

Multiple witnesses report that it was the Jones and Crow families who spread the false and malicious rumors about Daniel Shepherd and Annie Wheeler in order to cover up their own culpability in the tragic deaths of these two young teenagers and to distract from any potential investigation into the recent series of sexual assaults.

Multiple sources confirm that J.C. Jones and Lester Crow then became Conspiracy Entrepreneurs, knowingly promoting the false narrative of events in order to take advantage of the situation to further their personal business interests by facilitating the removal of Mark Shepherd from his pastorate and by lobbying against the very corruption they knew their families had caused in order to jockey for lucrative positions of influence and power within Riverside Community Church which they have wielded for their own personal financial benefit.

Reed Jones and Aden Crow have been arrested in connection with these events. J.C. Jones and Lester Crow have yet to be brought to justice. Other perpetrators of sexual assault may still remain at-large. If you have any information about these crimes, please come forward to report it to the local police, the county sheriff's office, or this newspaper.

For ten years, the graves of Daniel Shepherd and Annie Wheeler have been routinely desecrated and their families, as well as the Farmer family, and multiple sexual assault victims have been unduly ostracized by the rumors recirculating throughout this town. Conspiracy Entrepreneurs perpetuated these falsehoods to protect themselves, to further their own self-serving agendas and to pad their pocketbooks. We felt it was time to set the record straight. Now that you know the truth, reader ask yourself: Could it be possible that some people in this town were quick to believe the lies about Annie Wheeler and Daniel Shepherd because of their own underlying prejudices?

Whatever may happen in the courts, the important thing was that the town knew the truth. They knew of the innocence of Daniel Shepherd and Annie Wheeler and of the depravity of the Jones and Crow families. They learned that Hannah Farmer and Gabby Shoemaker had not thrown an irresponsible rave. They knew that Pastor Mark Shepherd had not been an inept father and had in fact, acted honorably and they knew that Freddy Fisher and Charles Carpenter had tried to help the crash victims and had been threatened, which garnered a measure of empathy from most folks.

Country Comeuppance

The wheels of justice turn more swiftly in small country towns than in the big cities and things moved along rapidly after the arrests of Reed Jones and Aden Crow. The story on the front page of the news created an urgency and the lawyers earned their money that Thursday.

That afternoon, with all of their homework completed, Benny and Lucy were allowed to go down to the police station as promised.

Inmates Jones and Crow were brought out of their holding cells at the local police department and into separate interrogation rooms with their respective attorneys. Nick escorted Benny and Lucy into a narrow surveillance room in between where they could monitor both spaces from behind one-way mirrors. Once they were inside, he announced "I've got some news. We were able to get good fingerprints off of the brake lines from Daniel's truck. When we took Aden Crow's prints after his arrest, we discovered they were a match. He's going down."

"What about Reed's fingerprints?" Benny asked.

"Unfortunately, only Aden's prints were on the brake lines. We've got quite a bit on Reed as it is though."

Lawyers from the firm that represented both Jones Properties, LLC and Crow's Car Palace had been called into a strategy session all night Wednesday and Thursday morning, tasked with corporate damage control and handling Reed's and Aden's individual cases swiftly.

The Prosecuting Attorney, the young, talented and clever Stanley Marshall, played his cards carefully, hoping to frighten Aden Crow and Reed Jones into taking plea deals. Reed's lawyer argued that there is a fine line between a ticket for following too closely and reckless endangerment, but the prosecutor kept the manslaughter charge in his hand to keep the heat on anyway, though it was more of a bargaining chip than anything else.

Lucy noticed, "The lawyers sitting with them are wearing Whitfield College pins on their designer suits."

"Do they look like *Gentlemen of the South* to you?" Benny asked. Lucy nodded in agreement.

The lawyers had the two men well prepared and the Prosecuting Attorney's attempts to turn them against each other were futile.

Facing such formidable foes, Stanley Marshall was forced to weigh his options carefully. The defense attorneys questioned introducing a diary into evidence written by a young man who had been deceased for a decade. They had to concede that the blue paint transferred onto Reed's truck, along with witness corroboration, provided strong proof that he and Aden were at the scene and involved in the accident, but they pointed out that the crash itself was initiated by a third vehicle, which limited the prosecutor's choices.

While waiting for Stanley Marshall to craft plea arrangements to offer both men, Benny went to the restroom. On his way back down the hallway, he overheard Lester Crow and J.C. Jones speaking around the corner in hushed tones with the lawyers who warned them of what could be revealed if this matter went to trial.

Reed Jones was eighteen at the time of the accident, legally an adult. With the testimony of three men hanging over him, two of whom witnessed his reckless chase-down of Daniel and three of whom witnessed him leaving the scene of the accident, with the fear that his old pal Aden Crow might yet flip on him, with formidable young prosecutor Stanley Marshall waving pictures of the blue paint from his truck grill in his face, and with the looming threat of a much steeper prison sentence, Reed Jones reluctantly agreed to plead guilty to the charge of leaving the scene of an accident.

Reed claimed that his gun had been unloaded when he used it to threaten Freddy and Charles that night and his lawyer insisted that without shots being fired there was no way to prove otherwise, so Stanley Marshall offered to let him plead down to a class A misdemeanor charge for unlawful use of a weapon and he did.

The sentencing ranges for those two crimes were far less than what Reed could have been facing. In exchange for his plea, Prosecutor Marshall agreed to take manslaughter and the other charges off the table (charges that would have been difficult to prove anyway).

After Reed cracked, Aden Crow was a sitting duck. Like Reed, he agreed to plead guilty to a class A misdemeanor charge for unlawful use of a weapon. Since, he too was eighteen at the time of the accident, he would face the full consequences of his actions as an adult if the case were to go to trial. He broke down as the Prosecutor showed him the severed brake lines bearing his fingerprints. Facing the potential of five to fifteen years in prison for voluntary manslaughter, he practically jumped at the opportunity to plead down to involuntary manslaughter with the shorter sentencing range for that crime.

Nick explained to Benny and Lucy "There is a difference between what a person knows to be true and what can be proven beyond a reasonable doubt in a court of law. The plea agreements establish that both men contributed to and fled the scene of a deadly accident, engaged in a cover up and threatened witnesses with lethal violence. That's something."

That evening, Coop and Mason sent Benny a text message asking him to come hang out. He replied that he was on a tight leash, but they wouldn't accept no for an answer.

Later that night, after his parents were sawing logs, Benny gingerly tiptoed down the stairs, quietly clicked the front door closed, put his shoes on and descended the driveway by moonlight. A twinge of guilt mixed with excitement surged through his body as he crossed the line past the stone gateway and reached the road. Benny wasn't one to disobey his parents, and *don't go sneaking out of the house in the middle of the night* was certainly implied with all of the extra precautions they had been taking, but he had been neglecting his buddies and was concerned that they might get themselves hurt or into trouble if he wasn't around to watch their backs and prevent them from taking things too far. As Benny climbed into Coop's car, Mason offered him a dark glass bottle from a six-pack of Sassparilla and slice of pepperoni from Mr. P's which he quickly devoured while the guys told him all about their trunk full of supplies for late night shenanigans.

Friday, November 9

After Benny and Lucy's news article was released, there was intense pressure on the leadership of Riverside Community Church to take action. Having the pictures of two men whose families were so deeply involved in this mess displayed prominently on the church website and listed as Consulting Elders was a public relations nightmare.

J.C. Jones was asked to resign from his consulting elder position first thing Friday morning. He refused, so the deacons, already gathered for an emergency breakfast meeting before work, voted him out. His various donors and backers steadily began withdrawing their support and distancing themselves from him, so with his mayoral campaign in shambles, J.C. Jones removed himself from the race in disgrace.

Lester Crow was also asked to resign from his lucrative consulting elder position based on his actions on the night of the accident. He threw quite the temper tantrum that day, coming down to the church late that morning to "have a talk," with the pastor, who refused to see him. He stormed out past a ladies' luncheon in the Atrium while shouting expletives and turning red in the face. His wife quietly excused herself from the table and followed him out the door.

Benny and Lucy were the only members of their families planning to attend court to see Reed Jones and Aden Crow plead guilty. Their parents felt like they had been through enough, but the persistent pair needed to see the results of their investigation all the way through. Due to the potentially volatile nature of the day's events, Nick picked them up. They were expecting to ride in the Mustang, but Nick was on duty and on high alert, so he drove them in a patrol car instead. Benny rode shotgun until they got to Lucy's house, then they both rode in back. They felt a little bit like outlaws, locked in the back seat with no door handles and bullet proof glass separating them from their driver, but it was kind of exciting.

"Do you mind if we take a little detour to the edge of town?" Nick asked. "There's something you two have just got to see."

"Sure," they both replied with anticipation.

"Can you imagine the look on J.C. Jones's face when he stepped out onto the porch to pick up the newspaper this morning?" Nick asked.

"Whoa," Lucy exclaimed.

"Hmhmhuhuhahahahaha," Benny cackled.

The flawlessly manicured yard of J.C. Jones had been staked with every size and shape of *For Sale* sign imaginable. Overnight, hundreds of beige forks had sprouted up in the perfectly landscaped flower beds. The lawn jockeys flanking the driveway had been toppled over and decapitated, their wooden heads now missing entirely (and halfway down the river).

"Now, the Good Book says that vengeance belongs to the Lord, and I would never tolerate violence or vigilantism, but I suppose we have to let folks have a little harmless fun...*just this once*. Down at the station, we're considering this a *peaceful* protest," Nick explained. "I heard they got Lester Crow's house as well."

Benny nearly busted a gut laughing so hard.

"Isn't that vandalism, though?" Lucy asked.

"Well, they used biodegradable forks, so they were environmentally conscious pranksters," Nick added, "and they didn't cause any property damage except for those awful lawn jockeys which were an eyesore and an embarrassment to our town, so I consider what they did...*town beautification*. Sheriff Potter called it *community service*."

When they arrived at City Hall, Nick released them from their temporary backseat prison and they marched up the steps holding hands. While Nick headed into the courtroom to secure seats, they stopped in the entranceway to view the spectacular murals depicting the history of Lost Valley. The building smelled faintly of linseed oil and cedar and still utilized the original benches where county judges had dispensed justice for well over a century.

Entering the courtroom, they spotted Nick over to the left, gesturing for them to sit beside him. Gabby and Hannah walked in and sat in the row behind them with three other women Benny didn't know. Nick hugged each of his former classmates and spoke with them for a few minutes as they waited for the hearing to begin. Benny heard him call one of them Cindy Spicer as he congratulated her on her recent promotion. She was wearing pink surgical scrubs and a nametag that indicated she was the head nurse in the traumatic brain injury recovery unit at Ridgeview Regional Hospital led by Dr. Jonah Blumenthal.

At the last minute, the rest of the Shepherds, Wheelers and Bakers entered the courtroom and sat on the back row. Pastor Dave and his wife Judy were with them. Benny's father gave him a strong and affirming nod. Benny nodded back, his eyes practically gleaming. They decided to come after all.

Since these proceedings were expected to go quickly, both Reed Jones and Aden Crow were led into the courtroom together. They entered the hearing wearing three-piece suits and were seated facing the judge, flanked by their high-powered attorneys. Reed wore his usual arrogant smirk. Aden looked worried with dark circles under his eyes.

The Honorable Judge William R. Bean was an old-fashioned, no-nonsense type of judge. Having issued the arrest warrants and after thoroughly studying the brief that Stanley Marshall supplied to him along with all depositions, he was well-prepared for this case. An intimidating figure, the silver-haired and well-bearded judge entered the courtroom and every observer instinctively rose before the bailiff even had to tell them. Judge Bean loudly gaveled the last session of the day into order saying "It is my understanding that the attorney's for each of the two last cases of the day have reached plea agreements, Is this correct?"

"Yes, your honor," answered the attorney for Reed Jones.

"Yes, your honor," answered the attorney for Aden Crow

"Reed Jones is charged with leaving the scene of an accident, a class D felony and with unlawful use of a weapon, a class A misdemeanor. How does you client plead?"

"My client pleads guilty your honor."

"Aden Crow is charged with unlawful use of a weapon, a class A misdemeanor and involuntary manslaughter, a class D felony. How does your client plead?"

"Guilty your honor."

Both of the attorneys for the defense expected the judge to set a date for sentencing at this point and had exchanged looks at the way the judge was handling things.

Judge Bean was an honest man and he ran a tight ship. He was known for being straight forward, fair, decisive and extremely well prepared.

"I have extensively reviewed the facts of this case presented in the superb brief prepared by the prosecuting attorney's office. I see no need to waste the taxpayer's money or anyone's time by postponing my judgement. And I am certain that no one wants to put the victim's families through more than they have already endured," he said pointedly as he looked down upon the lawyers.

"Mr. Crow, Stand. You tampered with the brakes of a vehicle, knowingly endangering the driver and any potential passengers. You then willingly participated in the coverup of a deadly automobile accident, even threatening witnesses with a firearm to prevent them from coming forward. For the crime of unlawful use of a weapon, I sentence you to serve one year of incarceration and to pay a fine of $5,000. For the crime of involuntary, criminally negligent manslaughter, I sentence you to an additional four years, bringing your total sentence to five years in prison.

Mr. Jones, Stand. You acted with wanton disregard for human life, failing to show any hint of remorse or human compassion even after you caused a fatality crash. For the crime of unlawful use of a weapon I sentence you to one year of incarceration and a $5,000 fine. And for the felony of leaving the scene of a fatality accident, I hereby sentence you to pay a fine of $10,000 and to serve the maximum sentence allowable under the law of seven years in the state penitentiary. The sentences are to be served consecutively for a total of eight years.

The court recorder will note that all fines in these cases are to be divided between the families of the victims. Bailiff, remand both men into custody." He then declared "This court is adjourned," as he hammered his gavel down.

The attorneys jumped to their feet as one shouted, "Your Honor! This is h..."

"Order," Judge Bean cut him off commandingly, slamming his gavel down five times. "I will have order. One more word and I will hold you in contempt of court. These proceedings are concluded." He cracked his gavel one last time and it echoed off the wooden walls of the courtroom as he rose to his feet and retired to his chambers.

J.C. Jones and Lester Crow were up in the lawyers faces, whispering furiously and spitting all over the place as their heads turned red like the bricks on the outside of the building. Their wives cried as they watched their sons taken away. Benny felt sorry for them, the wives that is. Aden was not married and Reed was divorced, so the Jones brothers were the only other family members present. Riley Jones stared daggers across the courtroom at Lucy and Benny as his brother Rhett held him back.

Benny and Lucy hugged. Nick shook both of their hands and gave them a wink. "Nice work detectives. Congratulations."

Gabby, Hannah and the ladies sitting with them hugged and shed a few tears. This wasn't nearly enough justice for what had been done, but it was something.

J.C. Jones turned from the lawyers to glare at Benny and Lucy and growled, "If it wasn't for you two meddling kids..."

Sarah Shepherd, Karen Wheeler and Donna Baker immediately stepped between their children and J.C. Jones and Lester Crow. The looks on their faces silenced the two men. It was like three angry mama bears staring down a pair of coyotes. Nick walked over to have a word with Riley while the trio of dads somberly approached J.C. Jones and Lester Crow. Benny and Lucy couldn't hear what they were saying, but by the way their fathers were gesturing toward them, they got the sense that they were having a long overdue conversation with the patriarchs of the Jones and Crow families. Those bullies were finally being put in their place. They began slowly backing away like a couple of cowardly coyotes.

The mamas turned to give big bear hugs to their children and then to Gabby and Hannah and each of the other ladies. Pastor Dave and Judy stood on alert, watching over their flock like shepherds, lest anyone try to harm them.

Successful Prosecutor Stanley Marshall, his face aglow with the thrill of victory, strutted over to Benny and Lucy and introduced himself. Shaking both their hands vigorously, he said "Really fine work you two. I know the sentences aren't as long as you probably hoped for, but the discoveries you've made and the evidence you provided helped to secure meaningful penalties that have brought a measure of justice to all of the people these men have hurt. Now that we've got them in prison, if further evidence surfaces on the charges that were dropped, or *if additional crimes are revealed*," he emphasized by slightly raising his voice and leaning ever so subtly toward the ladies in the row behind them, "you have my word that I will relentlessly pursue justice in such matters."

"Thank-you, sir," they both said together.

"Thank *you*," he emphasized, flashing them a broad smile before nodding to the next row on his way out, swinging his square cornered, mahogany leather briefcase, it's golden latches gleaming in the soft light of the hallway.

As Nick escorted Benny and Lucy out of the courthouse, Sheriff Andrew Smith stopped them. He looked Benny straight in the eye and said "Young man...I owe you an apology. I saw how upset you were in the assembly a few weeks ago. I am sorry for the way I spoke about your brother. I was wrong. I had never witnessed anything as horrible as that crash and it affected me profoundly. I swore I would do everything within my power to make certain it never happened again. But using your brother as a cautionary tale was thoughtless, and I now know, completely wrong. Please accept my sincere apology." The sheriff extended his hand, and Benny shook it in acknowledgement. "If either of you ever want a job in law enforcement, give me a call. I could use some investigators like you."

"Thank-you sir," Benny replied. Lucy nodded.

When Nick met them outside of City Hall, he was wearing an overlarge grin. He pulled Riley Jones's driver's license out of his pocket and showed it to them, explaining, "Mr. Jones received tickets this week for speeding through a school zone and running a stop sign as well as a traffic citation for reckless and imprudent driving. With his previous wreck, he has now accumulated too many points and has been forced to surrender his driver's license, which will be safer for everyone, himself included."

There would continue to be consequences and a special brand of country comeuppance in the following weeks and months.

A surprise inspection of Jones Properties, LLC's new housing division project, Prairie View Estates, revealed shortcuts had been taken, resulting in multiple code violations. The city pulled their permits and J.C. Jones was forced to sell the property to another developer at a significant loss. The new developer built an entire subdivision full of quality, affordable family housing.

Sales at Crow's Car Palace dropped off significantly that quarter as the townsfolk expressed their judgement with their pocket books.

Jones Properties, LLC also lost out on a bid for a lucrative contract to widen the highway East of town and eliminate Hell's Half-Moon. Rumor had it their application was filed directly into the garbage can.

The sting operation that caught Joe Gordon selling alcohol to minors didn't produce enough evidence to get him arrested, but Benny and Lucy's newspaper article, combined with Freddy's testimony about buying alcohol as a high school student, was enough for the local Chamber of Commerce to revoke his liquor license. He sold Gordo's Beer-Mart and it is now a clean, reputable convenience store called "Speedy-Stop," with a small delicatessen and a spectacular variety of snacks. They put in new gas pumps where they sell the cheapest gas around and the store is a favorite haunt of fishermen who stop by for bait on their way down to Lost River (or out to Miller's Bridge for the ones in the know).

The Shady Hill Cemetery installed a video camera at the entry gate, though Benny and Lucy suspected the vandalism would have ended even without the deterrent.

Saturday, November 10

Family Forum

Saturday, after lunch, Mr. Shepherd called a family meeting. "For the past few years, we have been using a portion of the tithe money we collect on Sundays to help support a food bank and clothing closet ministry together with Hilltop Bible Church. I have also been helping Pastor Dave with the church's finances and long-term planning. He is a good and sincere man and was wise enough to know that as his church grew, he needed some help and mentoring. We didn't publicize these things so that he wouldn't be hurt by association with me. For the past six months, Dave has been asking me to come on staff as the Executive Pastor. The rest of the church leadership is in agreement. Your mom knows all about this," he said as he looked at Benny.

"I have also been hesitant because we were not on good terms with the Wheeler's and I knew they attended Hilltop. But now that the air has been cleared, the truth is known and those relationships have been mended, especially after our dinner last week, we feel like it is time to join together with that church. We've prayed about it and several of our Bible study members have mentioned the idea as well, which we took as confirmation that the Holy Spirit is telling us the same things. We had actually just discussed the unification last week before everything happened at dinner.

Tomorrow morning, I will be officially voted on as the new Executive Pastor at Hilltop Bible Church, but it is just a formality. It will be announced that our Bible Study homegroup will be merging with that congregation as part of their church replanting strategy. I will have regular preaching responsibilities and be working in full time ministry again. I turned in my notice to the lumberyard on Friday and Josh Baker has agreed to hire Sam Weaver, who suddenly finds himself in need of a job, to take my place on Monday. What do you think Benny?"

"I think it's about time. You are a wonderful pastor and father. And I think you already know I really like it over at Hilltop. Should we celebrate?"

"We should. Let's go *out* for ice cream," his mom suggested.

The Shepherd men wholeheartedly agreed. There was something special about being able to go out in public as a family. They went to one of Daniel's favorite places in all of Lost Valley, Aunt Polly's Old Fashioned Ice Cream Parlor, down on the river. Benny had a double scoop of cookies-n-cream in a waffle cone. His mom had a single scoop of strawberry in a sugar cone and his dad splurged for a banana split in a little boat.

As the Shepherds enjoyed their ice cream, they watched a small flock of ducks paddle by on the river, occasionally diving for fish. They were quackless, Muscovy ducks, each with its own unique blend of black and white feathers, contrasted by a red face and beak.

"For some reason these town ducks never go south for the winter," Mr. Shepherd commented.

"They've been staples in Lost Valley for as long as anyone can remember," Mrs. Shepherd added.

Benny smiled when he noticed Nick and Gabby coming out of Tia's Cocina, Nick's aunt's restaurant, holding hands as they walked along the riverwalk. "Would you look at that?" Benny asked, nodding toward them.

"They were pretty friendly at dinner," his mom commented.

She and his dad asked Benny all about youth group and how he had liked his first two visits to their new church. He excitedly shared all about it for once. It was a lovely celebration.

As they strolled down the riverwalk back to their car, his mom mentioned, "Pastor Dave has asked if it would be alright to take some time during the service tomorrow morning to honor Daniel and Annie. How do you feel about that?"

"I love that idea. It's long overdue."

"He mentioned that he asked you to share a few words about your brother with the youth group," his dad added. "Have you been preparing?"

"Yes, I've got some pretty good ideas about what I might say."

"How would you feel about speaking tomorrow morning instead?" his mom inquired hopefully. "That way the whole church could hear."

"I would love to. I would *really* love to."

"Good, I think Lucy is going to speak as well."

Benny spent the rest of the day in the lower level of the turret, working on his speech, and praying. Ten years ago, as a housewarming present, Grandpa Tom helped them convert the room into a study library. He built bookshelves and cabinets below each of the five windows, ringing the room. The tops of the cases were covered with a beautiful mahogany shelf, wide enough to use as a writing desk and he had built in a few spaces for chairs to slide up underneath. In the corners between the windows, the bookcases extended to the ceiling. The lower shelves were filled with children's books and collections of classics while the middle shelves were occupied by Bible commentaries and Theology texts. The upper shelves displayed a variety of non-fiction books ranging from gardening to picture books, offset with family heirlooms and decorative tchotchkes.

The Shepherd family loved to read and the charming atmosphere in the library was the perfect place to curl up with a good book. Grandma Becky had fashioned new cushions for the antique wooden furniture that came with the house out of a pretty floral print. Benny's mom had tastefully arranged the loveseat and matching chairs around a coffee table in the center of the room to allow for reading and relaxing conversation with a stunning view. Side tables with lamps added a cozy feeling for nighttime reading. Benny lounged on the cushions and made good use of the rich collection of Bible study materials to aid in his preparations.

Sunday, November 11

The Gathering

It was incredibly special for Benny to be able to ride to church with his parents and enter as a family on Sunday. It had been nearly ten years. The question of the day was how would the people of God respond to all that had been, and was about to be revealed?

Since Benny would be speaking and his mom and dad were being introduced, they took their seats on the front row as the church began to fill up quickly. The Bakers sat right behind them, along with Benny's maternal grandparents, Tom and Rebecca Thatcher, who were also weekly attenders of the Shepherd's Bible study. The other members of the house church sat in the third row. Lucy came over with her parents to sit beside Benny. He was surprised to see Coop and Mason walk in and sit on the back row. They both gave him the thumbs up and he nodded in return. Lucy smiled.

"I've never seen so many people here before. I expected twelve new faces, but I see about thirty who have never been here before."

"That's awesome," Benny replied.

"Are you nervous?" Lucy asked.

"Very...you?"

"Very."

"You'll do fine Lucy. At least you're used to being up on stage in front of people. You're great at leading worship."

"Thanks. But this is different."

"I know. But you'll be excellent."

"So will you."

"I hope so."

"Are you playing the keyboard this morning?"

"No, I wanted to be able to focus on speaking, and we have some special music happening today."

As the hands of the clock reached 10:30, Pastor Dave stood at the pulpit to deliver a welcome. "Good morning. I am so thankful to each of you for being here. We have some special guests today. A house church that has been meeting in the home of Mark and Sarah Shepherd has gathered together with us for a joint worship service this morning. Please help me greet them."

As Dave led a warm applause, Benny was pleased to see the Bakers making their way up to the platform. Pastor Dave continued. "I have asked Josh and Donna Baker to lead us in a call-to-worship hymn. Please stand as we sing."

After the hymn concluded, Pastor Dave got back up to speak. "By now, most of you are aware of ongoing wrongdoing that has occurred within our community, beginning near the time of the tragic deaths of Annie Wheeler and Daniel Shepherd ten years ago. As you may know, some men from Lost Valley have committed a variety of nefarious acts including the terrorizing of families and the abuse and assault of young women. Coyotes in sheep's clothing managed to creep into positions of leadership at a local church which they used to advance their sinful agendas for personal gain. As a church family, we lament these wrongdoings and the malicious lies that were spread about innocent people. Leviticus 19:16 admonishes us not to go around spreading slanderous gossip. We repent of our part in perpetuating any such untruths.

Today, we are going to begin the process of making things right. Normally, we would sing worship songs and then I would deliver a sermon, but we have some family business to attend to this morning so we are going to be doing things differently. Our gathering today is going to look a little more like the first century church. You will be hearing short teachings from three individuals which are going to help us to heal and to grow and then we have a special musical treat for you. I have asked Mark Shepherd to join me on the platform to help oversee the proceedings and I am going to be inviting the speakers to come one at a time." As Mr. Shepherd took his seat back behind the podium, Pastor Dave said "The first person I would like to welcome to the platform is Gabby Shoemaker."

Unsilenced

On that Sunday morning, supported by her friends and family and emboldened by her faith, Gabby Shoemaker stood up to show the world the strength, intelligence and resilience of a God-fearing, Ozarkian woman.

"Good morning," Gabby began, "Some of you may be aware that Daniel Shepherd recorded the names of girls he believed had been sexually assaulted in his diary. I am one of those girls. At the beginning of my senior year of high school, I drank a glass of punch at a back-to-school party. That is the last thing I remember from that night. A month later I found out that I was pregnant at the Grace Pregnancy Center over in Ridgeview.

The ladies at the pregnancy center were so kind. They were empathetic and encouraging. The counselors understood the trauma I had been put through and how to help. The staff took care of my body and my soul.

They also took care of my baby, providing me with the prenatal care I needed and supporting me throughout the process. The atmosphere was so loving and Christlike that it strengthened and prepared me for what else was to come.

I only told my parents and my two best friends, but some members of our cheerleading squad were shopping in Ridgeview and saw me walking into the pregnancy center. They confronted me at the Halloween party on the night that Daniel and Annie were killed. They told me to "take care of it," or "get rid of it," pressuring me to get an abortion so that I wouldn't miss our upcoming cheerleading competition and so no one at church would find out and none of the boys at school would ever know. They told me I would swell up and not be able to fit into my cheerleading uniform, not be able to wear a prom dress. They told me this would ruin my future. It was like the devil himself was whispering in my ear trying to take me, an innocent rape victim, and trick and coerce me into killing my baby. How many women has our society manipulated and fooled into doing just that? They need our help, but I knew better because I had the Holy Spirit speaking to my heart. I wasn't going to let my attacker define the rest of my life or change the person I am. Those wise people at the crisis pregnancy center also reminded me of Psalm 139:13-16:

For you formed my inward parts. You knitted me together in my mother's womb. I will praise you for I am fearfully and wonderfully made. Wonderful are your works; my soul knows it very well. My frame was not hidden from you, when I was being made in secret, intricately woven in the depths of the earth. Your eyes saw my unformed substance. In your book were written, everyone one of them, the days that were formed for me, when as yet there was none of them. (ESV)

Those words helped me to realize that my daughter is not guilty of the crime her father committed against me. She didn't deserve the death sentence for his sins. I may have gotten pregnant as the result of a man forcing himself on me, but her soul was created good and knitted into her body by a loving God who has a plan and a purpose for her life. They spoke with me about the option of adoption, but I chose to keep my baby. My daughter is flesh of my flesh and bone of my bone and I love her with all of my heart and wouldn't change my decision for anything in the world. Nothing could replace the joy my child brings me every day.

The consequences for my right choices were severe. People jumped to conclusions and judged me without knowing any of the facts. My church disfellowshipped me and my parents were ostracized. It was a struggle just to graduate from high school. Dealing with morning sickness and then going to class was not fun, especially with people whispering behind my back and teacher's giving me the stink eye. I was forced to quit cheerleading when my uniform didn't fit anymore and I missed the prom. When the principal tried to stop me from walking in the graduation ceremony, someone intervened. I'm still not sure who.

But through all this my parents and my friend Hannah helped and supported me even though she was going through a difficult time herself. When I was called a slut and gossiped about, the Christ-like people from the pregnancy center stood by my side, lifted me up and provided me with baby clothes, formula, diapers, even a crib and a car-seat, all free of charge.

I had planned to go away to Whitfield College on a cheerleading scholarship and major in social work. That plan had to change, so I got a job at the flower shop and lived with my parents while I took classes at Riverbend Junior College. The owner was kind enough to let me bring my baby to work when I didn't have a sitter. I earned my Associates degree in small business management and now I own that flower shop. I have a precious daughter that I cherish, a lovely home, a pleasant job and a church family that loves me, and for that, I thank you.

So why am I sharing this today?

Firstly, so that you will understand the damaging effects of gossip and jumping to conclusions before asking questions. Talk *to* people rather than *about* them and ask questions before making assumptions.

Secondly, I am sharing this because God did not cause the horrible trauma that I was put through. He is not the author of sin and evil. But he has been faithful to me through it all and has sent people to minister well to me. Sins such as sexual assault are a violation of God's commands and because He himself is the avenger of such wrongdoing, I do not have to live my life thirsting for revenge or consumed with anger.

Thirdly, in my parents, my two friends and the staff at the pregnancy center, I had a safety net to keep me from falling, but not all women have such a support system. Today, you have the opportunity to do something about that. At the end of this morning's service, we are going to be taking a special offering as the first step toward beginning a ministry to pregnant women in our community. The church will be supporting this ministry with our tithes and offerings. We will be purchasing a variety of necessities to have in place for women in need. I am hoping to take some classes in ministry and counseling because I believe God is calling me to minister to women the way I was ministered to. I want to be there to comfort and assist women through crisis and trauma in the same way that others were there to help and encourage me."

At that point, Gabby stepped to the side and the audience applauded her courage as Mark Shepherd came to the microphone. "Thank-you Gabby for your incredible bravery and willingness to share with us today." Turning to the congregation, he said, "What happened to her and what was done to these other girls is an egregious evil. I am deeply disturbed at the way she was treated afterward by people claiming the name of Christ. Like the hypocrites of old, there were church leaders hiding their poisoned hearts behind a mask of righteousness. They used their positions of power to silence Gabby and other voices like hers. Today she speaks on behalf of many. First Thessalonians chapter four, teaches that it is directly against God's will for women to be harmed sexually."

For THIS is God's will, your sanctification; that you keep away from sexual immorality, that each of you know how to control his own body in holiness and honor, not with lustful passions, like the Gentiles, who don't know God. This means one must not transgress against and take advantage of a brother or sister in this manner because the Lord is an Avenger of all these offenses...

"To disregard the well-being of a person and use them for one's own selfish pleasure is unspeakably wicked and a direct violation of God's desire," Pastor Shepherd continued, "Rape is a sin that grieves the very heart of God. When a woman is hurt in this way, God is on her side, and His church had better stand with her as well. We must make sure that the house of the Lord is a safe place of refuge."

Pastor Dave returned to the pulpit as the congregation applauded in agreement. "Church family, we want to be a group of Christ followers that cares well for women in need and protects the vulnerable. We want to be a lifeline to those who need help and we want to bring the hope of the Gospel to them and I am going to be sharing more about how we are going to accomplish these goals at the end of the service. Can you thank Gabby once again for her courageous testimony?" The applause was immediate and robust. "Now, I believe there was one more piece of information Gabby wanted to share with us as her church family."

"Speaking of God's goodness to me. Ten years ago, my life got turned upside down. Little by little, piece by piece, God has been putting things back into order. I am overjoyed to announce to you that as of last night, I am engaged...to Nick Baker." All eyes turned to Nick who was sitting on the front row holding the hand of Gabby's daughter Maggie who was smiling from ear to ear. Someone hollered *Hallelujah* and then the congregation erupted into joyful applause.

A Lesson from the Departed

As the clapping faded away, Pastor Dave came back to the microphone "I would like to invite our next speaker, Lucy Wheeler to come to the pulpit and share."

As Lucy made her way to the stage, Pastor Dave explained "Many of us have learned this past week about the untruthful and unfair rumors that have circulated for the past ten years about Annie Wheeler and Daniel Shepherd. The injustices committed against these families are horrendous. This morning, I have invited Annie's sister and Daniel's brother to speak to us. I would like you to listen to what they have to say as we pay proper respects to these two innocent victims."

Lucy began "My sister Annie was a bright ray of sunshine to everyone who knew her. She was fun-loving, energetic and thoughtful. She was a wonderful big sister. She always made time for me. There was a big age gap between us, but she treated me like there wasn't. She loved to play make-believe and dress up, to fly kites and swing with me and she was so imaginative.

You should know that my sister hated alcohol. She had no idea the punch she drank that dreadful night was spiked. In her Bible she had highlighted:

Wine is a mocker, strong drink a brawler, and whoever is led astray by it is not wise. (ESV)

My sister had big dreams for when she grew up. Last night I had a sleepover with her two best friends, Gabby and Hannah and with Miss Maggie." Lucy gave a little finger bending wave toward Maggie, who smiled and waved back, happily swinging her feet on the front row between her mom and Nick. "In the hours before Annie died, her friends overheard her talking with

Daniel, sharing their hopes and dreams and hearts. Annie loved music. She wanted to go to college and study to be a music teacher or a music minister at a church. She wanted to work with people and to help them, to make their lives better, fuller and richer.

It isn't fair that Annie's life was cut short. It isn't right that she and Daniel were despised simply because their skin was a different color from each other and make no mistake, they were targeted for that reason. Those evil boys were enraged that Daniel and Annie were together, just because their skin had differing amounts of pigmentation. They set a trap for Daniel and Annie and chased them down to their deaths.

Talking with Gabby and Hannah last night, and looking through Annie's Bible in preparation for today, I found a marker she had placed and a thread of verses she had stitched together. My sister had come to believe that the purpose of dating was to find someone to marry, to become friends and really get to know a person's heart. She had placed a marker in 2 Corinthians 6:14:

Do not be unequally yoked with unbelievers. For what partnership has righteousness with lawlessness? Or what fellowship has light with darkness? (ESV)

She wrote a note in the margins. *Find a godly man to date who will make a good husband one day.* Annie and her friends had grown tired of the games and nonsense. They were sick of putting up with boys who did not honor God and certainly did not respect or honor women. She wrote another Scripture reference in the margin: *Galatians 3:27-28.* It reads:

For those of you who were baptized into Christ have been clothed in Christ. There is no Jew or Greek, slave or free, male and female; since you are all one in Christ Jesus. And if you belong to Christ, then you are Abraham's seed, heirs according to the promise.

This passage teaches that we are all equal in Christ. Our place in the family of God is not based on ethnicity, social status or gender, it is based on our relationship with Jesus Christ as our Savior. In the margin, Annie wrote, *find a man who respects women as equal heirs in Christ.* She noted *1 Samuel 16:7.* When I turned there, she had highlighted:

Man looks on the outward appearance, but the LORD looks on the heart. (ESV)

In the margins she wrote: *Daniel has a beautiful heart (and he's pretty cute too).* The congregation laughed in appreciation.

"Annie noted one more passage in the chain, *Galatians 5:22-23.* She highlighted: *The fruit of the Spirit is love, joy, peace, patience, kindness, goodness, faithfulness, gentleness, self-control. (ESV)* In the margin she wrote one word...*Daniel.*

My sister chose Daniel because he was a godly man. She chose him because she saw the fruit of the Spirit in his life and because he had a heart like Jesus...and racist, sinful men killed them because of it. Everything about her decision was right and just and godly and anyone who has a problem with her choice is in sin and needs to repent. If everyone took relationships as seriously as Annie and put the same level of care and prayer into choosing a potential spouse as she did, then families would be healthier, the church would be stronger and the world would be a better place."

The congregation applauded in agreement.

The Final Entry

Then Pastor Dave invited Benny Wheeler to the platform. As Benny came, his father stepped down from the platform to go hold his wife's hand while his son spoke. He gave Benny a strong hug as they passed by each other.

"Today would have been my brother Daniel's 28th birthday. My brother was kind and compassionate. He loved to spend time with me and he was always so much fun. Daniel hated teasing, so he never pestered or picked on me, but he would ride bikes or play catch, shoot hoops or play hide and seek. He never said no when I asked him to play. He was a wonderful brother. He put the needs and interests of others above himself and he was incredibly courageous.

Daniel was brave in love and it drew the ire of bigoted boys. He was dauntless in other ways too. It was that bravery in part that led to his death. My brother stood up to evil boys who were doing wicked, sinful, vile things. They were harming girls and he would not tolerate it. He was the hero of this story, not the villain as so many have made him out to be.

On the night that he died, Daniel brought pizza home for us to eat together. He dressed up like a cowboy at my request and took me out to collect candy. We met up with Lucy and Annie Wheeler and Daniel bought us all cinna-pecans and candied apples. When we got back home, while I was eating candy and watching cartoons, Daniel was writing in his diary. I begged him not to go to that party, to come to the Harvest Carnival at church with me, but he said 'I'm sorry buddy, this is just something I have to do.' He went to the party that night to guard Annie and the other girls from harm. Had he lived, I truly believe my brother Daniel would have become a pastor to watch over, teach and protect people. On the first page of his diary, he wrote his life verse, Jeremiah 23:4

I will raise up shepherds over them who will care for them. They will no longer be afraid or discouraged nor will any be missing.

In every way throughout his much too short life, Daniel lived up to the name of Shepherd. The last words he ever wrote were:

There is only one solution to stop the hatred people feel in their hearts toward their fellow man, only one remedy to the prejudice, the injustice and the violence in this world, only one way to prevent people from abusing and taking advantage of each other, only one way to escape from this nightmare of sin, and that way is Jesus. He is THE Way, THE Truth and THE life and no one comes to the Father except through Him. It is only through the change that the Holy Spirit brings about in our hearts, minds and lives that we can be delivered from sin's clutches. The good news is that there IS a way.

Daniel wrote down a Scripture reference below that final paragraph. I would like to read this pericope to you from 2 Peter, chapter 1, verses 3-11.

His divine power has given us everything required for life and godliness through the knowledge of him who called us by his own glory and goodness. By these he has given us very great and precious promises, so that through them you may share in the divine nature, escaping the corruption that is in the world because of evil desire. For this very reason, make every effort to supplement your faith with goodness, goodness with knowledge, knowledge with self-control, self-control with endurance, endurance with godliness, godliness with brotherly affection, and brotherly affection with love. For if you possess these qualities in increasing measure, they will keep you from being unfruitful in the knowledge of our Lord Jesus Christ. The person who lacks these things is blind and shortsighted and has forgotten the cleansing from his past sins. Therefore, brothers and sisters, make every effort to confirm your calling and election, because if you do these things you will never stumble. For in this way, entry into the eternal kingdom of our Lord and Savior Jesus Christ will be richly provided for you.

This passage is about becoming mature believers in Christ. I had many questions and there was deep pain in my life, but I have learned a lot and grown a great deal these past few weeks. Through the years I have watched my parents remain faithful and somehow manage to stay kind and not bitter, because of the love of God in their hearts. In recent days I have witnessed the reconciliation that has been brought about between all of our families and that is something only God can do. I have observed the change and the repentance the Spirit of God brings about in the hearts of men who once did terrible things. And in his life and through his diary, I have discovered the hope that Daniel had in the precious promises of God. I know beyond the shadow of any doubt that Daniel Shepherd and Annie Wheeler are in heaven. They are part of the everlasting Kingdom of God that we just read about. They are safe and at rest in the Father's arms and I find great peace in that truth.

We have experienced suffering inflicted by the actions of evil men. We have firsthand knowledge of the corruption caused by this world as sin eats away at the human heart. But there is a way, ONE Way, out. When we become partakers in the divine nature, God heals our hearts, cleans them up and makes them like new. We can escape the power of sin and live godly lives through faith. Peter listed seven virtues that God wants to bring about in our lives.

1. The first virtue is GOODNESS. Goodness is having a sense of morality based on God's word. It is knowing the difference between right and wrong and acting with integrity to choose the right things. Being good involves seeing after the well-being of others and never using them for selfish gain. We must take right action that is beneficial to the people in our lives.

2. The second virtue is KNOWLEDGE. Part of the Christian life is learning about God and getting to know him. This is about developing a relationship based on deep understanding and trust. Wisdom is the correct application of knowledge. The type of knowledge we are seeking here isn't just about memorizing facts, it is about gaining an understanding of morality that leads to wise choices.

3. The third virtue is SELF-CONTROL. We have all recently become aware of the horrors inflicted upon some of the women in this town due to the lack of self-control on the part of young men. Self-control means we don't give ourselves over to drunkenness, lust and evil desires that tempt us to consume, devour and otherwise use other people for our own selfish pleasure and benefit. Self-control is a fruit of the Spirit, something that God brings about in our lives.

4. The fourth virtue is ENDURANCE. Endurance, or long-suffering, is the ability to remain faithful to God and trust in Him even when things go wrong. I have watched the faithful endurance of my parents and have seen it in Gabby, the Wheeler's and others as they have remained unshaken in their faith, even in the face of injustice, shocking evil and unbearable wickedness.

5. The fifth virtue is GODLINESS. Godliness is becoming more like Jesus, being his disciples, learning his ways

and following his example in the way we behave and treat others. Godliness is about partaking in the divine nature. We have been cleansed from sin and are being conformed to the image of God. It is his power at work within us that is transforming us to be more like Christ. Praying, studying the Bible and planning fellowship with other believers are some of the ways that we can grow in godliness.

6. The sixth virtue is BROTHERLY AFFECTION. Having a genuine concern for members of the family of God means that we care for one another, look out for each other, hold one another accountable and lift each other up. Lucy read to us about being the true children of Abraham. As believers, we are the truest form of family there is. It is time to start acting like it. I have witnessed such affection between Christians these past few weeks, and it is a beautiful sight to behold that I believe is very pleasing to God.

7. The final virtue listed is LOVE. Love is self-sacrificial. Love puts others first. Love demonstrates genuine affection for our fellow man.

All of these seven virtues are prefaced with FAITH. Faith comes first. It is only after we place our faith in the saving power of Jesus Christ that we can experience these things in their fullest sense. Do you want to be forgiven and have all of your past sins wiped away like we read about? Then turn away from your sins and toward God. Ask him to forgive you and I promise He will. Do you want to come into a relationship with Jesus and experience this virtuous life? Invite him into your heart and welcome him into your life. Ask him to fill you with his Spirit and heal your heart and clean up your mind. Do you want to become more like Jesus? Read God's word. Pray. Spend time growing with other believers. Do you want to know for certain that your place in heaven as part of God's family is secure? If you have accepted Jesus into your heart then it already is. If you have questions, there will be an invitation at the end of the service. I invite you to come up and speak with a minister or speak with me and we will be overjoyed to help you."

Resolution

After Benny was finished, Pastor Dave returned to the platform. "We have learned how badly these families and individuals were slandered and mistreated. Their willingness to forgive and love for our community is truly remarkable. Most of you don't know this, but for the past few years, Mark Shepherd has been volunteering his time to help me with our church's finances and to craft a revitalization plan. He took no money and wanted no credit. As an experienced pastor, he just wanted to be a good mentor and to see our church prosper and he did not want my image to be tarnished by association with the very false things that had been said about his family. I stand here today, proud to call Mark Shepherd my friend. Under his guidance, I was able to develop a plan for paying off our church's debts and I am pleased to announce to you that as of this last week, we are now 100% debt free (massive applause).

For the past nine years, Mark and his wife Sarah have been hosting a Bible Study in their home each Sunday morning. In addition to lending his expertise to me, for the past couple of years their Bible study group has joined together with us in benevolence ministries by sharing a portion of their tithes and offering money that has helped enable us to provide a food pantry and clothing closet for families in need. As you know, the members of this fellowship are here today and I am thrilled to announce that their house church is going to be merging together with our Hilltop family. Please take a moment and make them feel welcome."

The congregation applauded and then took more than a few minutes walking the aisles, shaking hands, hugging and receiving the new families. Eventually, Pastor Dave continued, asking Mr. and Mrs. Shepherd to join him on the platform.

"Mark and Sarah Shepherd have endured nasty persecution. They have been lied about and mistreated, yet remained kind and faithful through it all. They resemble in every way what the apostle Peter wrote:

Conduct yourselves honorably among the Gentiles, so that when they slander you as evildoers, they will observe your good works and will glorify God on the day he visits. He went on to say: *For it is God's will that you silence the ignorance of foolish people by doing good.*

The Shepherd family has lived out this passage of Scripture, setting a tremendous example for us all. As our church has grown, the leadership team and myself have been discussing adding some much-needed staff positions and with our debts cleared, we now have the financial means to do so. It is my genuine pleasure and honor to present to you Mark Shepherd as a candidate for the position of Executive Pastor."

The pastor had to stop talking as he was interrupted with enthusiastic applause and a standing ovation. As the clapping slowly died down, he continued, "Pastor Mark will take on the stewardship of overseeing church operations and supervising the budget while I lead in the areas of teaching, ministry and outreach. Pastor Mark will be preaching to us regularly as well. I would like to take a moment to allow our membership to vote on this matter. All in favor of bringing Pastor Mark onto our church staff say, *Aye.*" A hearty unison *Aye* echoed throughout the building. "Any opposed say, *Nay.*" There was not a single person who voiced opposition.

"You have heard this morning what we as leaders have recently become aware of. We have been busy at work this week, planning our response and as a result I have some exciting things to tell you about. First, I want you to know that we will be hosting a Compassion Ministry workshop for area pastors and lay leaders to deepen their knowledge and develop their skills to be able to better counsel people in crisis, help individuals recover from trauma and comfort fellow believers who are in pain. This training will be free of charge to all members of our Hilltop Bible Church family.

The church leadership and I have also been discussing this and meeting with Gabby Shoemaker and it is our desire to bring her on staff immediately as our Minister to Women. Her first task will be to contact the other women listed in Daniel Shepherd's diary to identify those who are in need of counseling or assistance. She will run the new ministry just like she described to you and I have some very exciting news about that. On Friday, Judge Bean ordered that instead of going into the county coffers, the fines issued in the court cases dealing with the car wreck would be paid directly to the Shepherd and Wheeler families. They were awarded a total of $20,000 which they have generously and eagerly offered to donate toward Gabby's education as she attends Vista Point Bible College in nearby Ridgeview to complete her Bachelor's degree in Biblical Studies with an emphasis in Counseling and Compassion Ministries. As a church, will continue to support her with additional funding as she pursues a Master's degree, focusing on ministry to women."

Pastor Dave had to stop speaking for a moment as he was drowned out by a thunderous applause of acclamation. No one was more enthusiastic than Benny and Lucy. It had been their idea. They didn't want to keep a dime from the Jones or Crow families, but wanted to see the money used for good.

"Additionally," Pastor Dave continued, "I am happy to report to you that the Shepherd's house church has been saving up money to construct their own building. Due to their faithful giving and Pastor Mark's diligence and careful stewardship of resources, they have graciously agreed that the money should be used to build a ministry center right here adjacent to our church campus. Pastor Mark, would you come and tell us how this building project is going to work?"

Mark Shepherd explained "All of the materials for this project will be provided through Baker's Home Improvement at cost. The building will be of steel construction on a smooth, concrete pad. In order to save on construction costs, we have already been in communication with some of our contacts from the home store; fellow believers who own the necessary equipment and are willing to volunteer their time to complete the foundation work if we pay for the materials. Then the exterior walls, support posts and roof will be constructed by a group of Mennonite barn builders. After those steps, we would welcome volunteers with the skill to install lighting, fit the plumbing, connect the electrical wiring, frame, nail and texture drywall, lay carpet and tile, hook-up heating and air-conditioning units and put a drop ceiling in place. We even have Christian members of our community who are excited about this ministry and eager to share their masonry skills to apply a stacked stone exterior to match the chapel and create a building that will last for a very long time. We will contract out for any other work that is needed. You will have all have opportunities to assist. It will be like an old-fashioned community barn-raising, but for a ministry building.

Approximately one-third of the building will be utilized to enlarge our food pantry and free clothing closet. It will be a welcoming place for families in need to come and receive assistance with no strings attached. There will be plenty of opportunities for you to volunteer to help with the clothing and food distribution and to share love and the good news about Jesus with people who really need that hope. This will also be an important point of outreach to invite new families into our fellowship if they don't already have a church home.

The other side of the building will house a new women's health and pregnancy center. We are still working on ideas for the blue prints, but we plan to have a medical examination room equipped with ultrasound, two private offices for counseling, a comfortable reception area stocked with drinks and snacks and a larger room for hosting birthing classes, kindermusic and other activities. Initially, two days per week it will be staffed by volunteer doctors and counselors to provide pregnancy screenings and prenatal care free of charge for those in need. They will provide referrals when necessary.

This schedule will also allow our Minister to Women, Gabby Shoemaker, to complete her classes during the other days while her own child is in school. The offering you give today will stock our food pantry and clothing closet with formula, diapers, bottles, binkies, infant and toddler clothes, maternity clothes, baby food and all of the things a young mother might need at absolutely no charge and we have been working on building this into the budget. We will be accepting donations of items such as car seats and cribs. I will be helping Gabby to coordinate these efforts. Eventually, we plan to grow this into a full-time, fully staffed women's health and pregnancy center as an outreach to the community and as part of our comprehensive pro-life plan. For right now, it will offer pregnancy screenings, support, counseling and referrals for pre-natal care."

Pastor Dave returned to the pulpit and stepped up to the microphone. "You have just been given a vision of what the future could look like here at Hilltop Bible Church. Now you have the opportunity to set that future in motion by your vote. All in favor of bringing Gabby Shoemaker onto our staff as the Minister to Women say *Aye*." A boisterous, unison *Aye* resounded throughout the building and of course, no one was opposed.

Continuing on, Pastor Dave announced, "The new building will be called *The Annie Wheeler and Daniel Shepherd Compassion Ministries Building*. At each entrance we will proudly display the names of these new ministry endeavors with beautiful plaques. Beside one door will be the name *The Daniel Shepherd Food Pantry and Clothing Closet*. The other plaque will read *The Annie Wheeler Center for Women*. Will all in favor of undertaking this building project say *I*." The hearty *I's* were almost drowned out by the applause of overwhelming support for the idea. People even drummed their approval onto the pew backs. No one dared say nay.

Pastor Dave added "There are collection boxes attached to the wall on either side of the door at the back of the worship center. At the conclusion of the service, you may place your offering in those containers.

Some of you here today may be wondering how these families who were wronged so badly could show such forgiveness and you have heard the answer through Daniel Shepherd's own words as he described the need for God to change our hearts. It is

THE DIARY OF DANIEL SHEPHERD

only through the change that God works in our lives that we can be so forgiving. If you have never made the decision to follow Jesus, then I invite you to come as we sing a hymn."

The response was instant and sincere as families prayed together at the altar. Pastors Mark and Dave answered questions and prayed with people for a variety of needs and reasons. Mr. Baker sang a few verses and then Mrs. Baker continued playing softly. No one thought of sneaking out the back. This is what they came for. Then Pastor Dave quietly cut the music off.

"Now," Dave announced, I would like you to welcome *The Harper Family*." As the musicians came forward, they carried the instruments of a traditional mountain bluegrass band onto the stage with them. The dad played the banjo, the eldest daughter bowed the fiddle, the mom plucked the mandolin, the eldest brother strummed the guitar, the younger brother picked the dobro and the youngest daughter enthusiastically laid down the beat with the upright bass on one and three. They all took turns singing and harmonizing in that special way that kin can as they led the congregation in a mix of hymns and gospel favorites. It was a toe tappin' knee slappin' hand clappin' good time. It felt like a weight had been lifted off the congregation's shoulders. They rejoiced and worshipped and celebrated the goodness of God like never before. There was abundant joy in the house of the Lord on that day.

The church nearly raised the roof when they finished up with *When We All Get To Heaven*. Folks still had their hands raised in the air triumphantly or were still clapping in worship and shouting "Amen," "Praise the Lord," and "Hallelujah," when Pastor Dave came back to the platform, saying "Thank-you so much for being here. We are truly honored that each of you chose to come and worship with us today. Now, we invite everyone to stay after the service for a fellowship meal. If this is your first time here and you didn't bring anything, please stay as our honored guests. I snuck a peak before the service and it looks like there's enough food to feed the five-thousand back there, so be sure to stick around." He asked Mark and Sarah Shepherd and Gabby to stand in the back next to him and shake hands as the congregation filtered out before saying "Just exit through these back doors and turn left down the hallway to the stone chapel, which doubles as our youth ministry room and fellowship hall. Tables are already prepared for you."

Coop and Mason met Benny by the back doors of the church and he said, "Hey, do you guys remember Lucy?"

"Yes. I remember the golf-cart train rides we all took together at the Harvest Carnival...when we were little. It's been a long time," Coop said, offering his hand to shake as she nodded yes and everyone smiled. "You both did an incredible job today."

"Yeah, that was awesome," Mason agreed, also shaking Lucy's hand.

"Thank-you," she replied.

"Thanks. I appreciate you guys being here. It means a lot," Benny replied. "Are you staying for lunch?"

"No, our parents are expecting us," Coop explained.

"But we might invite them to come with us next week. I love it here. Everyone's so...real," Mason added.

"Our parents stayed home this morning after what went down at Riverside this week, but I think they might like it here," Coop said.

"I'm sure they would," Benny suggested.

"It's really great. You should come back Wednesday night," Lucy invited.

"Yeah, definitely."

"For sure."

"Will we see you at school Monday?" Coop asked.

"Yeah. I'll be back," Benny answered.

They said their goodbyes and Benny and Lucy joined the quickly growing dinner line. Benny had never shaken so many hands in his life.

Potluck

There really is nothing quite so fine as a church fellowship dinner. The line went all the way down the hall, but everyone was so engaged in conversation that no one seemed to mind. In fact, some of the senior adults intentionally placed themselves at the back so they would have more time to visit. "This is the best part," said one elderly gentleman with a long, white beard.

As he and Lucy entered the chapel, Benny noticed that the foosball table had been pushed into a corner, the café style tables of the coffee area had been moved into the back for overflow seating and the room was filled with long folding tables set end to end and surrounded by metal folding chairs. The coffee bar was covered with glasses of lemonade and sweet or unsweet tea and there was a table next to it filled with desserts.

In front of the stage were tables draped in red gingham and decorated with a cornucopia of serving dishes, pans, bowls, bake wear and baskets, each filled with a family's best offering. There were crunchy, crumbly, cheesy chicken casseroles galore with meatloaves, lasagnas and plenty of potatoes scalloped or mashed, bowls of noodles, sweet and spicy meatballs, smoked or sugared hams, crisp colorful salads, hot rolls, country cornbread and a variety of other delicious dishes.

Benny and Lucy sat in the middle of a table with the Wheelers on their right and Nick and Gabby to their left. Tony and Bella from Wednesday night youth group waved from across the room and Lucy exuberantly waved back while Benny gave a little wave with a head nod. Hannah and Freddy sat across from them with Hannah's parents to her right and the Shepherd's to their left, along with Benny's grandparents. This was the first time Hannah Farmer and her parents had attended church together in ten years. Gabby's daughter Maggie had been allowed to fix her own plate. She sat between her mom and her grandparents, enjoying a hot roll and one chicken tender. "I've gotta save room for dessert," she whispered enthusiastically to Lucy as she walked by with a big grin. The Bakers came in and sat down next to the Farmers, warmly engaging them and the Shoemakers in conversation.

Lucy indulged in Mrs. Baker's homemade brisket tamales while Benny decided that her famous meatloaf was his favorite. "You know, God has really blessed us abundantly," Benny reflected. "Even in the middle of life's complications, we have always had plenty to eat and a safe, clean place to live. Our needs have always been taken care of. I have a lot to be thankful for."

"Here, here," said Freddy through a mouthful of cheesy broccoli casserole.

"Amen," agreed Nick in between bites of handmade dumplings Pastor Dave's wife Judy prepared from a special family recipe. "Dim Sum fine dumplings," he joked.

Only Gabby laughed, "Of course they are. Her parents own Bonzai Gardens restaurant."

Everyone was impressed with the squaw bread Gabby brought.

"This is incredible," Hannah said.

"Thanks, it's my great-grandmother's recipe."

Maggie made sure they knew that she helped, "I mixed it up," she said between mouthfuls of casserole her mom had added to her plate, saying, "Yum, sweetie, try this, it's sooo good."

"So, who's going to run the flower shop now that you're coming to work for the church?" Benny asked Gabby.

She and Hannah exchanged a giggly smile. "Hannah is."

"I am moving my business here to Lost Valley and into Gabby's main street storefront. One side of the store will remain devoted to flowers and gifts, the other side will display an eclectic collection of vintage clothing and jewelry. I'm having the sign repainted 'Water's Edge Floral *and Boutique*.' Diversification is key for a small-town business. I can sell gently used fashions for half the price which is something this place needs. In the springtime, I will stock up on vintage formals for girls to get beautiful prom dresses at super low prices."

"We've been talking about combining the two businesses forever," Gabby added, "and now is the perfect time to do it."

"We always thought we would run it together," Hannah added. "But this will be good too."

"And we will live in the same town again and can hang out any time we want to," Gabby concluded.

After plates were cleaned and seconds polished off, steaming cups of coffee were poured and the church family continued their lively fellowship over dessert. Lucy nearly spit-taked her sweet tea when she saw Maggie coming back wearing a giant smile as she used both hands to carry a plate containing a brownie, a dollop of apple crisp, a spoonful of chocolate pudding and a slice of carrot cake. "Is that for all of us?" Nick asked.

"Nope," she answered, "This is for me." Everyone had a hearty laugh.

As Maggie dug in to her dessert plate, Nick raved about the delicious blackberry cobbler, sharing a bite off his fork with Gabby, who closed her eyes and said "mmm." While Lucy indulged in a heapin' helpin' of peach cobbler, Benny enjoyed a thick slice of pumpkin bread to finish the meal. After they were done eating, as their parents lingered at the table with their coffee, Lucy asked Benny, "You haven't been out back yet, have you?"

"What's out back?"

"Come with me and you will see," Lucy replied as she took his hand, pulled him up out of the chair and led him through the doors and around behind the church.

The front side of the building boasted a sweeping perspective of the prairie. The back side gave way to a panoramic view of the Lost River Valley. Capped by a large outcropping of solid rock was a lovely prayer garden. Approaching the overlook was a winding pebble pathway hemmed in by colorful creekrocks. The walkway was surrounded by fall-blooming native wildflowers such as lavender asters, pink turtlehead flowers and white ox-eye daisies with their happy yellow centers. The vibrant hues of dark purple love grass and three-foot-high goldenrod added depth to the landscape. A colorful assortment of pumpkin and ornamental gourd vines provided groundcover and the edge of the garden was bordered by the orange blooms of trumpet honeysuckle bushes. The tranquil trail led to an oval area with a bench for enjoying the breathtaking lookout.

Lucy shivered as they walked, so Benny put his coat around her shoulders. The couple sat on the bench with their arms around each other for a few minutes, quietly taking in the beauty of their surroundings. Then they offered a prayer of thanksgiving, expressing their heartfelt gratitude to God for the truth he had brought into the light, for the restoration that had been given to their families and for His protection and their safety.

"And I am thankful for you," Benny said.

"And *I* am thankful for you," Lucy replied. "And I'm very proud of you Benny. I'm proud of you for your courage during our investigation and I'm proud of how well you spoke today. You did an excellent job of explaining the Scriptures and sharing the good news about Jesus."

"Thanks Lucy. I'm really proud of you too. Without your insights, our quest wouldn't have gotten very fair. And I love to hear you teach. You did such a fantastic job in church this morning, in front of *all* those people. I hope to hear much more of that."

Benny took her hands into his own, looked deep into her eyes and expressed the words that had been overflowing in his heart, "I love you, Lucy Wheeler."

Without a moment's hesitation, her eyes locked into his, Lucy requited, "I love you too, Benny Shepherd."

The couple shared a warm embrace, the kind of affectionate hug that communicates emotions words find difficult to express. Benny Shepherd had found his best friend, the woman he would spend the rest of his life with and his love was reciprocated. In her arms he felt safe, warm, and loved and he knew she felt the same. A sense of happiness, peace, purpose and fulfillment that had been lacking in his life came over him. It was Lucy. It was their families and their friends. It was God with them, watching over them. He realized in that moment that he was blessed beyond measure and despite the difficulties of this life, he always had been.

They went back inside, helped fold and put away chairs and wiped down tables, exchanging the most joyful of smiles as they did.

When it came time to leave, as Lucy hugged Benny goodbye, she whispered in his ear "Ask your dad what we talked about, ok?"

"I will," Benny promised.

The Mystery of the House

After the potluck, as the Shepherd family loaded up the car, Benny's dad mentioned, "You did a really outstanding job this morning."

"We're very proud of you," his mom added.

"Your Granny June and Papa Floyd wished they could have been here. They would've driven down to hear you speak if they would have known in time," his dad assured him.

"I promised to send them a video and they asked me to tell you how very proud they are of you," his mom added.

Most Sunday afternoons were for relaxing, but the Shepherds felt particularly energized that day. As they pulled into the driveway, Mr. Shepherd said "It's long past time we finish fixing this place up. What improvements should we make?"

"I think we need a proper front porch. We could move the steps back and have a wooden porch built across the front of the house and cover it. We could even have a little gable in the middle over the door," Mrs. Shepherd suggested.

"I think that's a marvelous idea," her husband answered.

"It's so flat over on the right side, it looks like an old farmhouse with a turret sticking out on the left. A covered porch and gable would definitely tie it all together nicely," Benny agreed.

"And inside the house, we could paint or refinish the wainscoting," Mr. Shepherd suggested. His wife nodded in agreement.

"We could put a wishing well over the ugly concrete pad where that creepy fountain used to be," Benny requested.

His parents exchanged bemused looks. "Son, did you know that there used to *be* a well right there? It was part of the original property," his mom explained.

"That concrete pad was put down over the hole so no one would fall down into it. I think installing a decorative wishing well on that spot is a perfect idea," his dad concurred.

"Yes, it complements the property and it could have a gabled roof to match the new porch," proposed his mom.

"That would look fantastic," Mark Shepherd agreed. "We can build the porch together."

"But we should definitely hire a contractor to build the roof over it," Sarah Shepherd hinted.

"And we can build a wishing well with stones."

"Or buy a pre-made one."

Both parents laughed. "For today, why don't we start simple and work our way up to the big stuff?" Mr. Shepherd recommended.

While Mrs. Shepherd went out to work in the potting shed, the first item on the agenda for the Shepherd men was to fix the noisy newel post at the bottom of the staircase. The decorative handrail had been knocking anytime someone stomped up the stairs for as long as they had lived here. As they worked, Benny asked, "Dad, am I still under lockdown?"

"No, I think all of that is behind us. You should be safe now. Just don't initiate any more stand offs with Riley Jones."

"You heard about that?"

"Of course, I did. I understand why you did it, but I'm not sure it was the wisest way to deal with the situation."

"I probably should have asked to speak with him privately, rather than publicly humiliate him. I suspect this won't be the last time we have trouble with that family."

"I suspect the same. But I *am* proud of you for standing up for your friend, Lucy. That was the right thing to do and it took courage. And I am very proud of the way both of you stood up for Annie and Daniel."

"Thanks dad. Speaking of Lucy. Is it ok if I take her out to dinner tonight after church?

"I think that would be a fine idea son," Mark Shepherd said as he took out his wallet and handed his son a few folded over bills. "Here. Take her somewhere nice."

"Thanks. Somewhere like Tia's Cocina or Spicer's Smokehouse down on the river?" Benny asked.

"That would be good, or Mama Moretti's. I'm afraid you might get nervous and spill barbecue sauce on yourself or get a chunk of meat stuck in your teeth if you go to Spicer's and Tia's food is fantastic, but some of the dishes are pretty spicy, plus...beans. But if you go to Mama Moretti's, you could have a nice salad course and warm bread and then they have several delicious pasta dishes to choose from for a main course. Just about everything they serve can be eaten with a knife and fork, so you don't have to worry about awkward table manners and the cheesecake there is the greatest."

"Yeah Dad, I think you're right. Mama Moretti's is definitely the better choice for our first time out together as a couple."

"Just watch out for the red sauce. Hey, that's strange."

"What's strange?"

316

As father and son knelt down to examine the boards, Mr. Shepherd replied "It isn't just the newel post that's loose, the railing is detached right here from the first few stairs. Do you see these loose balusters?"

"Yes, but why is that strange?"

"It looks like they were pulled away from the steps and then hastily nailed back in place, see how these two nail holes are joined together? That's why this part of the balustrade is wobbly."

"Ok, I guess that's a little weird."

"Does this second step seem loose to you?"

"And a little crooked," agreed Benny.

"Here, let's get a better look at it, lift that up."

Benny pulled up from the top while his dad pried underneath with a large screwdriver. Both were surprised at how easily it popped out. Neither was prepared for what lie beneath. They looked up at each other with mouths agape. Underneath the missing stair step was a secret storage space filled with journals. As they pulled the leather-bound diaries out and began to look through them, Mr. Shepherd said "I recognize these names. They are in our family Bible."

Father and son exchanged looks of utter bewilderment as they realized they had just found the records left behind by generations of Shepherd men who had archived their life's work and adventures and it was all right there for them to read.

"I knew that preserving our memoirs was a Shepherd family tradition, but I had no idea these diaries were all in one place," said Mark.

"But why are they here?" asked Benny.

Before his dad could answer, Benny's mom burst in through the back door, looking excited and out of breath. "Quick, come with me, you have to see this." She took off trotting back out the door before they had a chance to show her *The Shepherd Chronicles*. The men promptly followed after her, right over to the shed.

When the Shepherds toured the property all those years ago, the shed door was padlocked and Mrs. Baker didn't have a key. After the doorknob and lock were replaced, the first people in the shed were the movers, who stacked the boxes two deep along the walls before the Shepherds had a chance to look inside.

"I was sorting through these boxes to see what might need to be moved into the new office at the church and I was looking through some of the containers of Daniel's old things to see what we should keep and what we might donate to the clothing closet and I found this," Mrs. Shepherd said, smiling as she gestured toward the back wall where there stood a wrought iron archway bearing the name SHEPHERD in large, elegant letters with a smaller inscription, *Jeremiah 3:15*, underneath.

Benny and his father exchanged looks of incredulousness. "Wow," they exclaimed in unison.

"That's the verse that's imprinted on the front of the Shepherd family Bible," his dad observed.

I will give you shepherds who are loyal to me, and they will shepherd you with knowledge and skill.

"It's our family verse," his mom added.

"We just found a cache of diaries chronicling the history of the Shepherd family underneath the stairs," Mr. Shepherd explained to his wife.

"Do you think our ancestors could have built this place?" Benny asked.

"Yes, I believe they probably did," answered his dad.

"They definitely lived here," added his mom. "And there's something else back there. Help me move these filing boxes." After the cartons of Mr. Shepherd's records on the side of the shed were moved, Mrs. Shepherd pulled away a filthy, moth-eaten drop cloth, causing a cloud of dust to fill the room. As the air cleared, another treasure was slowly revealed; two swinging, iron gates. When joined together in the middle, they displayed the Shepherd family crest with the family mantra: *Faith and Virtue.*

Mark Shepherd spoke first "The original Shepherd family crest, *Fide et Virtute*, translates as *Faith and Valor*. I wanted you to know that Benny, because you have shown such tremendous courage and strength of character. When they came to America, our branch of the family modified it and adopted the motto *Faith and Virtue*. I thought it was very fitting that you chose to preach on seven virtues this morning. Son, you have certainly lived up to those principles and we are very proud of you."

"What you have done for this town and for our family is truly wonderful," his mother added. "You have been a true shepherd."

"I believe God brought us back to this town years ago for a reason," his father continued, "and I believe He has now worked through you to restore our family to see that purpose fulfilled. The people of Lost Valley are lost indeed and it is our sacred responsibility to help them."

He asked his wife a question with his eyes. She nodded affirmatively before saying, "Benny, there is something we have prepared for you."

"A very special gift," added his dad.

"We think now is the appropriate time for you to receive it."

The family went inside and into the library in the lower level of the turret where the warm, afternoon sun shone cheerfully through the windows. Benny's dad walked over to a cabinet and pulled out a large family Bible which he removed from its protective covering and set down on the coffee table. He then retrieved a small package which he ceremonially presented to his son.

Benny tore into the heavy brown paper. Inside was a handmade, dark brown, oil-conditioned, leather diary, much like his brother's. It was filled with blank, deckled edge pages of hand-pressed cotton. Next to the journal was an inkwell and a beautiful quill pen made from the feather of a Muscovy duck.

"This is a Shepherd family rite of passage, son. Every member of the Shepherd family is gifted a journal and a quill at a time of great significance in their lives. One of the few mementos that I have from my birth parents is a diary like this. Your grandfather had prepared it before I was even born. It was given to my adoptive parents along with the family Bible and a scrapbook with instructions on how to make a journal like this. I presented one to your mom on our wedding day, as is our custom. Chronicling our history is a long-standing and important tradition in the Shepherd family. Each person picks a special verse or passage of Scripture and writes it on the first page."

"Which verse did you choose, dad?" Benny asked

Shepherd God's flock among you, not overseeing out of compulsion but willingly, as God would have you; not out of greed for money but eagerly; not lording it over those entrusted to you, but being examples to the flock. 1 Peter 5:2-3.

"That fits. It sounds like you."

"What verse did you pick, mom?"

He will tend his flock like a shepherd. He will gather the lambs in his arms. He will carry them in his bosom and gently lead those that are with young. Isaiah 40:11.

"Jesus is the Great Shepherd and this verse reminds me that it is his character I am supposed to emulate when I lead and care for others."

"That's really beautiful," Benny affirmed.

"Let me see here," Mark Shepherd said as he walked over to the staircase and reached down between the loosened steps. "Ah yes, here it is," he said as he pulled out a metal clamp with a stamp on one side and a crank on top. Coming back into the study, he said, "Hand me your journal Benny." Benny handed the book to his father who carefully placed the odd metal implement around the diary and squeezed, pressing it into the freshly-oiled leather. He then turned the crank which created even more pressure. When he loosened up the crank and removed the stamp, the leather had been imprinted with the Shepherd family seal. "This tool appears to have been missing for some time. When I saw the seal embossed into the other journals, I realized what this was. Your diary now bears the mark of our family crest." He then opened the family Bible to reveal a full color version of the image.

The shield was beautifully and meticulously designed in gold leaf. The family mantra that Benny had noticed on the gates, *Faith and Virtue* was stamped on a plaque across the bottom while the name Shepherd was emblazoned on a banner across the top. Leaves adorned the image from above. The crest was divided into four sections, each bearing its own symbol: a cross, a shepherd's crook, an ichthus, and a dove holding an olive branch in its beak.

The images appeared in vibrant color with metallic highlights as if they were set into stained glass windows. The empty cross stood still against the deep pink shades of sunrise. The shepherd's crook rested on a field of sparkling emerald grass. The ichthus glistened silver in a purple sea and the dove flew through the light blue morning sky.

"These are the same images we just saw at lunch in the stone chapel," Mrs. Shepherd observed.

"Could our family have built that church?" Benny asked.

"I think it is extremely likely that they did." Mr. Shepherd confirmed. "The cross stands for the cross that Jesus died on for our sins. This cross is here to prompt us to proclaim the good news about Jesus," he explained. "The Shepherd's crook reminds us that we must be faithful to protect, feed, provide for and otherwise care for God's people. Jesus is the Great Shepherd. We are the under-shepherds that care for *His* flock. The symbol that looks like a fish is the ichthus. It was used by early Christians to identify themselves and it encourages us to fulfill the Great Commission by becoming fishers of men. The dove with an olive branch reminds us that God fulfills his promises, just like he did to Noah. The olive branch causes us to reflect on the peace we have as believers because God reached out to make a new covenant with us. The dove represents the Holy Spirit, his presence and work in our hearts and in our lives."

"Do you remember that *poimen,* the word translated in our Bibles as *pastor* is actually the Greek word for a *shepherd?*" his mom asked.

"Yes mam, I remember you teaching me that."

Then Mr. Shepherd said "You delivered an excellent sermon this morning son."

"You have a real gift," added his mother.

"Thank-you both," replied Benny.

"Do you have any ideas about what verse you might like to write in your journal?" his mother asked.

Be on guard for yourselves and for all the flock of which the Holy Spirit has appointed you as overseers, to shepherd the church of God which he purchased with his own blood. Acts 20:28

"I think that is a fine choice," his father affirmed.

"I was reading that passage the other day," Benny explained. "It goes on to issue a warning, using savage wolves as a metaphor for men who do harm to the church, who will try to lure people into following them with lies, false teaching and deception for their own selfish benefit. That reminds me of Ezekiel 22:27 as well:

Her officials within her are like wolves tearing their prey, shedding blood, and destroying lives in order to make profit dishonestly.

"We've seen what happens when people in positions of influence are greedy for money and lust for power," Benny continued. "They are like tricky, vicious, predatory coyotes. That's what happened in our town. They preyed upon the church. Someone has to defend the flock from the coyotes.

I've been thinking a lot about my future lately. I want to help people, protect them and teach them God's word. I want to take care of them when they are hurting. I want to foster a culture that is safe and a community that is healthy. I want to care for those who are beaten down and mistreated and I want to help the bad ones too. I want to see them all be made new in Christ. I want to help people find hope and a future in Jesus. I want to be a Pastor. I am going to be a Shepherd."

Later that afternoon, before he went to pick Lucy up, Benny sat down in the library with his journal. He turned on a lamp, took out his special quill, dipped it into the ink and began to write down all that had happened over the past two weeks so that someday in the future, another Shepherd, perhaps his own child or grandchild, might come along to read the chronicles of their family and be encouraged.

-THE END-

Made in the USA
Middletown, DE
25 March 2023